SILENCED

BESTSELLING AUTHOR
LEDDY HARPER

Edits by: Josie Cruz Editing

Cover by: Wicked by Design

To my ASA girls.
You guys are my rock when I need it.

PROLOGUE

Killian–age 8

I HATED SCHOOL nights. Mom always made me go to bed early, even though I wasn't tired at eight o'clock. She said I needed to get sleep so I could focus in class, but it didn't matter how many hours of sleep I got, I could never pay attention the way all the other kids did. My teacher complained because I'd spend too much time doodling on my paper instead of doing the work.

Mom would get frustrated with me.

Dad would lose his patience.

But I couldn't help it.

I remembered everything I saw, like a picture in my head.

Sometimes I'd draw the milk carton, the one that always sat on the top shelf in the fridge. Next to it, the bottle of wine my mom used to cook with and a two-liter bottle of seltzer water. I'd add the labels exactly the way they were— sometimes turned, other times only the backs of the bottles showed. There were times I'd sit in front of a test, and instead of giving the answer, I'd draw the page of the textbook the information was on. I'd sketch the photo on the top right, and then add in squiggles beneath it, where I knew the answer was, but I couldn't remember the words.

The school counselor said I had a photographic memory.

I could physically see it in my mind, but rather than the information, I was left with images.

They tried pills.

Therapy.

Art classes.

Nothing worked.

Medicine made me feel weird. Mom told them I acted like a zombie. I was given several different prescriptions—again, nothing worked. One of them made me even more aware of my surroundings, adding more images to my mind I had to get out with a pencil and paper. The day I drew my mother's jewelry box, exactly the way she had it with every ring, necklace, earring perfectly in place, she stopped giving me the pills.

I'd only seen her jewelry box once.

She said it wasn't working.

Now she made me go to bed earlier, hoping more sleep would help.

But all I did was lie awake and stare at the ceiling. The muffled vibrations of the TV hummed through the wall. I pretended I knew what they were watching and created the entire movie in my head. Tonight, my parents were quiet, so I knew it must've been a movie about bad guys. Those never scared me, even though Mom and Dad wouldn't let me watch them.

When the house went quiet, I turned to the digital clock on my nightstand. The red numbers told me it was just after ten. I'd laid there for two hours when I could've been drawing. Or reading. Or watching TV.

I closed my eyes and pictured the container of Legos in my closet. They sat on the top shelf right next to a barrel of Lincoln Logs. My clothes hung beneath them, organized by school clothes first, by color, and then my nicer clothes for church. Everything else was folded neatly in my dresser. Thinking of those, I pictured each drawer, each T-shirt and pair of shorts. I conjured an image of my Transformers shirt—the one with the mustard stain near the collar. Mom had wanted to throw it away, but I wouldn't let her. I loved that shirt, and the stain reminded me of the birthday party I'd gone to and the hot dog I ate as I sat next to Lily.

Lily Rose—her real name was Lily Abernathy, but I called her Lily Rose. Because she was beautiful, and the first time I ever saw her, she wore red earrings in the shape of a flower. Whenever I called her that, she'd blush, and it made me smile.

My lips curled. With my eyes closed and the entire house quiet, I pictured her in my head. That's when I turned off my

2

brain and allowed myself to succumb to the daydreams of Lily. Of me going to school the next day and giving her one of my mom's flowers from the garden.

But just as my body grew heavy and my mind got lost in thoughts of sitting next to the prettiest girl in class while sharing my sandwich at lunch, something pulled me out of it. My eyes flashed open and my forehead ached with tightness as I lay still enough to make out what sound I'd heard. My chest felt tight, like someone sat on it, but my heart hammered away. Pressure grew between my ears until it thumped along with my heart, faster and faster, louder, angrier.

And then I heard it again.

A thud, muted by my closed door.

A creak from the stairs, followed by what I could only describe as air leaking out of a tire.

I lay still, frightened, my entire body trembling.

It's just Mom going to the kitchen.

But I knew that was a lie. Mom never went downstairs after she went to bed. She never left her room once the lights were off. And as soon as I heard their door slowly creak open from down the hall, I was certain it wasn't my parents.

I glanced at the clock again.

Eleven twenty-one.

I'd heard them close their door over an hour ago.

They never opened it again.

Someone is in my house.

I squeezed my eyes shut and pulled the blanket over my head. No matter what I tried to think about, I couldn't stop imagining someone breaking in. The bad guys from the movie I'd thought about earlier were back, and they were coming for me.

A muffled scream made my breath catch in my chest.

The sound of something heavy hitting the floor made my skin burn.

And then I heard my name.

"Killian!"

It was my mom, but it didn't sound like her. Her voice was sharp, yet deep. Not quite as deep as Dad's grumbling tone, but like her voice box had been swallowed up by her throat. I knew what that felt like, because it happened to me every time I got scared by a bad dream and cried out for help.

I threw off the covers and jumped out of bed. My legs shook like a leaf in a storm while I stared at my closed door, waiting to hear my name again. Fear coursed through my veins and set my skin on fire. It accelerated my heartbeat and silenced my cries.

I fisted my hands at my sides as I tried to convince myself I'd made it all up. The house made sounds all the time. Sometimes, noises from outside seemed like they came from inside. But before I could accept that theory, I began to imagine something worse.

I'd heard something heavy fall to the floor, the echo still resounding in my head. In my mind, my dad could've fallen off the bed. Maybe he'd had a heart attack like Grandpa, or rolled off and hit his head on the table next to him, the corner catching the tender part on the side. And my mom had called out for me because she needed my help.

I ran to the door and swung it open, not thinking twice about running to them. My dad was hurt and needed me. My mom was panicked, and I needed to be the man she always said I would become. I flew the few feet down the dark hallway and pushed their door all the way open, not coming to a stop until I was completely inside.

Invisible concrete weighted down my feet and kept me from fleeing.

Imaginary cotton filled my throat, preventing me from screaming.

My eyes were held wide open by sticks that didn't exist.

And in front of me was a scene so unreal it was unfathomable.

A scene I'd never forget.

A scene that would haunt me forever…

ONE
Rylee

SWEAT DRIPPED DOWN THE side of my face, collecting in the collar of my shirt. The heat was almost unbearable, but I didn't want to be inside. Mom was away for work again—this time for a full week—and Dad was stuck in front of the television set watching another football game. I hated it when Mom was gone, because my dad didn't really know how to handle me. He had no problem bonding with my brother, but where I was concerned, he acted completely clueless. So Sundays became the day I'd take a book and sit in the back yard beneath a tree.

I brought my water bottle to my lips when something caught my attention near the privacy fence, separating the houses in the neighborhood and the wooded area behind it. It ran up the side yard, offering us seclusion to the house next door. The young woman who lived there often had guests over, which made my parents uneasy. But now, someone was in her back yard, climbing her fence.

No...not just someone.

A boy.

His stick-straight hair, the color of sand, hung to the middle of his ears. But I couldn't see his face. He had his back to me as he climbed, just before jumping over to the side filled with trees. His black T-shirt was a blur. He was there one second and gone the next.

I stared at the barrier, wondering if I could climb over and follow him. I knew everyone in the neighborhood, but I'd never seen him before. I glanced over my shoulder and waited a moment, just to make sure my dad or my brother weren't on their way out. When I noticed no movement beyond the sliding glass door, I jumped up and ran as fast as I could. Without second guessing it, I began to scale the tall slats of wood.

Once I made it to the top, I looked down and realized it was much higher on the other side. I'd never been in the wooded area before, and for a second, I contemplated just going back to my yard. I thought about my book I'd left beneath the tree and my father who might've gone looking for me. But then I remembered the boy—and I so desperately wanted to find out where he came from.

Curiosity got the best of me.

I swung my leg over and, with the pace of a sloth, I used the wood between the slats to lower myself to the ground. Standing on my feet again, I searched through the trees, hoping to spot the boy with blond hair and a black shirt.

But he was nowhere.

I carefully walked farther into the trees on the soft dirt, keeping as quiet as possible. I didn't want to venture too far, because I worried I wouldn't be able to make it back to my house. From this side, I couldn't tell which house was which. So I made sure not to deviate too far from behind my back yard.

It felt like an hour, but realistically, it was probably closer to five minutes before I decided to give up. I thought it might've been better to have just waited until he came back. I turned around, ready to head home, when I spotted him.

Or…he spotted me.

He stood maybe fifteen feet away, staring at me. The first thing I noticed were his eyes—seafoam green, my favorite color, which I had my entire room decorated in it—locked on me, holding my gaze captive. I couldn't look anywhere else but into his intense, almost worried stare. It was as if he'd been caught doing something wrong—or criminal even.

I glanced over my shoulder, making sure there wasn't anyone else behind me. When I realized no one had followed us, no one had come looking for me, I faced him again, only to see he'd turned around. He sat down in the packed dirt, his back arched forward, shoulders slumped. His long hair hung in front of him, and I noticed the back of his head, beneath the veil of sandy-blond locks, was buzzed close to his scalp. I'd seen kids with the same cut, but they were all older, closer to my brother's age—sixteen. This boy didn't look that old. However, he didn't appear to be my age, either.

My feet carried me toward him. His body grew stiff just before I sat down, but I ignored it. I bent my knees to my chest and wrapped my arms around my shins, all while keeping my gaze on him. But he never looked my way. He sat with his legs crossed, his elbows on his knees, shoulders pulled up to his ears with his head down, his hair covering his face, like he didn't want to be bothered. A notepad sat in his lap, a pen between his fingers, but he made no move to write anything. Just sat there in silence, pretending I wasn't next to him.

"My name is Rylee Anderson. What's yours?" I asked with a shaky voice.

His hand moved, and the next thing I knew, he held up the notebook, still refusing to look at me. On the blank page, in black ink, written in chicken scratch was the word, *Killian*. At first, all I saw was "kill" and my breathing almost stopped. But then I read it to myself a few times and realized it was his name.

He had answered me.

"Killian," I said out loud, almost a whisper. It rolled off my tongue like a foreign language, one I'd never spoken before, yet it came out so effortlessly. "That's a really cool name. How old are you?" Again, he scribbled something on the paper, his face still hidden from sight. When he held the notebook back up, I realized he had answered me again. "Eleven? You're only a year older than me." Excitement took hold of my chest, knowing there was a kid around my age nearby. "What grade are you in?"

That time, he didn't bother writing anything down, and instead, shrugged his slouched shoulders.

"You don't know? Do you go to school?"

Tutor.

"Oh. That's cool. I wish I had a tutor. I don't like going to school." Silence fell upon us, which prompted me to ask another question. It didn't take long to understand he wasn't a conversationalist, but it seemed he had no problems answering when asked something. "Do you live around here?"

He grew so still I wondered if he'd stopped breathing. But then he glanced over his shoulder, away from me, and pointed through the trees. I studied the line of the fence, thinking about which direction I'd gone. When I realized he had pointed in the vicinity of my house, I took a guess and assumed he'd meant my neighbor's house, the woman who always had people over.

"Ms. Newberry's house?"

He nodded and went back to staring at his notepad.

"Are you just visiting?"

His hair swayed as he shook his head.

"You're living with her? Is she a relative?" I didn't recall her having any children, and if she did, they had never come over before, let alone ever lived with her. I knew for a fact I'd never seen Killian over there before.

He nodded, but didn't offer any other explanation.

I paused, wondering if I'd overstepped by following him out here. He wasn't speaking to me, and it seemed he didn't want to look my way. But I wasn't a sensitive person afraid of meeting new people. Sometimes I ended up making friends. Other times, they wanted nothing to do with me and I'd move on to someone else. I wasn't about to give up on Killian until he told me to leave.

"Are you shy? Or do you just not like to talk?"

Can't.

I stared at his messy writing, studied the way he crossed his T, the line long and drawn out. When he pulled his notebook back into his lap, it broke the spell and brought me back to his answer. "You can't talk? Do you know sign language?"

I stared at the paper, willing him to answer me, but instead of writing anything, he turned his head toward me. I glanced up, mesmerized by his eyes once again. They shone like a beacon of light, the pale green mixed with just a hint of blue. I started to smile at the sight, but as soon as I began to take in the rest of his features, wanting to memorize them all, I gasped and covered my open mouth with the tips of my fingers.

He immediately turned away and closed in on himself once more.

Go away.

8

"I'm sorry. I didn't mean to do that. Please, look at me again."

No.

I made no move to leave. Instead, I shifted in the dirt beneath my butt and leaned closer to him. I opened my mouth to say something but was stopped just shy of getting my first word out. His hand moved fast, the pen scratching furiously against the paper.

Do I scare you?

"No," I whispered, telling the absolute truth. I may have overreacted, but he didn't scare me. "I was surprised. I'm sorry. I didn't mean to do that."

Slowly, he lifted his face, his eyes meeting mine. I carefully scanned his features, taking in his straight and narrow nose, his nostrils prominent only when they flared. His top lip was thin with a deep V in the middle, the bottom plumper and glossy from where it appeared he'd licked it before turning to face me.

I'd never seen a boy so *pretty* before.

What had caused me to gasp before were the scars on his cheeks. They started at the corners of his mouth and extended toward his jaw about two inches on either side, creating the illusion of a smile.

My fingers reached up, almost on their own accord, until his hand wrapped around my wrist and pulled it away. His eyes flickered between mine, and then briefly dropped to my mouth before looking away. However, he didn't let go of my wrist. He looped my arm beneath his, where he held my hand in his lap, on top of his notebook.

"Is that why you can't talk?" My voice came out hoarse, sounding like I'd somehow caught a cold in the last ten seconds. When he nodded, I felt the need to ask another question, to prod him for another answer. "When did that happen?"

When I was 8.

I moved closer to his side so I could see his answer, written next to where my hand rested. When I shifted, his body hardened, tensed, but I didn't let it stop me. "What happened?" It didn't look to me like an accident, but I couldn't imagine what might've caused scars like that.

My focus remained on the piece of paper, even though he made no move to write anything. As soon as I glanced up to look at him, he began to move the pen. But it wasn't to write in his notebook. Instead, tingles broke out on the skin on the back of my hand. When I peered over his arm to see what it was, I noticed he'd started to draw something on me.

I leaned my head against his shoulder to watch. He stilled for a moment, but when I didn't move, he continued. Line after line, stroke after stroke, he created a vivid flower in black ink, starting at the webbing between my thumb and forefinger.

Our conversation was apparently over.

TWO

Killian

I COULDN'T GET HER out of my mind.

I saw her face, whether my eyes were opened or closed.

Those big brown eyes that sloped just so at the corners. The color reminded me of my mom's clay pot she kept by the front door, full of red flowers that spilled from the top. Her eyebrows had this natural arch to them, which reminded me of the wings of a soaring bird. She had a dip in the center of the ball of her nose. I imagined a dozen times what it might feel like to touch it with my finger. And those lips…full and naturally pink, as if she wore lipstick that never rubbed off. I wanted to know what they'd feel like pressed against mine.

But that'd never happen.

She may have looked at me like she would anyone else, but I'd never be able to forget the way she gasped when she saw my face. When she saw the scars left behind as a reminder of the worst night of my life. No matter what she said, I knew they terrified her.

They terrified *me*.

But that didn't stop me from thinking of her, wanting to see her again.

The night after she found me in the woods, she came back. It was dark, with only the light of the moon peeking between the leaves. Elise had invited more people over, and I didn't want to be around any of them. They were nice, but I couldn't take the way they'd gawk at me. Not to mention, I didn't care to be locked in my room, listening to the laughs, the murmurs, the music through the door.

It was all too much.

So I'd decided to hop the fence and find some peace.

Minutes later, peace had found me, in the form of an angel.

She'd whisper-shouted my name. And I was done for. Not thinking of how she would react, I'd snuck up behind her and covered her mouth with my hand, only wanting to feel her lips just once. But then her body shook in fear, a whimper had escaped, and when I spun her around, I couldn't take my eyes off the few tears falling down her face. But then her gaze met mine, and without a second's thought, I took her hand and pulled her behind me until I found the clearing in the trees.

For at least an hour, we sat beneath the moon…in silence. She didn't bother to ask me anything—probably knowing I had no way to answer her without my notepad—and instead, rested her head against my shoulder while I doodled on her palm. The only thing I had on me was a thin red marker, and I used the moon to see the lines I drew. Eventually, her breathing evened out, and I realized she had fallen asleep.

I wanted to stay there forever.

To freeze time and never let her go.

If I could've, I would've stolen the moon from the sky.

Held it hostage.

And kept her with me.

But that wasn't a possibility. I had to give her up. She didn't belong to me, no matter how badly I'd wished for it. And the thought of her getting into trouble because she'd followed me didn't settle well. So I woke her and helped her back to her house. It wasn't until we'd made it to her back yard, to her window with the screen resting against the wall, before I realized she'd actually snuck out.

To see me.

She'd held her finger to her lips, and again, I wondered what her lips would feel like against *my* finger. Against my mouth. Against my tongue. But I had to ignore it when she pointed to the corner of the roof, just at the edge of the house. She whispered, "Motion detector light. You have to stay along the fence; otherwise, it'll go off, and my dad will see it."

Then I helped her back inside and adjusted the window screen in place, taking one final look through the glass at her shadow before heading back home. Since then, I'd done nothing but think of her, conjuring her image in my mind. Memorizing every detail, every flaw, every line.

"Killian!" Elise called out, interrupting my thoughts of Rylee. "You have a visitor!"

I threw my notebook onto the bed next to me and jumped to my feet.

Just then, the door opened slowly, time practically standing still. I never had anyone over; no one knew I lived here. My heart pumped so hard it reverberated in my ears as dark, curly hair came into view. Each curl wound tight like a spring I wanted to pull and watch it snap back into place. Even in the dim light of my room, it was shiny and looked smooth. And for the hundredth time, I pondered what it'd feel like to run my fingers through it while staring into her eyes.

"Are you thirsty? Can I get either of you anything?" Elise came up behind Rylee, but watched me, probably wondering why she was here to begin with.

"No, thank you, Ms. Newberry." Her voice was so sweet, so soft. I could've listened to her chat with Elise for hours about nothing. It was the only reason I bothered to answer her questions, when I never cared to answer anyone else.

Because I never wanted Rylee to stop talking.

"Okay, then I'll let you two...visit." Elise's eyes met mine, and I couldn't ignore the glimmer of bright hope. "If you need anything, I'll just be out here. Don't hesitate to ask." And then she walked away, leaving us alone, wrapped in silence.

Rylee stared at me for a moment before her lips turned up into the smallest hint of a grin. She had brief moments of uncertainty, but they were always quickly swallowed up by utter confidence. It was an amazing sight to behold—the inner workings of her psyche through her eyes. The way they squinted just the tiniest bit before flaring an almost golden color.

"Do you mind if I come in?" Her question broke my spell and forced me back a step until I ran into the bed.

I shook my head, and then nodded, unsure of how to answer. I vividly recalled my father correcting me several times, informing me how to properly respond to a "do you mind" type of question. But Rylee didn't seem to notice and stepped into my room, although she left the door open. For whatever reason, the idea of Elise being able to listen to us made me uneasy, so I moved around her and closed it softly.

A gasp behind me caught my attention. When I whipped around, I found her holding my notebook in one hand, the fingers of the other splayed over her parted lips. Her round eyes met mine and locked on me. I couldn't move, completely frozen in time, while my mouth opened and closed as if I had a verbal answer for her.

Finally snapping out of my daze, I snatched the pad away from her.

"You did that?" Her whispered words, filled with awe, surrounded me.

I held the book to my chest to keep her from seeing it again and turned to face her. It was like this unbearable need to see her eyes, watch her expression, understand her thoughts through her body language. What I didn't expect to find was the absolute wonderment—possibly admiration—I saw reflecting back at me.

I nodded slowly while the weight of fear settled into my chest.

"That's…unbelievable. May I see it again?"

Holding my breath, I slowly held it out for her to take, never breaking eye contact. I desperately wanted her approval, unlike I'd ever wanted it from anyone before, but I couldn't fight off the immense trepidation of her rejection.

Of how obsessed it'd make me seem.

How I'd just given myself away in more ways than one.

She sat on the edge of the mattress and held the pad in her lap, studying it with a careful eye. Her fingertips traced each line of my pen. The likeness I'd created of her jaw. Her chin. Around her lips, the bridge of her nose. Her eyes. Finally, once she'd followed along every contour, her finger stilled on the faint scar I'd added to her forehead—the one I'd noticed that night beneath the moon—and focused her sights on me.

"You drew me?"

I sat next to her and hung my head, offering her the slightest nod.

"Why?"

I balled my hands into fists in the space between my parted legs. I knew she'd ask that. It was the one question I could count on, and the one I prayed wouldn't pass her lips. Suddenly, the pad of paper slid into view and I took it from her. I found the pen I'd tossed to the side when she'd come in, and I picked it up, ready to give her an answer.

Why not? I wrote on a blank piece of lined paper.

"I don't know. I just don't know why you'd choose *me*." Her original question became clear. She hadn't meant to ask me why I drew it, which was good because I couldn't give her that answer. Now, knowing the true intention of her curiosity, I put the pen to the paper and began to scribble as fast as I could.

I see things and I have to draw them to get them out of my head.

"What kinds of things?"

Just things. Things that catch my eye.

As soon as she finished reading, I felt the need to add more. To explain further.

They're like photographs in my head.

She giggled and I immediately went rigid. I wanted to look at her, to ask her what she found so funny, but I couldn't lift my focus from the paper in front of me. My words stared back at me and I wanted to erase them all.

"You draw so beautifully. You seriously have such amazing talent...but your handwriting is awful." She giggled again, and had to cover her mouth with her hand to hold back the sound, which now was nothing more than a melodic hum. "I'm sorry. I just can't believe someone who writes so messy can draw something so..." She calmed and grew quiet for a moment, and then murmured, "So perfect."

I turned and met her gaze. The golden flecks trapped me inside their warmth and refused to let go. They were like rays of the sun reflecting off treasure at the end of a rainbow. Her eyebrows pulled together in concentration, which ended my worship of her.

"Are you okay?" Her breath filled each word and brushed them across my face.

I nodded, narrowing my gaze to silently question her.

"You just seem so...angry? Frustrated? I don't know how to describe it."

Refocusing on the paper, I gripped my pen and let my fingers do the talking.

I'm not used to talking to people. I don't have any friends.

"Why not?"

I shrugged, but decided to answer anyway.

I've moved around a lot, and not many people want to be friends with someone who looks like me. I scare everyone away. It's why I'm homeschooled. Well, that and because I'm behind.

"You don't scare me away." The way she leaned over to read as I wrote caused her words to cascade over my face like a gentle breeze. It made me turn to look at her, to catch her eyes as she spoke. "You said Ms. Newberry is a relative. How are you related to her?"

Aunt.

"Oh...so is your last name the same as hers?"

I shook my head. *Foster.*

"Killian Foster..." she whispered with a smile. "What's your middle name?"

Owen. I paused, and then decided to give her more. *Family name.*

"I like it. Sounds strong...I mean, it's a powerful name. You're going to be somebody one day, Killian Owen Foster. Mark my words. People will know your name." Her round eyes brightened impossibly more, and I so badly wanted to believe her.

But the truth was people already knew my name.

And not for anything good.

What's your middle name? I suddenly had a profound need to know.

"Scott. I know, it's a boy's name, but it was my mom's maiden name. She thought I was a boy, so I was going to be Scott Anderson. Then I came out a girl." She giggled, and I wanted to bottle up the sound to keep forever. "So...they mixed up their names—my mom is Holly and my dad is Ryan—and made my middle name Scott."

I stared at her, wishing more than anything I could say her full name out loud like she had with mine. I wanted to feel it pass between my lips, reverberate through my vocal chords, taste it on my tongue. But I couldn't.

She grew quiet with a weak smile. "It's a stupid story."

I couldn't take my eyes off hers, as if I were locked in a trance—a reverie woven by golden threads, filled with hopes and dreams I had no right to chase after. I so badly wanted to shake my head, to tell her she was wrong. It wasn't a stupid story. But I couldn't manage to do anything other than stare at her until she turned away, more than likely feeling uneasy.

"So do you like…live here? With your aunt?" She paused when I nodded. Apparently, my lack of further response spurred her to press on. "Where's your family? Your mom or dad? Are they here, too?"

I could only shake my head, unable to write anything down.

I wanted to hold onto her friendship for a little while longer.

"Oh. Your aunt seems really young to take care of you."

My gaze fell away as I thought about Elise and how much I'd disrupted her life. I didn't want to be such a burden, which was why I tried to stay in my room as much as I could. She loved me. I knew she did. But Rylee was right; Elise was far too young to care for someone my age, not to mention, someone dealing with my issues.

I wrote out the number twenty-six and let that sink in for a minute before offering her more. *She's my mom's sister. No one else could handle me, so she took me in. I'm pretty sure I make her sad.*

"Why?"

Tears lined my eyes and I had to swallow down the lump in my throat.

Because I remind her of my mom.

Thankfully, she didn't press for anything else. Rather than ask more questions, she suggested we watch a movie, and I couldn't have been happier. Elise came to check on us, and when she saw us sitting on the bed with our backs against the headboard, shoulder to shoulder, she simply smiled and closed the door behind her.

Content.

It was the first time in three years I'd felt it.

And I never wanted to let it go.

THREE

Rylee

"HEY, Daddy?" I sat at the kitchen table while my dad drank his coffee and read the newspaper before work. My cereal was now soggy, considering how long I'd sat there, finding the courage to ask him a question. I wasn't sure how he'd take it, but I needed the answer. "Why would someone have scars on their face in the shape of a smile?"

He lowered the paper and leaned forward, propping his elbows on the table. "I'm not sure, pumpkin. There are probably lots of reasons. Any half circle could look like a smile. Why?"

"No...I don't mean like that. I mean like if someone gets hurt—by someone else...maybe on purpose—and their mouth look like they're smiling." I used my fingers to draw invisible lines from the corners of my mouth up to my cheeks.

His eyes grew wide, then they narrowed a split second before his brows dipped with concern. "Why would you ask about that? Did you see someone like that?"

I shrugged and then offered, "On TV."

My answer must've settled his nerves because he blew out a long breath and relaxed in his seat. "Oh, honey...that's something bad people do. But not here. It's a European thing, I believe. I think it's called a Chelsea Smile, because it started a long time ago in Chelsea. You don't have to worry about that happening, sweetheart."

I wished his words could've soothed me, but they didn't. Because he was wrong. It did happen here. To Killian. Or...maybe he wasn't from here. That was a possibility. Since

I'd never heard him talk, I would never know. But it was definitely something I wanted to find out.

I finished my cereal while repeating the term in my head so I wouldn't forget. As soon as he checked his watch, I knew it was time for him to leave, and then I'd be able to use the computer and get the information I needed. He kissed the top of my head and repeated the same rules just as he did every morning: don't leave the house, don't answer the door, and don't tell strangers I'm home alone. I knew he hated leaving me without the supervision of my brother, but really…anytime Jason was home, he never paid any attention to me. Either way, I was completely unsupervised.

I waited until he backed the car out of the driveway before turning on the computer in the dining room. I had limited knowledge of the Internet, but I knew enough to understand the concept of Google—thanks to Mrs. Beatty and her constant research assignments last year.

In the search box, I typed "Chelsea smile." I had a friend at school with the same name so I knew how to spell it. However, what popped up on the screen was nothing like the girl with red hair and glasses. My stomach turned as I scrolled through each page, taking it all in, along with the pictures it provided.

I couldn't imagine Killian going through that.

And then I remembered him telling me it'd happened when he was eight.

Sympathetic tears fell into my lap.

In a hurry, I changed my clothes and headed next door. It was early, and I hadn't expected anyone to be up, so I knocked on what I assumed to be his bedroom window. I had to take a guess since I'd only been in the house once. But I remembered he had blue curtains.

It took me rapping on the window three times before the curtain pulled away, revealing a tired boy behind the glass. He rubbed his eyes and squinted against the sunlight, but as soon as he recognized me, a grin tugged on his lips. He held up one finger and then vanished again.

I stood against the back of his house, waiting for him to…do something. I wasn't sure if he'd come back to the window or not. It wasn't until I heard footsteps in the grass that I realized he'd come outside, and then he came around the corner. His long legs peeked out of the bottom of frayed cargo shorts, his plain white T-shirt wrinkled as if he'd grabbed it off the floor. His hair was all over the place, and I so badly wanted to tuck the wild strands behind his ears so I could see his face better. The notebook in his hand, tucked against the side of his body, made me smile.

He was going to talk to me.

Before I could open my mouth to say anything, he jerked his head to the side, gesturing to the fence along the back yard. Without a moment's hesitation, he led me to the woods. We didn't venture out very far this time before he sat in a small clearing with enough room for me.

"I looked your scars up online this morning," I blurted out.

His posture stiffened. Not even his shoulders or back moved with the exertion of breathing. I wished he would've looked at me so I could at least get an idea of how he felt, but he refused, keeping his attention on the dirt in front of him.

"I'm sorry. I know I shouldn't have." I sighed and dropped my head into my open palms. "I wish I hadn't seen that. I hate knowing what happened to you…without *actually* knowing. You don't even want to know the things I've thought of over the last thirty minutes. It's horrifying."

His hand moved frantically. *I think I can imagine.*

"Oh gosh, I didn't mean that. I'm so sorry."

Stop apologizing.

As he wrote—*talked to me*—he never once met my eyes.

"I just wanted to know what happened to you."

Someone broke into my house.

A gasp rang out before I could stop it. The words "I'm sorry" sat at the tip of my tongue, but thankfully, I managed to swallow them. "D–do you know who?"

With his gaze fixated on the paper in front of him, he shook his head.

"And your parents…?" I couldn't even finish my question. "That's so bad, Killian."

I don't want to talk about it.

I didn't blame him. I only wished my curiosity would die, because I didn't think I'd ever be able to fully let it go. And other than hearing it from him, I knew there was no way I'd get the real story.

"Is that why you can't talk?"

He nodded, but didn't write anything down.

"Does it hurt?"

Not anymore.

My breathing became labored while I sat next to him, suffocating in the silence between us. I understood his inability to speak—not that I'd ever encountered anyone like that before, but I understood it—however, it didn't get any better.

I touched his arm, making him jump where he sat. "Just know, Killian, that if you ever want to talk to anyone, I'm here. My friends say I'm a good listener. They share all their secrets with me because I never tell anyone."

Slowly, he faced me. A sheen of tears lined the faint green of his eyes, making them sparkle like murky pool water in that stage just before it needs to be shocked with chemicals.

"Can you draw something for me?" I whispered, unable to take his intense stare for another second. It consumed me and filled me with things I didn't understand. My heart raced and my head grew fuzzy, like a balloon without a string. Full of static electricity and air.

Instead of using the paper he'd brought with him, Killian took my hand again. I didn't fight him. I loved it when he drew on me. I never wanted to wash it off. This time, instead of flowers, he drew vines around my wrist up to my fingers, wrapping them around onto my palm.

I could've spent all day like that—my hand in his, resting on his lap, his pen creating beautiful lines on my skin—but it wasn't long before his aunt called for him. With an apologetic grin, he stood and helped me back over the fence.

• • •

THE HOUSE WAS DARK and quiet, but I couldn't sleep. My mind wouldn't shut down long enough to allow me to drift off into the daydreams I'd had all day. My hand still tingled with the remembrance of his pen, the black ink now faded, but the memory still vivid.

Sharp, quick knocks on my bedroom window startled me, forcing me to sit up straight in bed and flick my gaze toward the direction of the racket. The blinds were closed, so I couldn't technically see anything, but I waited to hear it again. After a few seconds, another set of raps resounded. For reasons unknown to me, I climbed out of bed and slowly moved the few feet to the window.

Peering through a small opening in the slats, I found a large shadow standing on the other side. It frightened me, but as my sight adjusted and settled on the outline, I realized it was Killian. I glanced down at my matching pajama set and tried my best to smooth down my unmanageable hair before pulling on the blinds, then opening the window.

"What are you doing here?" I wondered if he wanted me to sneak out. The thought crossed my mind, but all I could think about was how I'd have to change my clothes and put on shoes.

He held up a folded piece of paper. Then proceeded to slide it through a small tear in the side of the screen. Once I had it in my hand, he turned to walk away. My heart clenched and pounded simultaneously. I didn't want him to leave. I wanted to pop the screen out and run into the woods with him, sit beneath the stars and let him soothe me with his pen.

"Wait. Where are you going?"

Killian glanced over his shoulder, turned sideways, and pointed at the paper in my hand. I couldn't really see his face in the dark, so his expression was blank to me. His finger shook, as if prodding me to open it, and then he was gone. Over the fence and back to his aunt's house.

Stunned, I watched him leave in silence. I didn't move— not to close the window, lower the blinds, or even open the letter. I stared at the wooden barrier between us for far too long before snapping out of it. That's when curiosity got the best of me and I flew into action.

I switched on the lamp on my side table and sat on the edge of my unmade bed, the comforter bunched around my legs, and proceeded to open his letter. The paper was filled with his chicken scratch scrawled in black ink. Some words were crossed out, others were misspelled, but I was able to read through it all.

When I was 8, someone broke into my house. Three people to be exact. I was awake when it happened, but I wasn't sure what was going on. I thought maybe something had happened to my dad, so I went to their room. It was 11:29. I stood there and stared at my parents. I didn't scream. I wanted to scream, but I couldn't. Nothing came out. I wanted to run from the three men in their room, but I couldn't do that, either. My parents didn't look like my parents. They looked like they were wearing masks. My mom looked like she had a red scarf around her neck, and her eyes were wide open. She just laid there and stared at the ceiling. My dad was on the floor. Before I went to bed that night, I remember he had on his favorite shirt. It was white with the mascot on the front for the high school where he taught. A big tiger. At first, I thought he changed into a red shirt, but the more I stared at him, I noticed the picture of the tiger on the front. I didn't know he had the same shirt in red. He stared at me while opening and closing his mouth, like he wanted to tell me something. But I couldn't hear anything. I wanted to go to him to see what he tried to say, but I couldn't move. I couldn't even ask him if he was okay.

I was ten years old. My life had been rather sheltered, considering I was the baby and only girl. But there were some things I did understand. And death was one of them. Sometimes, when Mom and Dad were gone and left me at home with Jason, he'd watch scary movies in the living room. I'd see them from the kitchen when I ate. I tried to pretend like they didn't bother me, but they did. They'd make me scared for at least two days. And my grandma died a year ago. I went to her funeral and saw her in the casket. But she didn't look like the people in my brother's movies. She looked peaceful, as if she was asleep.

Reading Killian's words about his parents terrified me. They made me think about the horrible scenes on the TV, the blood, the screams. Not at all like Grandma. I didn't want to keep reading for fear it'd get worse, but then I remembered I'd asked him what had happened. He'd told me he didn't want to talk about it. Now, he'd given me his story. I couldn't stop, no matter how badly I wanted to.

I saw the men in the room when I first walked in. They were what made me stop as soon as I stepped through the doorway. But as soon as I saw them, I found my parents, and it was like the guys just disappeared. My dad made this really weird noise through his mouth.

Not quite a wheezing sound...but more like a long sigh when you're sick and have to cough. He no longer looked at me, but he didn't close his eyes, either. That's when I looked at the men. They all stood completely still and stared at me. I wondered if it was a bad dream. Mom and Dad were watching a bad movie before they went to bed, and I thought maybe it was a nightmare. No one moved, or spoke, or blinked. They all either lied there or stood in the room, staring at me. Mom stared at the ceiling, Dad stared at my feet, and the men stared at me.

They were wearing black clothes. All of them. Baggy jeans and black T-shirts that looked like they belonged to their dads. I know sometimes I wore my dad's shirts and they were really big on me, and that's what theirs looked like. One of the guys had a dog collar around his neck with pointy things on it. The one near my mom's side of the bed had red on his face, like her blood had splattered on him or something.

They started talking to each other, but I didn't understand most of it. I remember one of them calling me a boy and starting to freak out. He was arguing with one of the other guys. Something was said about my eyes, and cutting them out so I wouldn't see anything. But the one guy kept calling me a boy. Then the one who was by my mom came after me. I turned to run away once I saw the knife in his hand, but he caught me by the arm and threw me to the ground. He sat on my stomach and held me down.

I tried to scream, to move, to get away, but I couldn't. I panicked and started to cry. I begged him to let me wake up. Nothing worked. He held me by my face and told me I was to never say a word to anyone, and if I did, he'd do to me what he did to my mom. He said Mom would never talk again because she didn't have any vocal chords. He told me I was better off without my parents, and then started saying a lot of bad words I wasn't allowed to say. He made me promise I'd never tell anyone what I saw. And I did. I promised him. But that wasn't enough.

The knife cut into the sides of my face and I felt something warm run down my cheeks to the back of my neck. It hurt so bad. But nothing was as bad as when he pulled himself off me and kicked me in the stomach. I curled into a ball and screamed. My mouth opened wide, and my cheeks hurt so bad. They burned and I thought they were on fire. The pain was so bad I couldn't scream anymore. No sounds came out. The man closed my mouth and said "That's right. Never speak to anyone. Or I will silence you forever."

Everything after that is a blur. I've never felt so much pain before in my life. I think I found a phone and called for help, but I don't really remember. I just remember hearing someone asking me questions I couldn't answer. Because I couldn't speak. Policemen came in with guns. Then ambulance guys dressed in blue carrying a bed on wheels. The sheets were white before they lifted me onto it, but they turned red. I was in a hospital for a while. A lot of people tried to get me to talk, but I never did.

I went to live with my dad's brother, but that didn't last long because I scared my little cousins. Then I went to stay with my grandparents, but they were old. My grandmother, MeeMaw, cried when I left. She kept saying she was sorry she couldn't help me. I had to go to a lot of offices and sit with people while they tried to get me to talk, but I never did. Those guys told me I couldn't. So I haven't said anything. Not once. I went to stay with a few people I didn't know, but even they said they couldn't help me. That's when Elise stepped in. She said she was tired of seeing me bounce between houses, and she would do her best with me. She's never tried to make me talk or shove pills down my throat. I hate pills. They make me feel weird. I'm trying my best to be good for her because I don't want to leave.

You asked me what happened. That's the most I can tell you. I probably shouldn't have even told you that much, but I wanted you to have answers. I don't know why. I've never cared before about answering anyone. Not the doctors or the policemen or even the strangers I lived with. But for some reason, Rylee, I wanted you to know.

The paper fell into my lap and I stared at the wall across the room for what seemed like forever. Tears rolled down my cheeks as I thought about the horrific things Killian had lived through. Although his parents hadn't survived, I was thankful and happy Killian had lived. But I couldn't imagine the things he saw in his head. He said he saw pictures, and part of me wanted to know if some of those were from that night, but I didn't think I could ever ask him.

I ended up staying up all night. I couldn't sleep after reading his story.

My heart ached for him.
I cried for him.
But I didn't know what to do.

FOUR

Killian

I'D SCARED her away.

I knew it.

It'd been a week since I told her my story. I'd given it to her and then left, because I couldn't stand the thought of her looking at me as she read it. But now, I questioned if that was the right thing. Because I haven't seen her. Not once. I'd climbed the fence a few times, hoping she'd see me and follow me into the woods, but she never did. I saw her bike in her front yard so I knew she was home. I'd seen her blanket and book in the back yard beneath the tree she liked to read under. And at night, I'd peek through the slats of wood and see her bedroom light on.

But she never came for me.

I thought she was different.

Apparently not.

School was about to start in a few days. It was the first time with this tutor, and I grew restless the closer it got. I didn't like meeting new people. They stared and made me uncomfortable. That's why I hated it when Elise had people over.

I became agitated and anxious. Panicky. More withdrawn than normal. I spent more time in the woods than I had in the last few weeks, and I often debated about leaving altogether. Sometimes, I'd sit beneath the trees, drawing in my notepad, and wonder what it'd be like to never go back. To just run away. Be on my own where I didn't have to depend on others. But I knew that wouldn't happen for a while. I wouldn't get my inheritance until I turned eighteen.

Seven more years.

And then I'd be gone.

No one cared anyway.

The only ones who did were gone.

Night had fallen and I knew I needed to get back. I'd been out for a while. I'd eaten my dinner alone in my room, then headed into the protection of the trees. When I drew, I lost track of time, but I knew it was late. When I made it to the fence, I could tell by how dark all the houses were that it was more than likely past ten or eleven. But I wasn't sure.

At the top of the fence, I glanced over to Rylee's house. Her bedroom was dark and I wondered if she was asleep. I just needed to check on her. I don't know why I landed in her back yard or crept in the shadows until I made it to her window, but I did. Something pulled me to her, despite her withdrawal from me.

I only planned to peer into her room to make sure she was okay.

I didn't plan to knock.

Or help her get the screen off.

Or climb in.

I certainly didn't plan to crawl into her bed.

And lay next to her in the dark.

But I did.

"I'm sorry I haven't come to see you since you gave me your letter," she whispered with her face so close to mine. Her warmth flowed over my lips and made them dry. So dry I had to lick them. "My mom came home from work. She's an airline attendant. Sometimes she's gone for a few days, but last time she was gone for a week."

I didn't move, and could barely see her, but I remained still and watched her as best as I could in the dark room. I never wanted her to stop talking. I didn't care what she said, as long as she spoke to me in that whispered breath that fanned across my face and calmed me. I had no way of speaking to her, so I prayed she'd just keep talking.

"My brother, Jason, is sixteen. He has a lot of friends. So he doesn't like to stay home with me when my parents are gone. My dad hates it when I'm home alone. He's a car salesman, which means he works all day. When my mom is home from work, she tends to baby me a lot. So I haven't been able to sneak away."

I hated how that made me feel. Hearing her admit she had to sneak around to see me cut me deep. Like she was ashamed of me. Like she didn't want anyone to know about me. Just like everyone else. It hurt. Because I thought she was different, and once again, I was proven wrong.

"I was kind of their oops baby. Jason says I was an accident, but Mom says I was just a surprise. Sometimes I think she forgets I'm ten and not five. She doesn't let me leave the house without knowing where I am, and she doesn't like me hanging out with boys. There used to be a boy who lived down the street. He was my age. But Mom wouldn't let me go to his house. I don't know why. She just said he wasn't a good kid. So I didn't want to chance her telling me I couldn't see you. Because I don't want to stop seeing you."

That deep ache flourished into burning excitement.

Approval.

"School starts in a few days. I don't want to go. I was looking forward to it because I'll be in fifth grade. I'll finally be one of the older kids. But now I don't want the summer to end. I know I'll see you even less, and I don't want that."

I grabbed her hand and held it beneath the covers between us. I'd never been in a bed with a girl before, but I liked it. I liked being next to her. It erased the pictures in my head and calmed the anxiety running through me. It lessened the anger I sometimes felt when I thought about the night I lost my parents. Being with her just gave me…happiness. Peace.

"My parents go to sleep around ten. My bedtime is nine, but I can stay awake for you if you want to come over. We'd have to keep the lights off, so you wouldn't be able to talk to me, but we can just lay here together. Or I can talk and you can listen."

I squeezed her hand to offer a silent response, letting her know I was okay with that.

"When I looked on the computer about your scars, it said something about it being Scottish or Irish. It's called a Chelsea smile. Other websites called it a Glasgow smile. Are you from there? From Scotland or Ireland? I've wondered if you'd have an accent like they do."

I shook my head against the pillow.

"So you're an American?"

I nodded.

"Are you from Tennessee?"

I shook my head again, wishing I could've given her better answers.

She hummed for a second, and then asked, "More north?" When I nodded, I could sense her smile. This had just turned into a game for her. And I had to admit I began to enjoy it as much as she did.

After a few rounds of yes or no questions, she finally guessed Pennsylvania. That's when the game ended because there was no way she'd guess the town I'd lived in with my parents. Not to mention, I never would've told her the truth. I'd already given her more information about the guys who'd broken into my house than I had told anyone else, and I didn't want to risk her playing detective.

I *couldn't* risk it.

For me—or for her.

Our conversation began to slow, her voice becoming softer. Her words were more spaced out and I could tell she was falling asleep, so I ran my fingertips over the back of her hand until she stopped talking completely. Until her breaths deepened and evened out. I didn't want to go. I had no desire to crawl back out her window and leave her alone. But I knew I had to.

I gave myself a little while longer to watch her sleep. Listen to her soft snores. And then I carefully pulled myself from her bed, her warmth, the friendship she offered. The friendship I wasn't sure I deserved.

The friendship I refused to give up.

By the time I slipped inside through the back door, it had to have been past midnight. Most of the lights were off; the only one left on was the one in the kitchen over the sink. I didn't pay attention to it and made a move to head back to my room, but something stopped me.

Someone.

"Killian." Her soft, broken whisper froze me in place. It sounded so much like Mom—except sad. I'd heard Mom sad before, but it wasn't often. Most of the time, she was happy, always laughing. But this voice—the one so much like hers—made it feel like a bomb exploded in my chest.

I turned toward the kitchen and found Elise leaning against the counter. Her expression was horrifying, like she'd been crying...or on the verge of tears. I hated the way it made me feel. It reminded me of the one person I'd never get back. Elise and my mom only shared one parent, so most of the time, they looked nothing alike.

Except now.

They were spitting images of each other.

"Where have you been?"

I glanced down at the notebook in my hand and then held it up.

"You can't just sneak off like that without telling me where you're going. I've been worried sick all night. I thought you were in your room, but when I checked, it was empty. You can't do that."

I couldn't look at her, so I averted my gaze to the countertop between us.

"I don't know what I'm doing here with you. I have no idea how to raise a kid, let alone an eleven-year-old. I'm trying my best but..." She blew out a long sigh, and even though we stood across the counter from each other, I could feel it hit me with the strength of storm winds.

When I glanced up, my eyes met her glossy ones. And my heart sank. This was it. This was where she would tell me she couldn't handle me. Elise was my last hope—the last family member I had who hadn't already given up. And here she was, throwing in the towel.

I took the pen out of my pocket and flipped the page in my notepad.

Are you going to give me back?

Her whimper filled the room, but I couldn't look at her. I didn't want to see the truth in her eyes. The pain. The pity. It'd be worse than the words, the confirmation of her abandoning me like everyone else. They all had their reasons, and they were all valid. But that didn't stop it from hurting every time they told me I had to leave. I didn't know what I was doing wrong. I tried to be good. I didn't talk, didn't argue, kept my room clean, and never bothered anyone. But apparently, I wasn't good enough.

Mom thought I was good enough.

No one else did.

Elise stepped around the counter and reached out to touch my face. I didn't like it when people did that, so I turned my head. Her hand fell to the counter and she blew out a sigh once again. She wanted me to look at her while she told me she couldn't handle me, and I wasn't going to give that to her. I underlined my question a few times, angrily pushing the tip of the pen into the paper.

"Give you back? No. God, Killian...no." Her cracked voice, coupled with her shaky hand, led me to believe the question hurt her as much as it did me. But I wasn't ready to believe that yet. "Please look at me. Listen to me."

She waited while I slowly slid my eyesight up to her. We were the same height, so standing next to her, we were eye to eye. Her tears shone against the soft, yellow light in the kitchen. Her bottom lip trembled, the shallow dimples in her taut, quivering chin apparent. They made my breathing halt with anxiety for her next words.

"I'm not sending you anywhere. You're here...for good. This is as new for me as it is for you, but we're going to make the best of it. You hear me? It's me and you, kid. Against the world. I love you. I've loved you since you were a tiny little thing who'd fall asleep every time I held you. Your mama used to say we had a silent bond, you and me, and that's why you'd zonk out minutes after I picked you up. I told her you were a narcoleptic nugget and I was your trigger." She smiled shakily through the tears, and it wasn't long before I felt my own lips curl up. The damaged muscles in my cheeks hardened around the shadow of a grin I displayed.

You don't ever talk about my mom.

She read the note I'd pushed toward her. After wiping away a tear, she met my gaze again. "I'm sorry, Killian...but I'm not used to your tone yet. Are you telling me not to talk about her, or making an observation that I don't?"

I shook my head and began to scribble as fast as I could, needing to get my words out before the misunderstanding caused her more pain. *Observation. Why don't you?*

Her hand covered mine, stilling the pen between my fingers. "I don't know. I guess it's hard to sometimes. Especially with you. It's been three years, and sometimes, I question if I've truly dealt with her loss yet. When it happened, I was twenty-three and starting my own life. I couldn't give up, because I had no one to pick me up if I failed. My daddy is long since gone, and as you know, my mother passed when you were young. Your mama was the only one I had left…and when she was taken from us, I didn't know what to do. I think I suppressed a lot of the grief in order to survive. I know I dealt with some form of depression, because I buried myself in work and friends. That's why I didn't take you sooner. I think I just blocked out the world. And I'm so sorry for that, Killian. I wish I'd been better, *done* better for you and for her."

I'd like to hear about her sometime. I miss her.

A fat tear raced down her cheek, stalled at her trembling chin, and then fell hard to her shirt, where the material soaked it up and left behind a wet spot. It fanned out through the material, and in an instant, my mind had been taken back to the blood soaked into my dad's shirt as he laid on the floor in his room, staring at me.

"I miss her, too." Elise's soft voice drifted into my memories, as if she were there that night, standing next to me, holding my hand while my life fell apart around me. But then her hand moved up my arm, catching my full attention, and the horrific, imagined scene vanished. "I'd be more than happy to talk about her with you. She loved you more than life itself…you know that, right?"

I nodded, wondering why she was so blurry, like I was looking at her through a puddle of water. I turned back to my notebook, and that's when everything cleared. Drops of liquid fell to the paper and distorted the blue lines on the page. My hand was heavy, making lifting the pen difficult. However, I needed to push through. Mom told me I'd grow up one day to be a man, like Dad, and there would be times when things were hard, would seem impossible, but I had to keep going. She said persistence, determination, and hard work separated a man from a boy. At the time, I didn't really know what that meant…but now I do.

I know. I want to make her proud. I don't want her to see me and be upset.

"Oh, Killian. She'd never feel that way about you. You're remarkable. A survivor. I know she's proud of you every second of every day. And I know she's happy we're doing this together. I may mess up. You may mess up. But that doesn't define us. That doesn't mean we've failed. It means we're learning. And we have a whole bunch to learn about one another."

I'm sorry I didn't tell you where I was. I just wanted to be alone.

"I understand, and I'll do my best to give you space, and pull you back in when I think you've had too much. Just please, tell me where you're going next time. I think we can do this as long as we have rules and boundaries. Both of us. You should come up with a list of things for me, too."

I nodded and then wrapped my arms around her when she fell into me.

"I love you, Killian," she whispered into my ear.

I love you, too, Elise, I mouthed into her hair.

FIVE

Rylee

THE BUS SLOWED AS it neared my house. From the window next to my seat, I watched Killian hop over the fence into the woods. I hadn't seen him in several weeks. I'd gone to his house a few times, wondering where he'd been, but I was either met with silence or his aunt gave me some excuse why he couldn't come to the door. I'd knocked on his window, only to be ignored. I'd searched for him in the woods, yet came up with nothing. It didn't make sense.

Over the last year and a half, Killian and I had grown really close. After the night he snuck into my room and laid with me until I fell asleep, it became somewhat of a ritual for us. He'd crawl into my bed, hold my hand, and listen to me tell him stories of school, my friends, and what I was learning. Three or four times a week, he'd leave me letters between the screen and the glass. He never tapped on my window to let me know, so I'd wake up in the morning to his words. Sometimes they were short notes telling me about a dream or something he saw, others were longer, offering me a piece of him through a memory. And then there were his sketches. I had a drawer full of them. The moon, trees, landscape, a building...but most of them were of me. One time, he'd drawn himself—the way he saw it—and I cherished that one the most. It was a boy, a happy kid, without scars, without the heavy grief weighing down his features. He had a smile on his face, a real one, and next to him was the outline of a girl with curly hair. No face, no features, just this presence of someone next to him.

But all that stopped about a month ago. Without warning or cause that I knew of.

As soon as the bus came to a complete stop and the doors opened, I jumped out of my seat and bounded down the steps. I didn't even bother heading to my house to put away my book bag. I ran through his yard, followed his path, and dropped everything in the grass. My breathing had turned ragged and the cold air burned my throat. The sun had warmed the weather enough to tolerate the chill—nothing like the frigid temperature after night fell—but with as fast as my heart pounded in my chest and the anticipation rolling through my veins, I felt overheated beneath my hoodie.

I made it over the top and landed hard on the dirt below. The trees had lost their leaves, leaving the space more open this time of year. It shouldn't have been hard to spot him, although I didn't think he wanted to be found. Ever since he turned thirteen, it was like he wanted nothing to do with me. I thought it might've been because I was still eleven…but I'd be twelve in a few short weeks. He knew that. He didn't have any problem last year during the six weeks he was twelve and I was still ten. But for some reason, now it was an issue. An issue I was determined to squash.

I glanced at my watch, feeling like I'd been searching for him for hours. I had no idea what time I'd gotten off the bus and chased after him, but I knew it was generally around two thirty. If that were the case today, I'd looked for him for fifteen minutes. I decided to go a little farther into the woods, more than normal, desperate to find him. It wouldn't have been too hard to find my way back, but I still worried about getting lost. Mom was gone for two more days, Dad wouldn't be home for hours, and Jason was off at college. So I knew I had time, but it didn't stop the fear of being lost from consuming me.

Finally, I spotted his grey sweater behind a tree trunk. He was crouched down, probably hiding. He wouldn't get away that easily. I snuck up behind him, careful about where I stepped so I wouldn't break a twig beneath my shoes and alert him of my presence. I managed to make it to the other side of the tree unnoticed, but when I peeked around the trunk to see what he was doing, my gasp broke my cover.

He jumped up, turned around, and quickly pulled down the sleeve of his jacket to hide what I'd already seen. I couldn't speak as I stared at his arm, knowing what was behind the material. My mouth hung open, and something I'd never experienced before filled my chest, tightened it, and beat against it all at once. Killian only stared at me with hardened eyes. His nostrils flared, his lips flat and tight.

"Let me see." I reached out for his arm, but he pulled it away from my grasp. "Killian…let me see. Please." When he shook his head, I took a step forward, then another one to match his retreat. Eventually, I stopped and put my hands on my hips, offering him the sass he used to find so funny. "I won't make fun. I promise. Can you please show it to me?"

His chin dropped, his hair falling around his face to hide it. It was still the color of sand, but now it was longer. It reached just past his earlobes and usually curled out. I loved to watch him tuck it behind his ears. I don't know why, but I thought it was cute. My dad said long hair was for girls—and earrings—although there was nothing girly about Killian Foster. He now completely towered over me with much broader shoulders than before. His legs were long, and even though it'd been a while since I'd seen him in shorts, I knew he had curly blond hair from his knees to his ankles, and the muscles beneath it had become defined. I was no stranger to older boys, considering I was in middle school with plenty of kids Killian's age, but he didn't look like any of them. If I didn't know him, I would've assumed he was in high school.

I took a step forward, careful not to scare him off. He seemed so skittish, I wasn't sure what would make him run and what would make him stay. So I kept my hands to myself and stood directly in front of him. "Why don't you want to show me?"

His eyes met mine, but without his notebook and pen in his hand, he couldn't communicate with me. No matter how many times I'd suggested we could learn sign language together, he refused. He kept saying learning it would be pointless. I never understood what he'd meant, and he never gave me an answer.

Slowly, he pulled his sleeve back, just enough to grant me my wish. Black ink stood out on his light forearm, on the soft skin between the crook of his elbow and his wrist. It wasn't his typical handwriting—the chicken scratch most people probably couldn't read. It was neat and fancy, some lines thick and others thin and delicate.

Without thinking, I reached out to trace the *R* with my fingertip. He shivered as soon as I touched his skin, but I refused to let that stop me. I continued to follow the lines until I finished tracing my name. When I met his gaze, I found him watching me with bated breath. His greenish-blue eyes focused solely on me, narrowed and intense, regarding me with caution and maybe a slight hint of curiosity.

"I–I don't understand, Killian. Why are you ignoring me, yet you draw my name on your arm? I've tried to come see you. You've pushed me away. I don't get it. Did I do something wrong? Did your aunt say you can't hang out with me anymore?" Hysteria filled my voice with each scenario I threw out, worried one of them would be right.

Killian shook his head with enough force to cause his hair to whip across his face. He reached up with both hands to tuck the wayward strands behind his ears and bit his lip. His gaze fell to the ground between us while his shoulders lifted just enough to offer me a shrug. However, a split second before I gave up hope for a response, he bent down and grabbed his notebook.

It's not you.

"Then what is it?"

He glanced all around, as if searching for something. His nervousness worried me until he put the pen to the paper again. *I like you.*

I couldn't contain my giddy laughter from erupting. It'd be a lie if I tried to say I hadn't had some sort of crush on him since the day we met. But I was young, and our friendship wasn't what people would consider normal. My parents still didn't even know I knew him. Our meetings were always in private, behind their backs. And the thought of us ever being more frightened me. Because I didn't know how to have a boyfriend, especially one nobody knew about.

"You've been ignoring me because you like me?"

Something's happening with me and I don't know what it is.

"Like what?"

His cheeks flamed and he refused to meet my eyes. But at least he didn't stop writing. *I can't talk to Elise about it, and I don't know who else to talk to. I've tried to look it up, but I don't understand.*

"Maybe I can help. Tell me what it is."

When I'm around you, I feel good. It took him a little longer to write the last word.

"Okay…why is that a bad thing? I feel good around you, too."

He closed his eyes, frustration lining his lips and forehead. After a deep breath, he held his hand over his chest and shook his head, then paused before glancing down his body. I still didn't know what he meant, and was more confused than ever.

"Killian?" I took his hand in mine and forced him to look at me. "You can tell me anything. You know that, right? I won't judge you or make fun. But I need you to write it out, because I don't understand what you're trying to say."

He pulled the notepad in front of his face, preventing me from reading it before he finished. His brows knitted together while he bounced nervously back and forth on his feet. He'd write, pause, scribble something out, and then write again. Wondering what he possibly had to say, and how it could've been a bad thing, caused my heart rate to accelerate. As far as I knew, liking someone and feeling good weren't bad things.

But then he showed me his words, scribbled so atrociously it took a second to read them.

I don't know how to explain it, but something is going on down there. It tingles and feels good. I've never thought anything of it before until it started happening when I'd be around you or think of you. It's messy but I don't know how to stop it from happening. I don't know what's going on. I think something's wrong.

My heart sank to my feet as I read his confession. Sometimes, it was so hard to see him as a sheltered boy when he looked so much older than his age. Then, after fully accepting everything he told me, an indescribable excitement filled me. It was mixed with some fear, a little worry, and with undertones of sheer panic, but overall, the thought of him thinking of me and no one else, made me almost giddy.

"Killian…what you're describing sounds like puberty."

His gaze narrowed even more, confusion deepening his features.

I shook my head and tried to come up with another way to explain it. I thought about how it'd been taught to me through my mom and at school, what some of the kids in class said, and the things I'd read in books.

"Our bodies go through changes at this age. It's hormones or something, and things happen. Boys get erections. Your…" I pointed to the spot between his legs, unsure of what word to use. "…gets hard. That's normal. And when you say it's messy, I think you're saying you're ejaculating. That's how people have sex—that's how babies are made. The man ejaculates and the sperm fertilizes the egg in the woman. And then they have a baby."

By the time I finished, his cheeks were bright red and he couldn't even look at me. He sat down in the dirt with his hands twisted in his lap, his gaze set firmly on the ground. I hadn't meant to make him uncomfortable, but I didn't know how else to explain it so it'd make sense. I felt sad for him. I'm sure this wasn't the way he wanted to learn about the birds and the bees. So I sat down, my feet tucked beneath me, and faced him.

"It's normal, Killian. There's nothing to be embarrassed about. I'm sure this would've been something your parents would've taught you, or maybe you'd learn it at school. I don't know everything about it, only what my mom's told me and what I've heard in health class. But I can tell you about it if you want."

He shook his head, but kept his focus in front of him.

"There are videos online I'm sure you can watch."

Slowly, he took the notebook away from me and began to write again. It pained me to see how hard this was for him. *Does this mean I want to have babies with you?*

I giggled softly, catching his attention. It was clear he didn't appreciate it, although I wasn't making fun of him. "No. I think it's just a normal part of life. I think boys feel that way about a lot of girls. My teacher said sometimes boys can't help it."

Do you know about sex?

"Not much…just what my mom told me when I asked about it. She said I'm supposed to wait until I'm married. That once I give away my virginity, I can't get it back. My teacher said girls have something inside them that makes them a virgin, but boys don't. So I don't think boys can give theirs up, because they can't be virgins like we are."

Have you ever kissed anyone before?

"No. Some of my friends have. But I haven't. Have you?"

No. But sometimes I want to kiss you.

"Sometimes I want to kiss you, too."

Is it bad if we kiss?

"I don't think so." My words were nothing more than a hoarse whisper. My heart thrashed against my ribs and made my chest ache like I'd been hit with something hard. I never thought something could be so scary. I'd seen my parents kiss all the time. It couldn't have been that bad, so I didn't understand why I was so afraid of it.

He nodded and a hint of a smile shadowed the corner of his mouth. *Then maybe someday I'll kiss you. As long as you're not grossed out by what I told you.*

"I'll never be grossed out by anything you do or say, Killian. We're friends, right? We support each other. No matter what. I'll do my best to teach you things, as long as you stop ignoring me."

When he looked at me, his attention steadied on my lips, and it made a tingle spread within me. I'd never wanted someone's mouth on mine so badly before. He didn't say he'd kiss me now, but I couldn't help the desire rolling through me that he would.

I held my arm out to him and pulled back the sleeve of my hoodie. "Can you draw your name on me?"

His eyes lit up, the color turning into what I imagined the ocean would look like. He held my fingers and began to scrawl his name on my wrist in fancy script. *Killian.* I never wanted to wash it off, but I knew I wouldn't be able to let my dad see it. I planned on wearing long sleeves until it vanished, needing some part of him with me.

It'd have to hold me over until my lips met his.

SIX

Killian

I'D TRIED TO STAY away from her, but I couldn't. She was like a magnet I couldn't pull away from. I was drawn to her, always had been. At first, I enjoyed her comfort and company. I liked how she talked to me, even though I'd never spoken a word to her—other than my words on paper. She didn't seem to mind. And not once did she ever judge me.

She accepted me.

All of me.

Rylee truly was my friend. The one person I could go to about anything. I should've known she wouldn't have looked at me differently when I told her about my problem. She'd never seen me any other way than she always did. But I'd been scared. I couldn't tell anyone. I felt ashamed, like something was wrong. Everything I found on the computer made it seem like I had some kind of disease caused by sex. I'd always assumed sex was being in bed with a girl, and I'd been in Rylee's bed. So I thought it was a bad thing.

After she told me what was happening to me, I went home and looked it up—I learned we hadn't had sex. It took more than being in bed with someone for that to happen. I learned a lot about sex that day. I found videos I never knew existed, and even though it seemed wrong to watch them, I couldn't help but play one right after the other.

For a week, anytime I was alone in the house, I searched for more videos. I'd watch until things settled down in my pants, and when I felt the urge again, I'd watch more. Each time, I thought of Rylee. I'd think of her in the shower, before bed, in the middle of the night when I'd wake up hard. Every time I slipped my hands into my boxers and wrapped my fingers around my penis, her face flashed behind my closed eyelids.

One morning, I came out of the shower and found my sheets missing off my bed. Elise was in my room picking up clothes off the floor, and when I stepped through the doorway, her wide eyes rose to mine.

"I was doing laundry and decided to wash some of your clothes. Your sheets looked like they needed to be cleaned." Her voice was unsteady, nervous almost. It made *me* nervous, panicked. I wanted to hide. And then I noticed my computer on my dresser, open and on. Then I not only wanted to hide…I wanted to run away and never be found again.

I turned around to leave, but I didn't have my shoes and it was too cold to go outside barefoot. I couldn't go back into my room to get them from my closet. My heart squeezed tight and the backs of my eyes burned.

"Killian, I think we need to have a talk."

I shook my head and continued down the hall, away from Elise.

She chased after me, calling my name until she cornered me near the kitchen table. "If you don't want to talk to me about it, I'm sure I can find someone you might feel more comfortable with. A guy maybe? Steven could talk to you. But either way, I think there are things you're finding out that should probably be explained in a better way than how you're learning it."

Feeling defeated, I slumped into one of the chairs and dropped my head into my hands. I didn't want to talk to her about it, but it was better than discussing it with her boyfriend, Steven. He was a nice guy; however, I had no desire to hear about sex from the man sleeping in my aunt's bedroom.

Elise took the seat next to me and lowered her voice to a calm, reassuring tone. "I never thought I'd have to have this talk with anyone, let alone a boy. But here it goes…when a man and a woman love each other."

I raised my head and held out my hand to stop her.

"Okay…you're right. That's just lame. And I don't think anyone actually listens to that crap. Let's try it this way.

Sometimes we get urges. When we act on them, whether it's by ourselves or with someone else, they feel good."

I stood up and searched around the room, not finding what I was looking for. I headed down the hall, ignoring Elise's pleas for me to stop and come back. Once I found my notebook and pen next to my bed, I returned to the table and reclaimed my seat.

I already know about this.

"From the videos you've been watching?"

I shook my head, pushing down the humiliation over having this conversation with her. This was worse than hearing about it from Rylee. *I looked it up online. I know about puberty and sex.*

"Do you know about protection and diseases? About the consequences of sex?"

My aunt then went on to explain condoms, birth control, and babies. She went into great detail about how difficult life would be if I acted on my urges and got a girl pregnant. She never said Rylee's name, but I wasn't stupid. Rylee was the only girl I knew. It was rather transparent when she went on to explain how young "we" were, and how that added a whole new level of danger. It wasn't the most comfortable thing to listen to while she explained how it's hard to think about protection in the heat of the moment, and that's how accidents happen. I didn't want to hear this from my aunt. However, these weren't things I'd been able to find on the Internet.

In the end, Elise left me in fear of something that had, at first, made me feel so good following Rylee's explanation.

That night, after my aunt had gone to bed, I snuck out the back door. This time, I wasn't on my way to the woods. I needed to see Rylee. Other than two notes left on her window, I hadn't seen her since the day behind the house. I was torn and confused about how I felt, and she was the only one who made everything better.

"You must be freezing. Get in here," she whispered after pulling open the window for me.

When I left the house, I hadn't thought about putting on real clothes, so I only wore my flannel pants, a short-sleeved T-shirt, and my tennis shoes. The chill cut through me before I made it to the fence, but I was on a mission. I couldn't turn around and get dressed knowing Rylee was so close.

She knelt on the floor in front of me to untie my shoes, just like she always did when I snuck in at night, and then helped me into bed like I was a child. She'd gotten a TV in her room for Christmas. It sat on her dresser across from her bed, the volume on low, but the light brightening the room. After she locked the door, she crawled beneath the covers and faced me.

It was our ritual.

I took her hand and stared at her. This was the time she'd usually start talking about her day, but for some reason, she didn't say anything. Instead, she studied me in the glow of whatever she was watching before I'd knocked on her window. Her throat worked hard with her swallow, and she licked her lips.

Those lips.

That mouth.

Her tongue.

For a week straight they were all I could think about, and now here she was. In front of me. And I couldn't think about anything other than what they'd taste like. What sound she'd make if I kissed her. I gripped her hand tighter and held my breath.

The space between our faces disappeared, and then my mouth was on hers. It wasn't like the movies at all. Nothing like I expected. My lips pressed against hers hard. I could practically feel her teeth behind them. But she didn't push me away. I couldn't move, my mouth glued to hers. Her hand gripping mine. Our breaths rushed and desperate between us through our noses.

It was nothing like the videos.

But so much better.

Because it was with Rylee.

She finally pulled away, probably to catch her breath. I knew I was winded, like I'd just run around the neighborhood during the summer. My body was warm and every muscle was strained. *Every* muscle.

"I'm sorry…" I didn't think about it until it was out. Too lost in the moment, in what just happened, I didn't realize what I'd said until it was too late. I only thought it, and then spoke it, not paying any attention to the reality of my actions.

She sucked in a sharp breath and stared at me with wide eyes. The light from the TV screen made them glisten as her sight flickered about my face. "W—what did you say? Did you just talk?"

I didn't know how to respond, so I simply laid there, staring at her.

"Killian. Did you just speak to me?"

Feeling my words being sucked back in, I nodded.

"But…but I thought you couldn't talk?"

I shook my head and closed my eyes. I only opened them again when I felt her fingertip trace the scar on the right side of my face. No one had touched them, not even her. But right now, I couldn't pull away. I couldn't remove her hand from me.

Panic filled my veins, pumping through me with each intense beat of my heart. I couldn't hear anything over the rush of blood in my ears. Then suddenly, she smiled, and everything else faded away. The whooshing sound disappeared into the distance, the pressure against my chest eased, and as if her breaths along my face gave me air, I inhaled deeply.

I was safe with her.

"I was told not to talk. They told me not to talk to anyone. And I haven't. I don't know why I said that to you. Or why I'm talking now." They were whispered words, only audible by the air serving them to our ears. But that was more than I'd been able to utter in the last five years.

"So this whole time, you've been able to, you just haven't?" When I nodded, she gently ran her palm over my cheek and brushed the pad of her thumb over my eyebrow. "Does anyone know you can talk?"

I shrugged, and then thought better of it. I liked speaking to her. I liked how it made me feel for her to hear my voice— whispered or not. "I don't know. After it happened, I was sent to a lot of doctors. Some of them were like therapists. They all said there wasn't a reason for me to be unable to speak."

"So you haven't said anything because those men told you not to?"

"They said if I did, they'd do to me what they did to my parents."

"You were just going to keep silent forever?"

"Until I found my voice again."

She smiled and traced my lips with the tip of her finger. "I think you just found it."

"Don't tell anyone. Please."

Her brow grew tight and it cast a shadow over her brown eyes, making them indistinguishable. "Why? I mean, I won't...but why? I'd think now that you've found your voice, you'd want to use it."

With my hand on her shoulder, I pulled our foreheads together. "I only want to talk to you. If I could, I'd steal the moon from the sky. I'd still the earth and keep it from turning into day. I'd stay here with you, talking to you, listening to you...kissing you. Forever. I don't want to talk to anyone else, say anything else. I don't want to *be* anywhere else except here. With you. You make me feel safe."

She covered my lips with hers. Although, this time, it was softer, slower. Our mouths weren't pressed together in a race against time. She somehow slowed the clock, drug out every possible second of the kiss, and made it mean so much more.

"You make me feel safe, too," she whispered. Her weak voice and airy words billowed against my lips until I inhaled them, swallowed them, made them part of me. "I won't tell anyone. I promise. You can talk to me anytime you want. You can still write me letters and draw me pictures. I don't want anything to change between us."

At her last sentence, I closed my eyes and just allowed myself to feel her presence. I wanted things to change between us, even though it was scary. I wanted to keep kissing her. I wanted to kiss her the way they did in the videos, but I thought it'd scare her off if I pushed my tongue into her mouth. There were so many things to change between us, but she didn't want that. She wanted to be friends, and I understood why. I had to sneak into her room, and barely saw her when her mom was home from work. Her parents wouldn't approve of me.

And I didn't want her to get pregnant.

But that didn't mean I didn't want things to change.

Maybe when she was older. Maybe when her body went through the things mine did, things could be different. And until then, I had to settle for my imagination. I had to be okay with the meetings beneath the cover of night, beneath the stars, and the written words we'd share in between.

One day, it'd all be different.

I'd find my voice in the real world.

And then we'd be together.

Like my parents.

SEVEN

Rylee

KISSING KILLIAN WAS NOTHING new to me. He was the only boy I'd ever kissed, and even though he'd never told me, I was sure my lips were the only ones he'd ever tasted. I had to say though, he'd gotten a lot better since the first time. No longer did he press his mouth so hard into mine it made my lips and teeth hurt. He'd long since learned how to be gentle. And I'd never forget the first time he shoved his tongue into my mouth.

I wasn't even sure what he meant to do. But after a few tries, we figured it out. But now, it was so much better. I couldn't help but compare then to now as he propped himself over me in my bed, his tongue melding with mine, his mouth swallowing my whimpers.

We'd improved a lot over the last two years of making out.

I was still the only one he talked to. He continued the silent game when it came to everyone else. At first, I didn't understand why he couldn't just tell people what had happened. They never did catch the guys who killed his parents and hurt him. But anytime I'd bring it up, he'd shut it down and tell me not to worry about it.

My parents now knew about him. My dad had come home one evening from work—earlier than usual—and found me walking out of Killian's house. When Dad questioned me about it, I couldn't lie. Needless to say, I was grounded for a week. He didn't know how to handle the situation, so we waited for my mom to come home. Of course, I never told them about Killian sneaking into my room at night, us making out, or anything about his past. As far as they knew, he was just Ms. Newberry's mute nephew who'd lost his parents when he

49

was eight. Once they knew his story, their attitude began to change, but they still didn't like the idea of me being in his house without adult supervision. I wasn't allowed to be alone with him in the house. And so far, I hadn't broken that promise, because anytime he was in my room, they were technically home.

Loopholes. They made the world go 'round.

Killian broke the kiss and rested his forehead on mine. This was usually the time he'd say goodnight and go home. After a few nights, I figured out why he had to leave, and it had nothing to do with being tired. His tented pants gave away his secret. We'd never gone further than kissing—although he did touch my boob once. I panicked and he stopped. Since then, we'd kept it to just our lips. Little did he know, when he left my room to go take care of his business, I'd flip onto my stomach and handle my own.

It was a dangerous game we played, but neither of us seemed capable of stopping.

I'd just started my freshman year of high school, and even though I was only fourteen, I had friends in some of my classes who admitted to already having lost their virginity. The thought of going that far with Killian made me nervous. I wasn't ready. He was fifteen and might've been, but he never pressured me for anything. He said he was content with what we'd been doing. Although, it seemed to have been progressing toward something else. *Slowly.* I mean, it'd been two years. At this rate, by the time we end up having sex, I might be in college.

"I hate taking a shower after I leave here," he whispered against my lips.

"Why? Isn't that like the best part for you?" We'd become so comfortable with each other that my teasing no longer bothered him. He used to get embarrassed and his face would brighten into a fiery shade of red; however, now he just laughed at me. I think he liked it.

"Well, yeah…I like that part. But I don't like washing off your scent. I wish I could fall asleep with your smell on me. It's not fair you get to lay here and smell me all night and I have to go home and wash it off." He straightened his arm and pulled away from me.

SILENCED

In the light from the flickering candle on my bedside table, I found my name scrolled across the inside of his forearm. He used to draw it there every now and then, but it seemed recently, he'd redo it anytime it started to wear off. Whenever I'd ask him to put his name on me, he always put it in a spot hidden by clothes. It would've been hard to convince my parents we were only friends if I had his name in marker on my skin.

"When I turn eighteen, I'm going to get it permanently put there." I loved the gruff sound of his voice. The first time I'd ever heard him speak, it was a bit higher, like the other kids I went to school with. But over the years, it'd deepened, and when he'd whisper-talk like he was now, it sounded abrasive and rugged. It did things to me. Things I shouldn't have even known about at fourteen years old.

"You don't really talk about the future much. What are your plans? How will you work if you don't talk?"

He shrugged and then settled into the mattress next to me. I remained on my back, but turned my head to face him. "Hopefully, I'll be able to talk by then. I don't know what I'll do for a job, but I'm sure there's got to be something out there for me."

I giggled and pushed a few strands of hair off his face. Most of the time, he wore it pulled back, showing off the shaved parts underneath, but when he was in bed with me, some of the front pieces always fell out. "What do you mean you'll be able to talk by then? You already can."

"You know what I mean, Rylee," he said with a huff of air.

"No…I don't, Killian. You've never explained it. All you've ever said is you were told not to speak, so you don't. You've mentioned finding your voice, but I don't know what that means."

"They took so much from me. My parents, my childhood, my voice. I won't let them win. Some how, some way, I'll take back what's mine. I haven't even been back home since I left seven years ago. I've never been to their gravesite. Never seen their headstones. I was taken from my house on a stretcher, brought to a hospital where I stayed for weeks, then I was shipped off to live with other people. I was never given closure."

"So you plan to go back there? For closure? And then you'll feel okay to talk in public?"

He laid his arm across my belly and pulled me closer to him. "That's the plan. I need to see it. I can't explain it, Rylee, but I need to be where they are. I need to know they're okay. There's this fire inside me when I think about what those bastards did to my parents—this intense anger I've never been able to deal with. I just want to feel normal."

"I thought I made you feel normal."

He huffed and pulled his forehead to my shoulder. "You do. And then you don't. You yourself, yes, you make me feel like I'm okay. Like I'm not living in the middle of some unsolved mystery. A never-ending crime drama where the murderers are roaming the streets and the victims are either six feet under or hiding out in his neighbor's bedroom with a permanent smile on his face for the whole world to see. And then when I take a step back and look at more than just you, I realize I'm your secret. I'm Elise's secret. I'm still stuck in this hole, the endless abyss of reminders. I need to escape that."

"You're not my secret, Killian. My parents know about you. All my friends at school know about you. I don't hide you. I'm not ashamed or embarrassed of you. You shouldn't feel that way, because I don't."

He pressed his lips to my bare shoulder where the sleeve of my shirt rode up. "I know. That's not exactly what I meant. You may tell your friends about who we really are, but you've never told your parents. To them, I'm the pathetic boy who lives next door. The one you hang out with because you feel bad for him."

I rolled onto my side, into him, to fully face him. "Because if they know, this will all end. They've gotten more lenient with me since I've started high school, but if you think for one minute they won't assume we're doing stuff, then you're wrong. Right now, they're okay with us hanging out alone outside. If I tell them you're more than a friend, they'll probably find an issue with that and put an end to us seeing each other completely."

"And if you think your parents believe you when you say we're just friends, then *you're* wrong." When he kissed me again, slow and careful, I forgot all about our conversation.

"Killian," I breathed out. "I don't even know what in the heck we are."

"We're friends." He pressed his lips to mine again. "Who happen to make out." Another peck. "In bed. At night." He wrapped his arm around my lower back, which caused my chest to collide with his. "You're the friend I think about in the shower." His lips trailed along my jaw until they reached my earlobe. "And I'm the friend you think of when you have your hand between your legs."

I gasped and my face burned with the heat of a thousand fires.

"Thanks for the confirmation on that," he said with a peck to my flaming cheek.

Pushing him away, I asked, "Do you plan on getting all the names of your friends tattooed on you? Right on your arms so everyone can see?"

"Yup." His smile took over his face and he wagged his brows at me. "You're the only friend I'll ever have."

"I don't believe that for a second. I might be your only friend now because you're homeschooled and don't really go anywhere—*because you refuse to talk to people*—but I call BS that you'll never have other friends for the rest of your life."

"No other friends like you."

I melted into his soft lips as they consumed mine.

When he pulled away, he glanced over my shoulder at the clock on the nightstand. "I should get going soon. It's after midnight. I've been here for over an hour." His gaze met mine again, and something wicked glowed in the pools of shimmering green. "But before I leave…can you at least show me how you look when you *think* of me?"

"No." I pushed him away even more and tried to laugh through the embarrassment.

"At least show me so I have something to think about in the shower. Are you on your back when you do it? Your legs up? Straight? You don't have to actually do it; I just want to see."

I sighed, but relented, rolling onto my stomach. However, I kept my arms by my pillow so it wouldn't look like I was touching myself in front of him. To my surprise, he leaned over me, practically pinning me to the bed, and blew out the candle. The room turned completely dark.

He didn't remove himself from me. Instead, he pressed his chest to my back and moved the lower half of his body to match up with mine. His hand pushed beneath me, between the mattress and the apex of my thighs—on the outside of my pajama shorts. I held my breath, unsure of what was happening, but not wanting it to stop.

"Like this?" he whispered into my ear while moving his fingers back and forth.

I couldn't respond. My eyes were closed so tightly, light bubbles floated behind my lids. My breaths filled my lungs but never made it back out through my dry lips. His body began to move with his hand, his obvious erection in the crevice of my backside.

I couldn't think.

Couldn't speak.

The only thing I could do was lift my hips and roll them into his hand. It took roughly thirty seconds for the explosions to rocket through my body. It was more intense than anything I'd ever felt before. No matter how many times I'd brought myself to this same place, nothing had ever felt as amazing as when he did it.

He ground into me, his mouth falling to my shoulder and his face buried in my hair, and a rumble ripped through his chest. My body muffled the sound, but it reverberated through me as his arms and legs began to tremble. He'd gone completely rigid on top of me.

Once the waves of a summer's heat settled, he moved away, leaving me cold and alone. His whispered voice floated over me as he said goodnight and kissed me on the cheek. But I still couldn't move. I remained on my belly, my face pressed into my pillow, while I heard him sneak out through my window. The screen groaned softly as he put it back into place.

And then I was alone.

My lower back was wet, my panties were damp, but inside, I was cold.

I didn't even know what to think of it, or how to handle what had just happened. So I closed my eyes, pulled my blanket to my chin, and laid there for however long it took before sleep pulled me in.

• • •

"YOU KNOW THE rules, Rylee. Stay outside. I shouldn't be gone long, so please don't leave the yard." My mom threw her purse into the car and waited for my acknowledgment. As soon as I nodded, she got in and closed the door.

I watched as she backed out of the driveway, unable to meet Killian's stare. It'd been four days since the night he touched me in my room. We hadn't even spoken since then. I knew I'd been uncomfortable after that, and by his silence, I assumed he had felt the same way.

As soon as her car rounded the corner, I turned to Killian, although I averted my gaze. "We should probably go sit in the back yard. I wouldn't put it past her to circle the block and come back to check on us."

He followed me to the shade tree I often sat beneath. It was strange he didn't hold my hand, considering he always held my hand. But I couldn't put too much thought into it, because it's not like I reached out for his, either. Awkwardness seemed to have wrapped us in its wings, smothered us in its cocoon.

"I'm sorry, Rylee." His voice sounded so grim. So deep and distant. "I didn't mean to do what I did. I shouldn't have."

"It's okay. I didn't tell you to stop."

"But it's made things weird between us."

Finally, I glanced at him, finding his eyes settled on me. "It scared me."

Every emotion between fear and sorrow flashed across his face in a split second, and it nearly gutted me. "I didn't mean to scare you."

I placed my hand on his bent knee for comfort. "No, Killian. *You* didn't scare me. It's not like that at all. It's just…" I focused on my fingers while getting through what I needed to say. "When it was about to happen, I couldn't think of anything other than it happening. And how much I wanted it. Then during it…I only thought about how good it felt. How I didn't want it to stop. Nothing else entered the equation. But after it was over, I realized how dangerous it was. What if it'd gone further, and neither of us stopped it? I'm not ready for that."

He picked at my nail polish and pressed his lips together.

"I just think maybe we got carried away," I added.

He cleared his throat, and I waited in fear of what he'd say. "I know. And I'm sorry. You go to school, around other people, so you get to figure these things out. I don't. I feel like I'm learning everything as I go, and you're the only one I'm learning anything with."

"Well…you're doing a fantastic job for not knowing what you're doing."

He smirked and turned to me. "I watch videos."

"You learned how to do *that* from a video?" And then I realized what kind of movie he was talking about. "Oh…you watch those?"

His shoulder lifted in a lazy shrug. "Yeah. Is that wrong?"

I thought about it, unsure of what to say. "I don't know. I've never seen one before. A girl in my class said she found one in her parents' room once, but she never told me what was on it. She said it was gross."

"Do you want me to stop watching them?"

I met his gaze and paused for a second to appreciate the youthful quality in him. There were moments when he seemed so assertive—like the other night—times he'd utter things I assumed only grown men would say, and then moments like these when I realized he was just a kid, figuring everything out as it came. "No. You can watch whatever you want."

"I promise I won't do that to you again."

I laughed and dipped my chin so he wouldn't see the inferno blazing in my cheeks. "Don't promise that. Maybe just say you won't do it for a while…until we're both ready for it."

His tone lightened with hope when he asked, "When do you think that'll be?"

"I don't know…after I turn fifteen maybe?"

He turned his attention to the sky and scrunched his face. "So in like…five more months? That's doable. Not too far away." We both laughed in unison. "I probably shouldn't come back to your room before then, huh?"

I hated the thought of not lying beside him for the next five months, but he had a point. There was no way I'd be able to turn him down if he came back and tried it again. I still felt the tingles of what he'd done to me...*four days later*.

"That's probably smart," I concluded.

"Can I still kiss you?"

I turned my narrowed stare on him. "You better."

And then wisps of laughter seeped past his lips as they descended to mine.

EIGHT

Killian

"HAVE YOU GIVEN ANY more thought to going to school this year?" Elise cleared the table after dinner, but I wasn't done eating yet. She walked away from me, turned her back to me, as if she could've read my mind to get my answer. "It's your junior year. I thought you might want to attend a real school for your last two years."

I sat in my seat and waited for her to face me again. She'd been doing this a lot lately, expecting me to suddenly start talking. She'd ask me a question, or just make a statement, but wouldn't look at me to answer.

Finally, she turned around and leaned against the counter. "Rylee wants you to attend school with her. She thinks it's a good idea. And I have to be honest, Killian, I agree. You're completely caught up to your grade level now, and you only have two more years before you graduate. I'd like to see you go off to college, get a degree, and do something with yourself."

Choosing to ignore her, I went back to finishing the food on my plate. She'd hinted at things before, and as of lately, she'd been trying to convince me to go to a real school. Rylee had mentioned it once as well, but I told her I wasn't interested in being the freak. It didn't matter what she said, she'd never be able to convince me I'd fit in with everyone else.

I no longer hid myself away anymore. I'd go to the grocery store, run around the neighborhood, and even visited the library sometimes. I saw the way people continued to gawk at me, and I wasn't interested in dealing with that on a daily basis. Deal with the other kids asking me questions, seeing the pity on teachers' faces. Not to mention, I knew they'd make me learn sign language, and I refused. I knew I'd find a reason to speak again.

I only had to wait a few more years.

But I'd find it.

Talking with my hands would no longer be necessary.

"It's nice you have someone to talk to, but I think it'd be better if you were around more kids your age. I think Rylee has been an amazing support system for you, and I can see how much she cares. I think you'd be surprised to find more people like her. More people you can open up to and talk with." She didn't move away as I locked my sights on her.

I couldn't wrap my head around what she'd said. I never spoke around her, or loud enough for her to hear. There's no way she would've known...unless Rylee told her. But I trusted Rylee. I knew she wouldn't say anything. At least...I hoped she wouldn't.

Elise rolled her eyes and waved me off, as if she hadn't just dropped a bomb in my lap. "Killian, I wasn't born yesterday. I know you talk to her, more than in written words. I'm happy you can do that with her. I wish you'd talk to me, but I understand. Hopefully, one day you'll get out there and learn it's okay to trust other people. You don't have to be silent all the time."

My brow tightened and it became harder to breathe through the anxiety coursing through me. This was my secret. No one was supposed to know. Especially her. She'd try to get answers, get me to talk about who killed my parents. And I refused to tell anyone.

Elise moved around the counter until she stood in front of me. "It's not a secret you can talk, Killian. I've heard you before. When you first moved here, you'd cry and talk in your sleep. You'd call out for your dad, beg your mom to wake up. Your words weren't clear, mostly sobs and heartbreaking cries for help, but you spoke. I heard you. The doctors informed me you were capable of speech, but either you chose not to, or it was the trauma keeping you from doing it. So please, don't look at me like I have two heads. Just because you haven't talked to me doesn't mean I'm unaware you have the ability to. I'll continue to let you do this at your pace. Speak to me whenever you want, or continue writing everything down for the rest of your life. It doesn't matter to me. I only want what's best for you, and I think it's time you start living in the real world. Around real people. Some good, some bad, some ignorant or sheltered. People will say mean things, make bad choices...but then there are people like Rylee."

I shook my head, because there weren't people *like* her. Only her. She was one of a kind. Rylee was my person, my best friend, the only one I could be me around. No matter what Elise said, she'd never convince me.

I didn't want anyone else.

I only wanted Rylee.

"Just think about it, okay?" She took the plate from in front of me and carried it to the sink. Despite her cool and calm demeanor, acting as if none of this bothered her, I saw the hurt in her eyes. I could see how my silence and avoidance bothered her. I never wanted to cause her any pain, but I didn't know how to give her what she wanted without sacrificing what I'd promised.

I promised *them* I wouldn't talk.

But I promised *myself* I would—eventually.

When the time was right.

"I'm going over to Steve's for a bit. He got a new big screen for his living room and wants to watch a movie. Did you want to go?" Her and Steven were now engaged. Elise still had people over from time to time, but nothing like it used to be. Now, they were couples who came over to play games and have a few drinks. I knew them all, and didn't mind them being around. Especially Steven. I admired the way he loved my aunt, and I had no problems being around him. I'd even gone to his house several times with Elise, but I wasn't up to it tonight.

I wanted to be alone.

As soon as she faced me again, I shook my head.

"Okay. Maybe I'll just reschedule."

Elise kept notepads and paper in every room, along with pens and markers. We even had a whiteboard on the fridge. So I stood and made my way to the counter next to the phone and began to jot down a note for her.

No. You should go. I'll be fine.

"I don't feel right leaving you alone."

I raised an eyebrow at her and smiled. *I'm sixteen. Not six. You leave me alone all the time. What's different about now?*

"I feel like I've upset you, and I don't want you thinking I'm running off to be with Steve instead of you. You'll always come first, Killian."

I knew that much. She'd been engaged for almost a year, but they hadn't made any plans to actually get married, and I knew why. She wanted to wait until I was out of the house, on my own, until she knew I was okay before making that commitment. She wouldn't let him move in with us to keep me from being uncomfortable regardless of how many times I told her I was okay with them getting married or him being here. I wanted to see her happy, and Steven made her happy. But for some reason, she wanted to wait.

She was choosing me.

And I appreciated that.

Go. Have fun and enjoy the movie. I'll just watch TV in my room.

"I won't be out late."

I huffed out a laugh and shook my head. *Stay out as late as you want. Just don't get pregnant. Make sure he uses protection.*

Elise jokingly slapped my shoulder as she laughed along with me. "What am I going to do with you? Trust me, you're enough for me. I don't want any more kids."

My heart warmed at her sentiment, but it didn't last.

Not long after she left the house, I thought about what she'd said. It made me think about my parents, and I wondered why they never had other kids. Why I didn't have brothers or sisters. The question sparked anger in my chest. It was a question I'd never be able to ask them, an answer I'd never hear them tell me.

Because they were taken from me.

Brutally.

The more I thought about that night, the hotter the anger became until it festered into a rolling wave of fury. I grabbed the sketch pad I kept under my bed for times like this when I couldn't suppress the rage and blinding heartache. Before I knew it, I had colored pencils, thin-tipped markers, pens, and charcoal sticks laid out around me, my hands moving along the paper of their own accord.

I'd done this so many times, drawn the same features, same scenes so often, I no longer needed to think about the lines as they formed. It was like autopilot. I'd lose myself in the memories, the pain, the images I'd never be able to forget, until they were brought to life on paper. The colors, the lines, the details visible for anyone to see.

There had been three guys, and I'd never forget their faces. One of them, the one who'd stayed in the corner and reminded his friends I was only a boy, was always the easiest to draw. Maybe it was because he didn't have any blood on him. I never thought he really had anything to do with it. Although, it didn't prevent me from hating him.

He could've stopped it.

Could've told his friends no.

Could've kept the one from cutting into my face.

But he didn't.

He'd only stood there, arguing, but doing nothing to help me or my parents. He didn't come forward and turn his friends in. He remained silent. Like me. So as far as I was concerned, he was just as bad as they were. However, when I sketched him, I didn't put in as much time as I did with the others.

The one who stood next to my dad was always second. I spent longer on him than the first one. Each time, his face was always the same. The same scowl, the same dark, angry eyes. His lips tight and thin, his nostrils flared. He had a crooked nose and an earring in one ear. A scar ran through one eyebrow, and after drawing him so often, it now resembled a scar instead of a smudged line. And I always took extra time to color in the blood that dripped from the small knife in his hand.

But I spent the majority of my time detailing the guy who'd left my mom's side, held me down, and cut my face. He was the one I remembered the most. The one I'd paid more attention to. His sketches always had more color than the others, and not just because of the picture on his shirt. His eyes were bright blue. Even in the dimly lit bedroom all those years ago, his eyes pierced through the darkness. Evil shone bright within them, the devil peeking out through the narrow slits of his lids. They were distinctive eyes—big and round, although he'd kept them partially closed. It was as if he had too much eyelid—they were too heavy—and it prevented him from opening them fully.

His hair was dark brown and shaggy, wavy, and too long to appear manageable. But his eyebrows didn't match. They were lighter, noticeably lighter. I remembered thinking over the years about it and wondered if he'd colored his hair darker like my mom used to do. Now, I no longer cared.

It always took more red pencil on his picture, because he was the only one completely covered in the thick maroon. It splattered on his face and neck, smeared next to his eyes. Maybe that was why the hue was so noticeable—the contrast stark against my mom's crimson blood on his pale skin. He had a gash on his nose, although I had no idea where it had come from. It bled, so I knew it was fresh, and as I'd gotten older, I often wondered if maybe my mom had fought back. With all the gore on his face, it would've been indistinguishable, except it was the one thing I'd stared at as he sat on me, holding my head still. I'd focused intently on that mark while pleading for my life.

I'd never forget that gash.

Those harsh blue eyes.

The hideous sneer on his uneven lips.

Sitting back on my bed, I took in the full picture. The one I'd drawn of the man I hated most in this world. I hated them all, but he was the worst. He'd looked in my mom's eyes and slit her neck, and then stared into mine while cutting my face open.

Evil.

That's what he was.

Every finite detail of his smug face was carved into my memory like words etched in a tombstone.

I slammed the pad closed, unable to see him any longer. My blood boiled and it became harder to breathe. The room felt as if it had closed in on me. I was suffocating, dying, my pure hatred and blind rage taking over.

I needed out.

I needed air.

After shoving everything under my bed where I kept it, I quickly put on my shoes and left the house. The air was still humid, but it was better than being trapped inside. The neighborhood was dark and quiet; most were probably asleep or in bed for the night. But not me. I broke out into a sprint, needing to release some of this energy and anger.

As I rounded the corner, my house behind me, a car turned onto the street, its lights blinding me. I squinted against the high beams and kept going, ignoring everything and focusing on my feet. My shoes slammed hard onto the pavement, one after the other. I felt it in my heels, my knees, my lower back. I knew I was running too hard, but I didn't care.

Suddenly, I heard my name called out. Not just my name, but the sweet voice that belonged to only one person. *My* person. I skidded to a stop and turned around just in time to see Rylee step out of the back seat. She closed the door and stood still, staring at me as if waiting for me to make a move.

Without turning back, she jogged toward me and put her hands on my heaving chest. "What's going on? Why are you out here so late? Is everything okay? You seem pissed off or something."

I wanted to look at her, but I couldn't take my eyes off the car she'd just gotten out of. I knew she had friends, hung out with people I didn't know, but it didn't stop the jealousy from wrapping itself around my throat and squeezing until I couldn't breathe.

The driver's side door opened and a guy stepped out. "Rylee, are you okay? Do you know him?" His words were white noise in my head. Static. The edges of my vision blurred, and all I could see was his shirt.

A black T-shirt.

A triangle in the center.

A bright rainbow extended from one side.

And my mind instantly went to my last sketch. The guy in my parents' room. The one with the gash on his nose. His knife. Him sitting on me. The pain in my cheeks.

The scars he left behind.

His black T-shirt with the same triangle and rainbow.

"Killian! Stop!" Rylee's voice drifted through the muffled sounds around me. It was enough to pull me back just enough until I understood what I was doing. "Killian…stop, please. Look at me. Stop."

I blinked and the world became clear again. I was no longer across the street. I now stood near the open car door, the driver pressed against the red paint with my hand around his neck. I dropped my arms to my sides and took a step away.

"What the fuck, man?" His question was hard and his voice hoarse while he sputtered and coughed. "You know him, Rylee?"

"Yeah, I do. Please, don't tell anyone about this. Please, I'm begging you, Ross."

"He comes at me for no reason and chokes me, and you don't want me to say anything?"

"He's not like that. I've never seen him hurt anyone before. Let me handle it." She peered over her shoulder at me, but I was paralyzed. I couldn't look at anything other than the fuzzy image of the kid in front of me. I was lost in a daze, unable to recognize what went on around me. "Please…let me handle it. I'm sorry. I swear, he's not a bad person."

Not a bad person.

I couldn't stop replaying her words in my head.

The next thing I knew, the car was gone and Rylee stood in front of me, my face in her hands. "Killian, what was that? What came over you? He's just a friend, I swear. I went out with him and his girlfriend, Malika—she's a friend of mine. He was just bringing me home."

She thought I was jealous…which I was, to a certain extent. But that wasn't why I'd attacked him. Honestly, I wasn't sure why I'd gone after him, other than the shirt. I knew he wasn't the same guy from my parents' room, but I attacked him anyway.

My shoulders deflated and I was finally able to take in a deep breath. "I'm sorry," I whispered to her. She couldn't know what triggered my response to her friend, so I decided to let her believe it was envy. "I don't like seeing you with other guys."

"I have several guy friends from school—*just friends*. You can't go attacking them all."

"I know. I'm sorry." It was all I could say. I didn't have any other excuse.

"Come on, let's get you back. We can talk about it there."

"Aren't your parents expecting you?"

She shook her head and held my hand before she started walking toward our houses. "I have a little over an hour before curfew. Malika had to be at her front door by ten, so we all left early. We have time. Is your aunt home?"

"No," I said as I walked beside her. "I don't know when she'll be back, though."

"That's okay. We'll just talk."

We ran as we passed her house just in case her parents were up. Now that we were older, they had an even harder time with us hanging out. Rylee said it was because her mom was paranoid we'd have sex, but I always wondered if it was more. If I scared them and they didn't want their daughter associating with me.

Once we made it to my house, I led her inside, and then back to my room.

She said we'd talk.

I didn't want to.

NINE

Rylee

HIS LIPS CRASHED TO mine, and I had no willpower to push him away. There was something going on with him, but I had no clue what it was. When we passed him on the road, he seemed pissed off, his feet pounding the pavement like I'd never seen before. Then, when I called out to him, he just seemed lost. But nothing compared to the way he took off, pushing me aside as if I hadn't been standing in front of him, and went after Ross.

I'd never seen him act like that before. So angry. So full of…hatred. And it didn't make any sense. He didn't know Ross, never bothered to meet any of my friends, so his attack confused me.

I wanted answers, but I couldn't pull myself away from him to ask the questions. The way he held me, kissed me, was like he needed me. It was desperate, which only confused me more. This wasn't the first time he'd ever shown me so much eagerness with his body, but right after witnessing his struggle, I knew there had to be more to it.

He pushed me backward until the backs of my legs hit the bed, but he didn't stop there. He continued to lean into me, and with nowhere else to go, I fell onto the mattress with him on top of me. His arms caged me in and propped him up enough to keep his weight off my chest, although he didn't take his lips from mine.

Killian moved me up until I had one of his pillows under my head and he was situated between my legs. His hips rolled, his obvious erection pressing against me. I moaned into his mouth as he ran his covered desire along mine. We'd never done this before. Ever since my fifteenth birthday, we'd grown more comfortable with each other, but we always played it safe.

This wasn't safe.

I was used to him bringing me to orgasm with his hands—always on the outside of my clothes. He never let me return the favor. I'd tried twice, but he told me no because it was messy. He didn't want to get his "stuff" on me, which didn't make any sense. There were countless times he'd ejaculate just by touching me—I could feel it through his shorts, or he'd leave a small wet spot on my bed. But for some reason, he never wanted me to.

Now, he was on top of me, moving against me like we were having sex. I didn't want to stop. It felt too good. But I was scared of where this had come from. Although, it wasn't totally unlike him to do something out of the blue, much like the first time he touched me.

"Killian," I whispered between kisses while I ran my hands down his chest. I didn't stop until I reached the hem of his shirt, which had ridden up with his ministrations. Along with his shirt, his movements also caused the band of his exercise shorts to lower. My fingertips grazed the coarse hair low on his abdomen, and we both stilled with a gasp.

"Rylee." My name was throaty, moaned along the sensitive skin beneath my ear.

I ignored his desperate plea and carried on. My hormones had taken over, and I no longer cared about talking. The way he made me feel as he ran himself against me, pressing into my eager bundle of nerves, took over my rationale. I hooked my fingers beneath the waistband of his shorts and boxers, and then pushed them down. He grunted, and it ignited something in me. I'd never heard that noise from him before. I wanted to make him do it again.

I pushed against him, just enough to sit forward and flip him onto his back. I don't know where the motivation came from, what came over me, but I took control and led the way. I straddled his hips and kissed him before trailing my lips down his neck, his chest, his stomach, until I reached his erection.

Saliva pooled beneath my tongue at the anticipation of what I would do. This was all new—for him, too—but at least he'd seen graphic videos. I hadn't even done that. I was completely clueless, other than the little I'd heard from kids at school. I was only fifteen, so it wasn't like I knew too many kids with this kind of experience. But I wanted to do it.

"Rylee, stop. Don't. You don't have to do this." His voice sounded strained, and I knew how much control it took him to stop me.

I glanced up and met his heated gaze. The pale green had darkened and fused with the blue until it was almost a passionate turquoise color. I knew he didn't really want me to stop, but had said so because he knew me. He knew my wishes and my comfort level. Normally, I'd be the one pausing and taking a break, saying we needed to slow down. But not this time. Not now. The way he moved on top of me had done something to me. Changed me.

Provoked me.

"I want to, Killian."

"I can't handle you ignoring me after this." The pain in his expression nearly gutted me.

I placed a soft kiss on his bare hip. "I won't. I promise. Let me do this for you."

He blew out a steady stream of air and relaxed into the bed with his attention turned to the ceiling. I looked down at the throbbing pulse in his hard length and the thick vein running along the underside of it. This was the first time I'd ever seen one—not counting the drawings they'd used in health class. I wanted to take it all in, savor this moment, remember every second of it.

I held his hard shaft and lowered my lips to the tip. Liquid beaded at the top, and I slowly raked my tongue over it, needing to know what it tasted like. The subtle saltiness didn't turn me off. In fact, it encouraged me to go further. Just knowing I did that to him, that I brought it on, made me soar with confidence.

His fingers threaded through my hair as soon as my lips parted around the crown. I flattened my tongue over the tip, taking in his flavor. I had no clue what I was doing, but I decided he'd either tell me or I'd figure it out as I went.

"Rylee..." he groaned out and tilted his hips up, pushing himself farther in.

When I lowered my mouth onto him, he hissed, and then sucked in sharply through his teeth. I loved how I made him do this. I set this in motion. I turned him on. It was a high unlike any other, and I never wanted it to stop.

I took him in as far as I could and then slowly pulled back, hollowing my cheeks as much as possible. I loved the feel of his hardness in my mouth, on my tongue, tasting every bit of him like no one else ever had. I savored every second, drawing it out slowly.

Suddenly, on my way down for the third time, his grip tightened in my hair. He held my head down and pushed deeper into my mouth. He went farther than I'd taken him in the first two passes, and I choked, trying to pull back. But he wouldn't let me. He held me against him, the tip of his penis hitting my gag reflex. I thought I was going to throw up. Tears filled my eyes, and before I knew it, something warm flooded my throat. His hold on me fell away, and I was able to back away from him. I swallowed and coughed, choking on bile and his ejaculation.

He pulled his shorts back up as I jumped off the bed. I wiped my mouth with the back of my hand and turned around, not facing him. I couldn't. The thought of looking at him soured my stomach. It rolled and felt weak, as if I were on the verge of vomiting. A few of the girls in school talked about how great it was to please their boyfriends, but I didn't understand. It was nothing like that for me.

His hand came down onto my shoulder and I jumped away from him. The movement caused me to whirl around until I faced him. And my heart immediately fell to my feet. He had no idea what he'd done. He didn't understand my reaction. The creases in his brow, his narrowed gaze and wrinkled nose, gave him away. He was concerned for me. Frightened. Worried.

"What's wrong, Rylee? Did you not like it?"

Words failed me. I couldn't form enough to explain it to him.

"I'm so sorry." He closed the gap between our bodies and wrapped his arms around me, pulling me into his chest. His face fell to my shoulder and his breath heated my skin through the cotton of my shirt. This was his way of comforting me. It almost worked, until he slid his hands to my front and tried to unbutton my shorts. "Let me make it up to you. I want to do it to you, too."

"No." I pushed against him. Tears lined my face, but I didn't bother to wipe them away. I didn't know what was going on with him, and a part of me didn't care. I'd told him I would always accept him, but at some point I had to draw the line. "I don't want you to return the favor. That's not how you make it up to someone, Killian."

"What did I do?" Apprehension flooded his tone, deepening the pitch into a desperate rumble.

I met his sad stare, his sorrow practically tangible. "I just don't need you to reciprocate right now. That's all. We should talk, not do…*this*. What's going on with you, Killian? What happened tonight?"

"Nothing's going on with me. Nothing happened." He fell to the edge of the bed and dropped his head into his hands. This was him shutting down. I knew it. But I couldn't do anything to stop it. God, I wanted more than anything to pull him back out of this hole, but I didn't know how to remove the anger roaring to life inside me.

"Something happened; I'm not an idiot. I saw you running down the street. It's late, and you never run this time of night. It looked like you were running *from* something. I only want to know what it is so I can understand this better."

He didn't speak, didn't look at me, only sat hunched over with his elbows dug into his thighs, furiously shaking his head back and forth.

"You choked my friend, Killian!" My voice rose and shook, despite the control I tried to keep. I balled my hands into fists in an effort to rein it back in, although I wasn't sure how successful it'd be. "You charged after him, put your hands around his neck, and *choked* him. Then you take something that's supposed to be good, something I wanted to do for you, and *hurt* me."

Killian finally glanced up, his eyes wet with unshed tears.

"Not only did you choke Ross with your hands, but you choked me with your dick. I may have never done that with anyone before, but I don't think that's normal. I don't think that's the way it's supposed to be."

"I didn't mean to," he whispered in a low, gruff tone.

"It doesn't matter. Whether you meant to or not doesn't change the fact you did. Which means something's going on with you. Something happened tonight, and I just want to know what it was so I can help. Please, Killian..." My voice cracked and a wave of tears threatened to break through at the sight of his palpable pain. "Tell me what it is. Let me help you. Let me be there for you."

Silence filled the room while we did nothing but stare at each other. My heart pounded so hard I was sure he could hear it. Seconds passed before the first tear fell free, slipping down my cheek. And then another. More followed, no longer trailing from my eyes to my chin, but cascading in rivers of pain, grief, and helplessness. Pouring from my face onto my chest in waves of vulnerability. Just before I opened my mouth to plead with him one more time, his bedroom door creaked open.

"Is everything all right in here?" Elise stood in the doorway with one arm crossed over her chest, her eyes soft.

I glanced at Killian once more, but he had his sights set on the floor in front of him, refusing to meet my gaze, refusing to acknowledge his aunt's presence. I closed my eyes, inhaled deeply, and then turned to Elise with as much of a smile as I could muster.

"I should get going. It's late." I didn't bother looking back or saying goodbye before squeezing through the opening between her and the frame and heading for the front door. No one stopped me. They both let me walk away.

• • •

I BARELY SLEPT all night, unable to control my emotions. Anytime I fell asleep, it wasn't for long, and it wasn't restful. I tossed and turned, cried, spent far too long thinking about Killian and what he could've possibly been going through. I hated how obviously he struggled, yet couldn't come to me. Refused to open up when it was clear he needed it the most.

After I climbed out of bed, I went to the window to see... I didn't know what I went to look for. It wasn't like I could see his house, but I guess part of me had hoped I'd catch him on the fence. Instead, I found a folded piece of paper slipped through the screen, resting against the glass pane.

I'm sorry. For everything that happened tonight. About your friend, about you. About the fight. I never meant for any of it to happen. Before you found me running, Elise tried to talk to me about going to your school. Then she brought up me talking to you. I don't know how she knows, but somehow, she's aware I speak to you. And I hate that she knows. She didn't seem mad or upset, but it doesn't change the fact my secret isn't really a secret anymore. And you're no longer the only person who knows. I guess that set everything into motion. She left the house and my brain started going. I couldn't stop myself from remembering it all.

Then your friend got out of the car. I swear, Rylee, I don't remember going after him. You were in front of me one minute and then trying to break it up the next. His shirt triggered something in me—a memory. It was identical to one of the guys in my house. My mind had already been back to that night, and seeing it must've snapped something inside me. I can't explain it. And I can't excuse it. It was wrong to go after him. I just want you to know I'm aware of that.

I only wanted to kiss you. Only wanted to hold you and feel you for a few minutes, knowing you can calm me unlike anyone else. I don't know how we went from kissing to you going further. I've never felt anything like it before and I guess things got out of hand. I can't apologize enough. I need you to know I didn't mean for any of it to happen. I never want to hurt you. Ever.

And I'm sorry I couldn't open up to you tonight.

He signed it the way he did every letter he left me: *With the moon and the stars, Killian.*

I stood and wiped away a tear I didn't know had escaped. My mind was made up, even before getting dressed. Before heading out to the kitchen. I knew what I needed to do—what I had no choice but to do. I had to see him. Had to know he was okay. Had to let him know I forgave him.

I'd forgiven him long before I read the letter.

Before I woke up.

Before I left his house last night.

"Where are you off to so early?" my mom asked from the kitchen table with a coffee cup in her hand. She slid her glasses off her face and set them down, along with her tattered paperback. She always used bookmarks instead of bending the pages, which I found comical, considering she bought books from used stores, and most of them were already creased and very well worn. But she believed you had to take care of everything, regardless of how abused it was when you got it. To her, the book was new, and she'd treat it as such.

I sat down across from her and met her brown eyes, the same as mine—except smaller and less droopy. "I'm going to see Killian. We kinda got in a fight last night, and I want to make it right."

She studied me for a moment, blinking more than normal. "I thought you were out with Malika. Did he go, too?"

"No. I saw him when Ross brought me home." When her gaze hardened and her breathing slowed, I knew I needed to give her more information. "Mom, he was outside. When we pulled down the street, he was running. He looked mad or upset…or something. So we stopped and I got out. It was just three or four houses down."

"So what kind of fight did you get into?"

"I knew something was going on, but he wouldn't tell me."

She cocked her head to the side and squinted her eyes. "Does he run with a notebook?"

I knew what she was getting at, and I hadn't realized the trap I'd fallen into when I opened up to her. She didn't know he spoke. Like everyone else, she was under the impression he was mute, silenced. And although I trusted my mom, I couldn't betray Killian.

"No, he doesn't. But he refused to answer me."

"How's he supposed to answer you in the middle of the night, on the side of the road, without a pen and paper? Did he finally learn sign language? Did you read his mind?" She wasn't rude in her questioning; she simply wanted me to see things from a different point of view. Anyone who knew my mother, knew she played the devil's advocate, and she played it well.

"Mom…" I shook my head and lowered my gaze to where I ran the tip of my finger in a circle on the glass tabletop. I wasn't so much deflecting as I was buying time. "We walked back home together, but he refused to go get a notebook. He wouldn't tell me anything, just kept shaking his head anytime I asked what was wrong."

"Did you go inside his house?"

I couldn't tell by her tone if she already knew the answer. She was so hard to read most of the time. Usually, if she asked a question point blank like this, she already knew, and lying would only make things worse. I wanted to go see him, to make things right, and if she caught me in a lie, that wouldn't happen.

I nodded, refusing to meet her burning stare.

"Was Ms. Newberry home?"

This time, I did look up, met her eyes, and saw the truth in the chocolate pools. She knew. I was busted. "No, but she—"

"You know the rules, Rylee. If I don't want you in his house alone with him during the day, what makes you think it's okay to be there without his aunt at night?"

"Mom…" I leaned forward and pleaded with her, holding her stare with mine. "She was on her way home. And I only went inside to get him to talk to me. I figured it'd be better inside than standing in the dark alone. Ms. Newberry came home and I left. If he didn't open up to me with her gone, he wouldn't tell me anything with her there. So I came back— *before* curfew might I add."

"I know what time you got in. I heard the door. But that doesn't mean I'm okay with you disobeying me, regardless of the reasons. Couldn't your argument wait until today?"

I shook my head and my shoulders drooped. Defeat weighed heavily on me, knowing she would put an end to my plans to see Killian today—and possibly for the rest of the week. My parents were tough…loving, but tough.

"I know you care a lot about him," she started and placed her hand over mine on top of the table. "He's not a bad kid. I don't know too much about him other than what I've seen, and what I've been told by you and Ms. Newberry. But it's enough to know he's a good kid. However…"

I knew there'd be some sort of objection. There always was. She had a way of seeing things from two perspectives, both sides—good and bad. Growing up, she never let me focus on the bad things. If something happened, if I got a low grade on a test, she acknowledged it, but always turned it on its head. There was always a positive side to every negative—and in turn, a negative to every positive. I huffed, but let her continue.

"He's sheltered, Rylee. He never goes anywhere, doesn't have friends other than you. I'd be willing to bet he's got the mindset of someone five years younger than you. He's been through a horrific ordeal, and sometimes, things like that change a person to their core."

"You don't know him, Mom. I appreciate what you're saying, but you don't get him like I do. Yes, he's sheltered. You got that right. But you're wrong. He *does* go out. He has his learner's permit and will get his license when he turns seventeen. He has a home tutor and has completely caught up in school—in fact, he's above grade level in half of his subjects. Killian is smart, not at all like you're portraying him to be."

"I never said he wasn't smart."

"You said his mindset is that of an eleven-year-old."

"That's not what I meant. I didn't mean when it comes to school. Life in general. His social skills."

I leaned back in my chair and stared at the ceiling. My mouth opened to say something, but she cut me off, silencing my thoughts. My heart. My breathing. All with one question I hadn't anticipated.

"Have you had sex with him?"

My chin dropped, mouth gaped, eyes wide open and set on hers. "No, Mom. I haven't."

She tried to play it off, but relief was palpable in her exhale. Her shoulders lost a little of the tension that pulled them back in her perfect posture. And then her eyes softened right before they closed for a beat, more than likely sending a silent thank you to the heavens above.

"Why would you ask me that? I'm fifteen."

"I know, honey. I was just making sure. I know you two are more than friends, but I don't know how much more. Because you don't tell me. You've tried to play it off for years, and maybe you *are* only his friend, maybe you care about him more than you're willing to admit, but I'm your mother. It's my job to see through your words. I'm allowed to be concerned."

"Well, we *are* just friends. I like him. I won't lie about that. I think he likes me too, but I don't know if that's because he doesn't really know anyone else." I patted the top of her hand and offered her a genuine smile. "I appreciate your concern, Mom. I really do. But I think Killian is as safe as I'm going to get. You don't even want to know the kinds of boys I go to school with. Be thankful I've chosen Killian to like and not someone else."

She nodded with lips curled into a hint of a grin. "Please, if he ever tries to pressure you into anything, come to me. I won't be mad. I won't punish you. And when you do have sex—be it with him or someone else—I need to know. I can't protect you from things if I'm unaware."

I knew what she meant. She'd mentioned it when I got my period for the first time, and again when I started high school. I knew all about protection and doctor's appointments and tests for diseases, although I hadn't had a reason to do any of that yet.

"I will, Mom. Can I go see him now? I need to apologize for getting angry with him last night. I wasn't very nice when I left."

She nodded, and then I kissed her cheek and fled from the house in a race against time to get to Killian.

TEN

Killian

"WHAT THE *fuck*, man? He has a kid!" The guy with the spikey collar around his neck gestured to me, his chest heaving, shoulders rising with every panicked breath.

"Take care of him," the one next to my mom said. His voice was even and calm, and when he held out his arm, pointing the knife in my direction, I noticed it didn't shake. It seemed odd; there wasn't a part of my body that wouldn't stop shaking, and it wasn't because I was cold. The heat in the room was stifling.

"And do what with him?"

My sight bounced around the room, the only part of me capable of moving. My mom stared at the ceiling, her mouth opened wide as if she were about to scream. But she was still. Completely still. Not even her red-painted chest moved.

I stared at her, willing her to get up.

Willing her to move.

But she didn't.

I became lost in memories of her singing in the kitchen, of her holding me to her chest and whispering how much she loved me. The pounding of her heart still rang through my ears...or maybe that was my own.

The man next to her shifted his stance. He was saying something, but I couldn't understand any of it. His words were muffled, like he had a sock in his mouth. I turned my attention from the rainbow on his shirt to his face, noticing his mouth was empty and wondering why he sounded so funny.

"Shut him up!" I was able to hear that, and it seemed everyone else did as well.

SILENCED

The one with the collar jumped at the harsh tone of the man next to my mom. I glanced between the two, feeling as if I were watching a movie. It was surreal. All of it. Like I was invisible, a fly on the wall as my mom always said.

The spikes on the collar caught a sliver of light through the window and gleamed when the man turned his head toward me. "He's just a boy."

Just a boy. I rolled my tongue around the words, though not speaking them out loud.

"I don't care how old he is. He's a witness."

"I'm not killing a kid." The collar must've restrained his voice, because he spoke in a low tone, not quite whispering, but not shouting like the man in front of him—the one with the knife. The man with the triangle and rainbow on his black T-shirt.

"Then gouge his eyes out. I don't care what you do. Silence him."

I turned my attention to my dad. I swore I heard him speak. But when I found him, I thought he might've fallen asleep, although I wasn't sure how he could've with people in his room. His eyes were open, and just like Mom, his chest was still.

The man standing over him didn't move, only stared at me with tight lips and stiff shoulders. He seemed angry. But I didn't know why. Maybe he was mad that my dad was asleep. I wished he'd wake up.

One constant noise kept pulling at my attention. I didn't know what it was, but I couldn't ignore it. It came from my dad, or near him. A muted tap, a muffled pat. It sounded like water dripping on something soft. I glanced down and noticed something shiny in the man's hand. I studied it more, only to discover where the noise had come from.

Paint dripped from the shiny object he held. I couldn't tell what it was. His fist clenched around the black handle until his knuckles turned white. And when I met his fierce, angry gaze again, fear nearly buckled my knees.

It wasn't paint.

Dad's shirt had been white.

He wasn't mad that my dad was asleep.

Because he wasn't.

It wasn't a movie or a nightmare or my active imagination. It was reality. As if I'd just smacked right into a brick wall, it hit me all at once. My parents were dead, and these men had killed them. I'd be next if the one by my mom had anything to do with it.

I stumbled back a step, but before I could turn and run, the man with the triangle on his shirt pointed his knife at me and crossed the room. He grabbed me by my shoulder and threw me to the ground. I tried to scream, but only air escaped. I tried to move, but he sat on me, preventing me from squirming away. My face was wet, my sight blurry, my lungs not working properly.

"He's just a boy! A kid! What the fuck are you doing, man?" I couldn't see him past the guy sitting on my chest, but I knew the frantic pleas had come from the one in the corner without any blood on him.

"Someone needs to make sure he doesn't say anything."

"I won't," I cried out, although it was choked with a sob and barely audible. "I won't. I promise. I won't say anything. Please, let me wake up. I want to wake up now."

"You think this is a dream? Your parents are monsters. They ruin people's lives. You're better off without them. This isn't a dream. In fact, I just saved you from your worst nightmare."

"No...no...no..." I kept repeating the word until my throat was scratchy and raw.

"They're fucking cunts. Both of them. Worthless pieces of shit. And I just saved you. You should thank me." He laughed, but it sounded off. Humorless. Not like he'd just told a joke. It scared me and I shook even more, sobbed even harder. "Yes...that's what you should do. Thank me, boy."

I couldn't. I shook my head and tried to free my arms from beneath his weight. But he was too big, too strong. I was stuck. Dad always said boys didn't cry, but Mom told me it was okay. She said everyone had feelings and emotions, and we were allowed to let them out any way we could, because holding them in was bad.

So I cried.

Out loud.

I didn't hold it in.

Because that would've been bad.

"Thank me!" the man on top of me shouted again.

"Th—thank you." Those two words burned my tongue, and I was scared my parents would be mad at me for saying them. I shook my head again, but the guy grabbed me. Hands on both sides of my face held me still. "Th—thank you," I repeated again, hoping he'd let me go.

"You won't tell anyone about this, right? If I let you live, you won't say anything?"

"N–no. I w–won't. I promise." My voice was airy, breathless, and with his crushing weight on my chest, the edges of my sight turned dark. My hands, feet, arms, and legs grew cold and tingly, like they were about to fall asleep.

"If you do…if you tell anyone—and I mean anyone—I'll remove your voice box like I did your mom's. Got that? Don't think the police can help you. They can't. They'll make you promises, tell you what you want to hear, but they lie. They're pigs. And they will lie to you. They won't be able to save you from me. Got it?"

I nodded, because I couldn't speak. My sobs choked me, and my tears blinded me.

"I'll know if you say anything. And then I'll come for you. Don't make me regret letting you live. If you do, I won't think twice about cutting you into pieces and making you choke on your own flesh through a hole in your throat."

I closed my eyes tight and shook my head, willing him to get off me so I could breathe. Praying he'd leave me alone so I could wake up from this nightmare. Warmth trailed down the sides of my face and pooled in my ears—and the world went silent. It sounded like I was in a bathtub, under the water, hearing things around me but unable to make out the words.

He let go of my face, and I thought my prayers had been answered.

But then came the searing pain.

My cheeks burned so badly I couldn't make a sound. My eyes popped open, and I found the man above me smiling, a wicked glint in his eyes. I couldn't even move my head, like it'd been superglued to the floor beneath me. My lungs shriveled up, on fire from the pain. My nostrils stung. There wasn't a part of my body not crying out in utter agony.

Then he stood up, but he didn't leave.

I tried to gasp for air, though I couldn't find any. It'd all been sucked out of the room. My body felt heavy. I couldn't move. Couldn't speak. Couldn't cry. Couldn't see.

But I could feel.

And what I felt next would be something I'd never forget.

The toe of his shoe crashed into my ribs. I felt something inside crack, snap, and blinding pain flooded me. My mouth opened wide in an effort to scream, but all it did was cause more torture. I didn't have a clue what he'd done to my face, but whatever it was left me choking on warm liquid. The taste of pennies saturated my tongue and dripped down my throat.

In my blurry vision, I noticed movement, but I wasn't sure what it meant. I couldn't see anything past the onslaught of tears, couldn't hear the words they spoke over the pounding in my ears. I don't know who or what gave me the strength, but I rolled onto my side.

And then darkness fell.

MY EYES SNAPPED open, my heart thrashing relentlessly against my chest. The ribs on my side that had once been broken throbbed in pain. And my cheeks, where I'd been granted a permanent smile, ached. My tight throat made breathing more difficult, but I ignored it. Without moving, I glanced around the room, taking it all in.

I wasn't eight anymore.

I wasn't in my parents' room.

I was safe.

It never failed—I always had the same dreams after sketching their faces. But if I didn't do it, the nightmares were worse. The residual pain I'd wake up with would be more severe. There was no escaping it. No evading *them*. They'd always be with me—in my head, on my sketchpad, in my dreams. Haunting me. Taunting me. Reminding me of the silence I promised to keep.

And I would.

I'd never tell a soul what happened that night.

Because no one could save me.

I settled onto my stomach, pushed my arms beneath my pillow, and closed my eyes. I'd barely slept a wink last night after Rylee left. Elise had wanted to talk. I wanted to be left alone. In the end, I wrote a letter, snuck out, and spent at least two hours beneath the moon and treetops out back. I didn't sketch, didn't do anything but stare at the silver disc in the sky and think about Rylee.

About the moon.

And about how one day, I wouldn't have to steal it from the sky.

I wouldn't have to stop time.

Because she'd be mine.

Satisfied with my resolve, I fell back asleep to the sounds of Elise moving around the house.

ELEVEN

Rylee

THE GARAGE DOOR OPENED as I ascended his driveway. Elise stepped out with her purse and car keys in her hand, a subtle smile on her face. "He's asleep, honey. I tried to tell him I was leaving, but he wouldn't wake up. Maybe come back in a few hours. He had a hard night last night. I don't know what took place between the two of you, but whatever it was, it didn't sit well with him."

I nodded and wrung my hands nervously in front of me. "I know. That's why I'm here. I want to apologize to him, maybe see if he'll talk to me today. If you don't mind, can I try to wake him up? I'd wait…but I really don't think I can."

Her chest expanded with her slow, deep inhale, and her gaze fell to my hands. "I won't be blamed. If your mom knows you're inside, in Killian's room, and I'm not home, I won't take the fall for it. I'm telling you right now to come back in a few hours after he's awake and can come outside. If you ignore me, and walk through the unlocked door, that's on you."

I heard her loud and clear, nodding enthusiastically.

When she started her car to leave, I hurried around to the front door and walked in. The house was eerily quiet—not that it was usually loud, but it wasn't often I was inside alone. The morning sun drifted through the front windows and brightened the living room. As I made my way down the hall to Killian's closed door, the shadows began to consume me, and I was left with a worried ache in my chest. Growing wider and deeper the closer I got to his room.

I didn't bother to knock. Instead, I twisted the handle and slowly opened it, taking in the dark space a little at a time until

I stood just inside the doorway. He was asleep on one side of the bed, the covers bunched around his waist. His back and shoulders moved up and down with each steady breath he took, his arms shoved beneath the pillow under his head.

Next to him was a yearbook, which I found odd since he didn't go to school. I carefully moved into the room and took a seat on the edge of the mattress, praying he didn't stir long enough for me to look at it. It was open, but I couldn't see to what page. The cover displayed a cartoon depiction of a tiger with the words "New Hope Tigers" in gold letters along the top. Beneath it, in scrolled font, read "Class of 2001." I couldn't imagine whose yearbook this was, or why he had it, opened next to him.

Just as I began to lift it, to see what he'd been looking at before setting it down, his fingers wrapped around my wrist, startling me. I gasped and dropped the hard book. Other than his hand, he hadn't moved. When I glanced at him over my shoulder, I found him lying in the same position, one arm still beneath his pillow, his face turned to the side. But his eyes were wide open, not a hint of sleep in them. The soft green completely contradicted the hard lines on his forehead as he took me in. His nostrils flared, making them more pronounced than usual, and his grip tightened.

I opened my mouth to say something, but he stopped me by pulling me toward him. I landed oddly on my side, although I didn't stay like that long. He simultaneously rolled me to my back and leaned up on his elbow to hover over my stunned body. It felt like he'd knocked the wind out of me. Even though I still had the ability to breathe, I chose not to.

He peered over his shoulder to his open door. His brow creased heavily in concentration, all while blinking toward the empty space, as if intently listening for something. I knew what, but it took me a moment to gather my thoughts and offer him the answer he sought.

"She's not here. She was leaving when I came in."

His eyes shot back to mine, and it concerned me when none of the apprehension left his features. "Did you get my note?" The way his voice came out sleepy and gruff, scratching over each syllable, sent my heart into an arrhythmic state.

I swallowed hard past the knot in my throat and nodded. Everything I'd wanted to say to him flew away, left my brain, and in its place, lust blossomed. I couldn't explain it. We'd been in this position before. He'd whispered hoarsely to me numerous nights in my room, beneath the covers, his body touching mine in one way or another. He'd brought me more orgasms than I could recall. And even last night, he'd ran his erection against the spot begging for him most. So it didn't make any sense to me why now, with nothing more than one question asked in his morning voice, I felt an ache so deep I wasn't sure it'd ever be relieved.

He crashed his lips onto mine. I couldn't close my eyes while his mouth took what it wanted from me. We'd kissed plenty of times, but never first thing in the morning. At first, I wanted to push him off me, tell him to brush his teeth, and then come back. But he didn't give me that option. Rather than letting up, he pushed forward, hungrier, more determined. His brows were knitted together and his nose pressed so hard against mine I could feel every exhale on my skin, peppering me with humidity I didn't often experience outside summer months.

By the time his tongue took over mine, I no longer thought about his morning breath, or asking him to brush his teeth. My eyes closed and a long, growly moan ripped through my chest. He palmed my breast, massaging it gently but with enough force to send shockwaves to the needy place between my legs. Though, it didn't last long.

He pulled away from my mouth but kept his body against mine while he trailed his lips and tongue down my neck. The moisture left behind on my collarbone cooled the farther down my body he crept, and it sent a new sensation through me. The nerves running down my spine, the ones that gathered at the base near the curve of my backside, burned like a trail of fire. However, my arms and legs tingled with a chill. My chest nearly exploded when he dipped the tip of his tongue into my belly button.

Desire pooled in the apex of my thighs, more than any other time he'd ever touched me. My hips rotated toward him, seeking him out. Needing him. Begging for his attention. I fisted the sheet beneath me in a desperate attempt to fight off the unknown cravings that ravished my logic.

"Wait...Killian..." I breathed out, forcing the words to come to life as soon as his fingers began to unhook the button on my shorts. "What are you doing?" Each heavy word was spaced with shaky breaths that matched the shudders overtaking my body.

He didn't lift his gaze to mine. Instead, he spoke with his lips against the soft skin below my navel. "Making you feel good. As good as you make me feel."

I ran trembling fingers through his hair, pulling the light strands away from his face. "You don't have to do this. I didn't come here for that. I only wanted to make sure you were okay after last night. That *we're* okay."

Finally, his eyes met mine. Desire enlarged his pupils until they were twice their normal size, almost taking over the color I loved so much. "I'd be a lot better if you let me do this. But we don't have to. If you're not comfortable, I can stop." Then he whispered, "Please don't make me stop," along my lower belly in heated breaths.

My legs tightened around him, squeezing his ribcage...in place of the words I couldn't speak. The approval I offered, but couldn't utter. It didn't matter we needed to talk, or that we still hadn't discussed the night before. My body wanted him.

My heart wanted him.

I wanted him.

Killian sat back on his haunches and pulled my shorts and panties off my legs in one swift move like he'd done this before. He lifted one of my legs from behind my knee and softly pressed tiny kisses up my thigh until he settled himself into place again. His breaths blew against my sex, a place no one other than myself had ever seen bare, had ever touched. And now here he was, his mouth, his lips, his tongue so close to my center I couldn't breathe.

When nothing happened, I opened my eyes to look at him, worried something was wrong. He regarded me with a soft expression, brows slightly knitted and lips parted just a bit. "I don't know what I'm doing, Rylee. I didn't know last night, and I don't know now."

We'd come a long way from the kids who mashed their lips together in hurried kisses. When it came to Killian, I didn't lack confidence. Maybe that was because for a few years, my maturity and knowledge of life surpassed his. But when it came to sex, I seemed innately self-conscious. I'd never watched the kinds of videos he had. Porn never appealed to me. But I knew that's where he learned everything, so I never questioned him. Seeing him now, so afraid, so insecure, my heart broke for him.

"It's okay, Killian. I don't know, either."

"If I do something wrong…tell me. I don't want to hurt you again."

I nodded and ran my fingertip down the side of his face.

His exhale hit me just right and caused my back to arch. Killian wound his arms beneath my thighs, bringing my legs over his shoulders, and gripped my hips to hold me steady. He took one last glance at me before pressing a kiss to my lower lips.

And then the room began to spin.

The dimly lit space darkened even more.

One swipe with the tip of his tongue sent me into orbit. The second lit my body on fire, charring me from the inside out. Then he flattened his mouth over the spot I needed him most, and the warmth from his lips pulled a long, deep growl from my chest. I shuddered as my orgasm licked its way through my body, down my extremities, and sizzled in the tips of my fingers and toes.

It felt like when he'd touch me through my clothes, and I began to settle into his bed. However, it didn't last long. Because a split second later, he licked me again. My eyes clenched tight, my thighs shook uncontrollably, and my fists gripped the sheet so hard my knuckles ached. Light exploded behind my eyelids, matching the eruptions going on inside. I was completely unaware of what my body was doing, never felt anything like it before.

My panicked breaths came out in harsh bursts of sheer desperation as he crawled up my body. Euphoria flooded my system with liquid heat and tremors I couldn't control. I grabbed the sides of his face and brought his mouth to mine. No longer did I taste his morning breath, but something hot and a bit tangy. His lips were wet, but I didn't care. The sweetness on his tongue left me begging for more.

More of what...I didn't know.

Just more.

As he deepened the kiss, I ran my hands down his chest, not stopping until I reached the elastic band of his shorts. The second my fingers dipped inside, he pulled away, his stare hard and unyielding.

"No, Rylee." It was meant to stop me, but the deep grumbles of his voice urged me on. He grabbed one wrist, using his other hand to hold him up. "This was for you. I don't want you to do anything for me."

"I know," I whispered, sounding far more confident than I felt on the inside. "This *is* for me." I wrapped my fingers around his hard shaft and pulled just enough to make him growl. When he lowered his mouth to mine again, feeding me his appreciation through moans and grunts, I used my hands and feet to push his shorts down.

With him completely bare to me, in my hand, inches from my aching core, I felt powerful. An illusion I never knew existed. It was what a few of my friends had talked about in school. The way it felt to bring a man to his knees. To be in charge of his wants, desires, thoughts, and actions. But Killian didn't do anything other than kiss me. He didn't push himself into the hold I had on his shaft. He didn't tilt his hips or press for more. Instead, he remained still and let me touch him, his lips working mine over with complete control.

In a move I hadn't expected, I lined the tip of his erection with my wet entrance. He stilled above me. His mouth left mine, but he didn't back away. "What are you doing?" he asked, his eyes hooded.

"I want to feel you. Everywhere. Inside me."

Killian shook his head slowly, never taking his attention off my eyes. "I can't."

"Why not?"

"After last night..."

"It's okay." I cupped his cheek and lifted my head until my lips landed gently on his. "I want this. I want you."

"We're not ready. *You're* not ready."

I hated how hard he tried to resist me. But that was my pride talking, bruised from his immediate rejection. I had to remind myself why. We were young. We'd agreed to take things slow, one step at a time. And he'd promised me he wouldn't hurt me.

None of that mattered anymore.

I stroked him a little more and ran the tip between my folds, my arousal coating him. Again, I placed him at my entrance. This time, I locked onto his eyes and nodded, silently telling him what I wanted most.

"We can't come back from this," he argued.

"I know. I don't want to."

He closed his eyes and blistered my face with his exhale. "I don't know what I'm doing."

"Neither do I. We'll learn together. Just like with everything else."

His hips bucked, which added unexpected pressure against my sex. I sucked in air through my teeth, the sound of a hiss forcing him to still.

"No...keep going. I'm fine."

"What if you get hurt? What if I can't control myself like last night? I hurt you, Rylee. I don't want to do that again."

"It's fine. It'll hurt, but I'm prepared for that. I wasn't expecting it last night, but I am now. Please," I begged, practically whining along his lips. "Please, Killian. I want this with you. More than I've ever wanted anything else."

He peppered kisses along my cheek and slowly rotated his hips toward me. I held him in place while he pushed against me. I wasn't sure if he was in or not, but it didn't feel at all like I expected it to. It was just pressure...a lot of pressure.

"I don't think this will work," he breathed against my neck where he buried his head.

"It will. I think you just have to push harder." I barely got the words out before he jerked his hips forward, pushing past the obstruction and entering me.

White hot pain seared through my lower half and I had to bite my lips to keep from screaming out in agony. I latched my wide-eyed gaze on the ceiling, and then his face came into view. Worry and shock lined his features, and his pupils were enlarged. His frantic breaths billowed past his parted lips.

SILENCED

We were skin to skin, his hips flush with mine. His heartbeat pounded through my chest, calling to me, syncing with mine. Beckoning every beat. Provoking every pulse. We were one, merged from our heads to our feet. Entwined. Linked together in the most intimate places.

"I didn't mean to," he rasped against my cheek.

"It's okay. I'm fine." My voice shook, unsteady from the dull ache throbbing inside. I urged him on with my hips, praying he missed the way my lip curled when I winced. Hoping he didn't think too much about how tight I now had my eyes closed.

Once again, he buried his face into the crook of my neck, and slowly dragged his erection out until only the tip remained. His entire body shuddered as he gently pushed back in. I held my breath until it turned stale in my lungs, setting a fire within my chest. I'd expected pain, but hadn't anticipated it to be like this.

After two more drawn-out rolls of his hips, his body turned rigid. His movements became harsher and his thrusts more punishing than the first one. He didn't pull back far enough to gain momentum, but what little advantage he did have, he took it, pushing inside me so hard his pubic bone slammed against mine with each plunge. Finally, he stilled, although his shoulders, arms, and legs tremored violently.

"I'm sorry," he rasped against my neck, his apology grating over my skin. "I'm so sorry."

"It's okay." My meek voice was barely audible, but I knew he felt my fingertips grazing his bare back, his flesh slick with perspiration.

"No, it's not. You're crying."

It only made the tears flow faster. I didn't know how he knew, how he could tell, but he did. Even without looking at me, without seeing my face, he understood my pain. And claimed it as his own. Blamed himself.

"I'm so sorry…" he repeated.

TWELVE

Killian

THE MIRROR WAS FOGGY from the shower as I slipped my white T-shirt over my damp chest. Ever since my eighteenth birthday, it'd been a struggle to stay here. I'd told myself for so many years that once I got here, I'd be gone. I'd leave to find my voice.

But I can't leave.

Not yet.

Not until I can take Rylee with me.

She's the only thing keeping me here. The only person capable of calming the storm inside. It'd been ten years since the night my parents were murdered. Ten years since those fuckers came into my house and stole the most important people from my life.

And walked away.

They'd never been found. Probably because I never talked. Never gave the police officers answers. At the time, I'd been too scared to say anything, even though I knew the answers. Now, my recollection would be of no use. Too much time had passed, too much evidence missed. The fuckers would never see the inside of a courtroom.

I opened the door and flicked off the light, ready to head for bed. But as soon as I stepped into the doorway of my room, everything stopped. The world quit spinning, my lungs refused to work, and my heart gave up pumping.

Elise sat on the end of my bed, my notepad in her lap. Tears lined her face and sobs racked her shoulders. I didn't need to see the sketch in front of her to know what she was looking at. I knew every single one of them by heart—some I'd drawn over and over again. But I glanced at it anyway, seeing the morbid scene, the colors bleeding on the paper from her errant tears.

I moved swiftly into the room and snatched the sketchpad away.

"I–I don't understand, Killian. Why would you draw that?"

I flipped the lid closed before she could look at it again. She didn't need to see in full detail what her sister looked like. The gaping hole in her neck. The blood. Her eyes wide in fear, devoid of life. Hell, I don't even know why I'd drawn it so many times. Maybe to remember the evil bastard who did it. To remember what he took from me—*and how*. Or maybe to alleviate my mind of the images, to get it out long enough to keep the weight of my memory from crushing me. Whatever the reason, there were dozens of them just like this one.

Of my father, too.

And the men who viciously stole them from me.

I turned around to leave. My face burned so hot it felt like I stood beneath the intense rays of the sun in the middle of a summer day…not in my room just after ten at night. I pivoted on my heel, not knowing where to go or what to do. Anger tightened my fists and the thought of punching a wall filtered through my head. Visions of breaking my silence to scream at her for invading my privacy flashed before my eyes. The need to leave, storm out the door, and never come back grew stronger, louder, more intense than ever before.

"Killian." Elise's feeble, shaky, uncertain voice stilled me.

I couldn't face her, couldn't look into her eyes. So I stood with my back to her and waited for what she had to say. Knowing I'd done this to her tore me up. She never needed to see those images. It was bad enough I had—then, and every day since. But it wasn't my fault she'd found them, wasn't my fault she'd seen my nightmare. I hadn't shown her. She did that on her own. And because of that, the rage inside wouldn't die, no matter the level of sorrow coursing through me for her.

"You need help, Killian. You need to see someone. Talk to someone. This isn't healthy—what you're doing. Had I known…" She inhaled slowly, deeply, and it shook, shuddered. Each slight hiccup hit me in the back, delayed my heartbeat, and wound tightly in my chest until I couldn't breathe. "Had I known this is what you were in here drawing, I would've sought help earlier. I would've taken you to see someone who could've helped with this."

A growl started low in my stomach, and before I knew it, I'd swung around to face her, inches from her face, and released the burning fury through clenched teeth. The roar pushed her back a step, her eyes wide in fear, her trembling hand over her chest.

I didn't want to scare her.

But I did.

And no matter how much pain it caused, I couldn't stop.

I followed her retreating form, taking a step forward to match every one she took back, until she fell onto the edge of the bed, exactly where I'd found her when I came in. I hunched my back with my shoulders pulled taut, my chest puffed out. My violent breaths wafted over her face, but she didn't move. She blinked her wide eyes at me. Her lips parted. But other than that, she didn't budge against my visual assault.

"Killian," she whispered and attempted to reach out to me, but I backed away. "Talk to me. On paper, with your voice…I don't care how you do it. Write on the wall for all I care. But don't push me away. I love you. I only want to help you. You shouldn't have to live that night over and over again."

I flipped the sketchpad open to a clean sheet toward the end. After so many years, there weren't many pages left, but I found one. A fat black marker sat on my dresser. I had pens and pencils scattered all over the room, but that was the first thing I went for.

You can't make it go away.

"If you talk to someone, it can help."

No talking!

She read my words and then turned her glistening eyes to mine. Her lips pressed together as her chin quivered, and I realized she'd misunderstood me. An ache started behind my sternum, low and deep.

I can't talk to anyone. No one can help me.

"They can, Killian. You just have to let them."

I shook my head, but that didn't stop her from continuing.

"You talk to Rylee. She helps, right? I've seen you with her. You're different. Calmer. She makes the images go away, doesn't she? But she's not a professional; she can't help you the way others can."

I've been to doctors before. They don't help. They only want to know what happened and I can't tell them that. I can't tell anyone. <u>*No one can help me*</u>. I underlined the last sentence a few times, reiterating it again. I'd write it a hundred times if it'd make her understand.

"Don't you see? You're drawing what happened. You have a notebook full of what happened. So why can't you talk about it? Why can't you tell anyone about that night? You remember…clearly you do if you're sketching it."

You don't understand. I showed her the paper, but quickly brought it back to add more. *You WON'T understand*.

"You don't know that because you've never let me. Try me."

My hand itched to write it out for her, to tell her why I couldn't say anything. But I knew that'd be useless. She wanted justice as much as anyone else, and she wouldn't stop until she had enough information. Until the *cops* had enough information. But she hadn't been there. She would never know the fear I'd felt, the rage I'd lived with, and the promise I'd made to myself.

I need to be alone.

She shook her head again and stood, her piercing stare preventing me from moving. "No. I'm not leaving. I'm not going to walk away when you need me the most. You're eighteen, Killian. You're an adult. When will you move forward? When will you be the man your parents hoped for…the man I helped raise you to be?"

I brought my shaky hand to the paper, my anger so deep it sent shockwaves throughout my body, but she stopped me by touching my arm.

"You complete high school in a month. What do you plan to do after that? You haven't worked through the worst night of your life, haven't dealt with the pain and resentment and grief the way you need to. You'll never be able to move forward until you do. And I don't want to see you stuck in this place…in this dark, silent, sad place. I want to see you go to college—a *real* college, not online classes like you've talked about. You need a job, a career. A life. That's all I want for you, Killian. I want you to be happy."

I will be.

"When?"

When I'm no longer silenced.

Her shoulders fell and she dipped her chin. She released a long exhale, and the sound penetrated me. Cut me open. Embedded itself deep within my chest until I felt like I was bleeding out at her feet. I loved her, and I'd hurt her. It wasn't my intention, but I didn't know what else to do. I couldn't give in to her. Couldn't give her what she wanted.

"You don't have to be. That's what I'm trying to tell you." When she glanced back up, fat tears curled over her high cheekbones, trickled into the soft, hollow spaces next to her mouth, and then hung from her dimpled chin.

I lowered my head and placed my lips next to her ear. "I'm working on it. My way. Let me do this the only way I know how," I whispered in the lowest, softest, quietest voice I could. They were nothing more than words floating on air, no hint of my voice present, but it was enough for her to gasp.

Elise fell into my chest. She covered her face with her hands and sobbed against me. I wrapped my arms around her, wanting to comfort her. It was the first time in ten years I'd spoken to her.

Her back shook with each hiccupping cry.

Her shoulders bounced uncontrollably.

Her entire body heaved with emotion I couldn't quell.

I held her for a while, stroking her back the way she'd done to me so many years ago when I first came to stay with her. At the time, I feared she'd give me back. I'd be too much for her to handle, and she'd give up, returning me the way everyone else had.

But she hadn't.

She'd kept me.

Supported me.

Loved me.

And here I was, about to turn my back on her.

I released her and pointed to a line I'd written a few minutes earlier. I took the marker and circled it, hit the paper with the tip until black dots lined it. I needed her to go. I needed to be alone. To think. To figure everything out. My heart and head were at odds and I wouldn't be able to make a decision with her standing in front of me. With her cries filling the room.

With her sorrow filling my chest.

Elise nodded, not once meeting my gaze. She backed away and took one step toward the open bedroom door. On instinct, I grabbed her arm and spun her around until she met my chest again. I wrapped my arms around her once more, squeezing her tight this time, and felt a sudden calmness overtake me when she did the same.

Maybe she knew. Maybe she didn't. But this hug felt as much of a goodbye from her as was meant from me. She didn't try to stop me, beg me to stay, say anything to change my mind. Which led me to believe maybe she wasn't aware of what I'd meant when I held her to me. Or, it could've been that she knew it'd be futile to hold me back.

After she pulled herself away from me, she looked into my eyes and cupped my cheek. "I love you, Killian. Never doubt that. Never question it. You may not have been my son, but in my heart, you always will be. I only want what's best for you."

I nodded, and then watched her walk away.

At least she didn't have to watch *me* walk away.

When the door closed behind her, I took a bag from my closet and began to throw a few things inside. I didn't have much. I didn't need much. Only my sketch pads, my dad's yearbook, a few pairs of clothes, and the withdrawal slips for my bank. Everything else I could figure out later.

I glanced around my room, the one I'd had for the last seven years. This had been my home, although it never truly felt like it. Elise had done everything she could to make me comfortable, make me belong. But no matter what, I was never able to shake the feeling of being a guest.

I had too much unfinished business.

As I snuck out the window, leaving everything else behind, I knew there was one more thing I had to get. One more thing I couldn't walk away without. One thing I couldn't leave behind. Everything I had was replaceable—including the sketches and bank slips. Everything except *her*.

Except Rylee.
I needed her.

THIRTEEN

Rylee

A THUNDEROUS KNOCK jolted me awake. I lay still for a moment to allow my mind the chance to comprehend where the sound had come from, even though my heart already knew. When it resonated again, I leapt from my bed and opened the blinds. Killian stood on the other side, pacing a few steps back and forth with his gaze set on the ground beneath his feet.

"What's wrong?" I asked once I lifted the window.

He glanced at me, and for the first time, I found myself hating the night. I couldn't see his expression, couldn't read him, but I could *feel* it. Devastation rolled off him in furious waves, blasting through the screen until they washed over me. Suffocated me. Drowned me in his pain.

"Killian," I whispered, although it came out slightly louder than I'd anticipated. I glanced behind me at my closed door, for no other reason than reassurance, and then popped the screen out like I'd done so many times to let him in. But he didn't come forward. He didn't make a move to crawl inside. That's when my panic increased, pushing me out the window.

He finally stilled once my bare feet landed in the grass. It took him two steps to make his way to me, where he grabbed my shoulders and stared into my eyes beneath the dark sky. If the moon was out, it was hiding. The only light available was the subtle glow from the stars, coupled with the streetlight on the other side of the fence.

"What's wrong?" Fear consumed me until my voice was shaky and breathless.

"Leave with me. Come with me."

I shook my head, hoping I'd heard him wrong. "Where are you going?"

"I can't stay here anymore. It's time for me to leave. But I can't go without you. I can't leave you behind. So please, come with me." The desperation in his tone frightened me. It hollowed me out and left me empty, confused, and utterly heartbroken.

"I can't, Killian. It's a school night. My parents will know I'm gone."

"That's okay. I can take care of you. It'll be me and you."

"I'm seventeen. I'm still in school." I tried to pull away, but his hold on me tightened. "*You're* still in school. We can't just run away. Where is this coming from? I don't understand. Why are you leaving?"

He finally released me and stumbled back a few steps. "I just… I can't stay here any longer. But I can't walk away from you. I need you, Rylee. Please, come with me. Run away with me."

"Killian, do you hear yourself? I can't run away. I can't leave my family behind. We had a plan. You stay and take college classes online while I finish high school, and then we go away together. Why are you changing this? Why can't you wait one more year?"

He fisted his hands in his hair and spun around in circles like a lost little boy in a grocery store looking for his mother. Fighting away the confusion and unanswered questions, I locked my arms around his neck, unconsciously offering him the comfort I knew he needed.

"Look at me." I kept my tone even, despite the uneasiness pumping through my veins. "We can still run off together…in a year. Let's stick to our plan. Just take a few deep breaths, think about what you're doing, and wait until I'm done with school."

He dropped his hands to my shoulders and grabbed a tight curl next to my face. It wound around his finger while he carefully studied it, as if memorizing it. "I don't know if I can wait. I don't know how much longer I can stay here, knowing I…"

"Knowing what, Killian? What do you know?" I asked when I realized he wouldn't finish his sentence. "What happened tonight?"

His hands settled gently on my hips, but then he gripped them tight, pulling my body flush with his. "She doesn't understand me like you do. No one does. I need you, Rylee…more than I need anything else in the world. You're the only one who can save me. I feel like I'm in a prison here. Trapped in my head, trapped in the nightmare I can't shake. But you…you're the only one who makes that go away. You erase the images. It's you. Only you. Don't make me do this alone. I won't survive."

I held onto his face and looked as deeply into his eyes as I could without sufficient light. Although, I didn't need to see them to know how he felt. It was in his voice, in the way he touched me. In his desperate breaths. The torture he'd hidden away for years had resurfaced and leaked from his pores, saturated him in agony.

I only wanted to make it go away.

Silence it.

So I pulled his face to mine. With our lips so close I could feel the heat from his, I whispered, "Then stay with me. Be with me. Don't leave. Don't walk away, Killian. I can't survive without you, either."

His mouth collided with mine with so much force our teeth clashed. It reminded me of our first kiss, the first time I ever felt his lips. It was hurried, desperate…needy. I wanted to evaluate the meaning, decipher the purpose, but he didn't let up. He took every ounce of oxygen around us until there wasn't enough left for my brain to function properly. Logic didn't exist. The where, when, how, why, wouldn't translate.

It was him and me.

Me and him.

No one else. Nothing else. Just us. On the side of my house with my back against the brick, his lips on mine, his tongue taking control—*demanding* control. For a brief moment, when he hooked his thumbs into the waistband of my cotton shorts, my chest constricted. Fear choked me. But it didn't last long, because he didn't take his time. My shorts and panties dropped around my ankles and his lips pressed against my neck.

"I need you, Rylee." It was all it took to wipe my mind clear of the entire world around us. He gripped the backs of my thighs and hoisted me, pinning me against the side of the house. My legs wrapped around his hips and I locked my ankles behind him.

Over the last year and a half, we'd been together so many times I'd lost count. It was awkward at first, neither of us knowing what to do, and both being completely inexperienced. But we'd learned together. We studied *each other*. And now, whenever he touched me, I lacked the ability to turn him down. My body knew what his could do, and craved it like a junkie.

Killian was my drug.

The only drug I knew.

I unfastened his jeans for him and pulled them down just enough to free him. He was hard, long, and throbbing in my hand. My core involuntarily clenched and pulsed, anticipating him inside me.

Not even a second after I aligned him with my entrance, he pushed in. His soft skin moved in and out effortlessly, slick with my need for him. His face remained buried in the crook of my neck—his favorite place—while he stroked every inch of my insides, bringing me to indescribable heights.

"I need you," he continued to growl against my skin. Over and over again he repeated the same sentiment, covering me with his demand, his promise, his devastation.

His hair twisted in my fingers, and I used the hold to keep him close to me. My eyes closed on instinct. Heat rolled through me like a storm cloud, slow and powerful, all-consuming. Heavy. Dark. Intense. It filled me on the inside and covered me on the outside. I tightened my legs around him as he lifted me higher and higher toward the proverbial cliff.

"I need you to be mine. All mine." His breath burned my shoulder.

"I am yours, Killian." I had to force the words out. He needed to hear them. But I was so lost in what his body gave mine, I wasn't sure they were loud enough, or clear enough for him to understand. "I'm yours. And you're mine."

With that, his pace picked up, his strength increased. I could feel him everywhere. Deep inside, licking the swollen need only he could reach. Outside, where his body met mine, where his pubic bone assaulted my aching clit, adding to the increasing sensations he delivered. Against me. Around me. There wasn't a part of my body, inside or out, that couldn't feel him.

But I felt him the most in my chest.

In my heart.

In. Every. Single. Beat.

The heat of his breath scorched the skin on my neck one more time, and his grumbling voice filtered into my ears. I knew he said something, but I didn't understand it. The tingles inside spread out, turning the heat to ice. The power in which I came deafened me to his words, numbed me to the harsh friction of the brick against my spine. I bit my lip to quiet the intense pleasure flooding me and held him tighter as his thrusts became shallow and rigid.

He finally lifted his face from my shoulder and pressed his forehead against mine. Our breaths mingled between us while we tried to settle down and process what had just happened. It wasn't the first time we fell into the need for sex before finishing a conversation. We both seemed to be so passionate about the other, we had a hard time fighting the desire to be together, despite the situation that laid at our feet.

This time was no different.

Except, this time, we weren't given the opportunity to finish our conversation.

Had we not been breathing so heavily, I might've thought more about the stray cat that raced past us. I might've contemplated it more than just realizing what it was. I wouldn't have ignored it. But I wasn't given the time to process it all before it rounded the corner of the house, tripping the motion detector light.

Instead of pulling away, Killian kissed me. Hard. His body shook and his hold on me tightened. It was unlike any other kiss he'd ever given me. Like he was telling me something in it. At the sound of the screen door opening, he pulled out of me and set me on the ground. He touched my face once more, lingering for a second too long.

"Go…before you get caught." I shoved him away with my heartbeat crashing in my ears. His mouth moved, but I couldn't hear anything, nor could I read his lips. Panic pushed me forward until I shoved him again. In an instant, he climbed the fence and hopped to the other side with a soft thud of his shoes on the grass.

I pressed myself against the side of the house, praying I was hidden enough in the shadows. My breathing was erratic, almost impossible to slow down. I closed my eyes and sucked in my stomach, as if it'd make me invisible, but the moment a bright light lit up the backs of my eyelids, I knew it was over.

"What are you doing out here?" My father's deep voice sounded closer than I thought it was. The light moved off my face and gave me a chance to open my eyes. I found him shining his flashlight into my window, where the screen leaned against the wall below it. He took an angered breath and growled, "Get back inside."

I couldn't move, frozen in fear. My shorts and panties still lay on the ground by my feet. My T-shirt hung low enough he couldn't see me, but I knew if he watched me crawl back through the window, he'd know. So instead of following his orders, I remained where I stood.

"Rylee…" It was a warning, one I knew better than to disobey. "I said to get back inside now."

Leaving my clothes behind, I shuffled along the brick toward my open window. It took three steps before his growl echoed in the night, sounding more like an incensed animal than my dad. The beam of light hit my bare thighs, then drifted to the grass. I didn't need to look to know what he found. The warm fluid along the inside of my thigh, cooling as it trailed down my skin, was enough to know how much trouble I was about to be in.

After the first time Killian and I had sex, we made sure to always use a condom. Always. I was too scared to tell my mom, even though she'd assured me she wouldn't be upset. I knew she'd make me stay away from Killian. So I never told her. I never went to the doctor or got on birth control. Luckily, I'd started my period two days later, so we didn't have to suffer long before we knew we were safe. But I knew now, standing outside in front of my father, half naked with come dripping down my leg…I wasn't safe.

At all.

Nothing could protect me.

• • •

A WEEK WENT by. Nothing from Killian. I'd been grounded, not allowed out of the house except for school. My parents had taken away my phone, so I had no way to get ahold of him. Every morning, I prayed I'd wake up to a note—even though my screen had been repaired and my window nailed shut. But every morning, I woke up to nothing.

A month went by. Still no word from him. My parents kept me under lock and key, and I knew my summer would be no different. I'd stare out the front window for hours, hoping to see him run by, or at the very least, just outside. But I never did.

The summer came and went. It was my senior year, a time I should've felt on top of the world. But I didn't. I couldn't. Not when Killian had practically vanished into thin air. I hadn't seen him since he jumped over the fence. Since the night he left me alone in the dark with nothing more than his come inside me. I knew it—had known it since that night—he was gone.

He wasn't coming back.

FIVE YEARS LATER

FOURTEEN

Rylee

"I'LL BE fine. Don't rush back. Drive safe." Josh's voice filled my car through the speakers, sounding more profound than usual. He had a deep voice, but not gravelly or heavy like other men. It was...normal. For some reason, when I spoke to him over Bluetooth in the car, it made him sound rougher, meaner. I liked it...and I didn't. I loved the sound of a man's voice, throaty and powerful. But I hated to hear it because it always reminded me of one person—the one I couldn't forget, no matter how long it'd been since I'd last heard it.

"I want to be there to support you, though. I feel bad I can't," I said.

"It's not even a real fight, babe. Just some kid who wants to make a name for himself. It's no big deal. I promise. I'll knock him out in two hits, he'll go down, the bell will ring, and it'll all be over. You won't be missing much."

I rested my head against the back of the seat and focused on the traffic in front of me. The drive from Smithsville, Tennessee, to Baltimore was long—about eight hours—and I still had at least two left, providing I didn't run into any more accidents along the way. I was tired of being in the car, but wanted to hurry and get home. Well, the place I'd called home for the last four years.

"I still don't understand how this fighting thing works."

Josh laughed on the other end. "It's fighting, Lee. You punch people until they're down or give up. It's not hard to understand."

106

I rolled my eyes. We'd only been dating for four months, and most of that I'd been in school finishing my degree, so we were still new to the relationship, but I hated how condescending he could be at times. Josh was older than me by nine years, and sometimes, it felt like he used that as an excuse to talk down to me. It didn't happen often, but when it did, it took everything in me to not argue back.

"You know what I mean, Josh. I'm not talking about fighting; I grasp that concept. I'm talking about the rules. How it all works. This isn't some bar brawl, a free-for-all." I sighed and switched lanes to get around a slow car, my irritation with my boyfriend bleeding into my driving. "Never mind. Don't worry about it."

"I'm sorry…I didn't mean for it to come out like that. Ask me what you want to know and I'll tell you." He'd explained it to me before—kind of. Josh had this way of talking to people as if they knew what he meant. He'd use terms and phrases that went right over my head, and when I'd interrupt him to ask him to clarify, he'd get frustrated. So eventually, I stopped asking, even though I had no clue what he was talking about most of the time.

"You said tonight isn't a real fight, that it's just some kid wanting to prove himself. I don't understand that. Why fight if it's not for real? And what do you mean by him proving himself? To who?"

"When someone wants to be picked up by a ring, they do one of two things. You either go to the team owner directly and hope they take you, or you set up what's called a bid. It's more or less like an application. From there, you go into the ring and fight. You don't get to pick your opponent; that's all chosen for you. The team owners come to watch—like scouting for sports in school. After the fight, if they want you in their ring, they bid on you."

"And then you can choose which team you want?"

His chuckle was soft and airy, but I heard it loud and clear. "No, Lee," he said with a bite of arrogance that made me want to end the call right then and there. "It's a bid, which means whoever bids the highest gets the fighter."

"Wait…you mean like money?"

"Yes. It becomes the fighter's sign-on bonus, I guess you could say."

"You make this sound so legit, Josh." I knew enough to know it wasn't. Legal, maybe—probably through loopholes. But definitely not legitimate. This may have been a business, but to a lot of people, it was a business for thugs.

"That's because it is. Say whatever you want, but these fights are regulated."

"Not by the Better Business Bureau." I shook my head, knowing I was seconds away from pissing him off. And I didn't want to do that while on my way to see him. It was bad enough he'd gotten mad when I went home to see my parents. It'd taken an entire day to get him to answer my calls, and I didn't want to start that all over again. "I'm just trying to understand why grown men would want to beat the shit out of each other. It would make sense if it was for a reason, like this guy stole from you or did something to make you angry, but he didn't. This guy wants a job—clearly—but instead of going and applying somewhere, he walks into a ring prepared to shed blood."

"You make it sound so violent."

"It is, Josh!" My fingers tightened around the steering wheel and my knuckles turned white against the black leather. I inhaled deeply to steady my voice before I continued. "I guess I just won't ever understand why you do this."

"Babe…fighting has been going on for centuries. This isn't a new sport."

"It's not a sport. I don't get how you can call it that."

"We train, we compete, we win and lose…it's a sport. I want you to understand it, because I want to share this part of my life with you. I love it when you show up to support me. I feel like a god when you're there watching me from the other side of the ropes."

"I know…I like being there, too. I'm sorry. I didn't mean for this to become an argument. It's just all so new to me. I'm trying to grasp it so I *can* support you. It's just hard when I can't comprehend why someone would be willing to get their nose broken for a few dollars."

His laugh filtered through the speakers again, this time softer, not at all condescending. "It's more than a few dollars, babe. The good ones will be around for a few years, and as long as they don't blow their money too fast, they could live off their earnings for a while. Then there are the greats…the ones who inflict more injuries than they get. They last longer, and most of the time, are set for life when they walk out of the ring for the last time. Dalton—my team owner and coach—was a great."

I smiled, thinking of Josh and the power he had behind his punches. "Which one are you?"

"Me? Babe, you should know that answer. I'm a great. I want to own my own team one day. Take this sport to a whole new level. And I will. Just watch. Which is why I need you to be completely on board, because you'll be by my side when I do it."

Butterflies erupted in my belly at his sentiment. We may not have been together for very long, but Josh always spoke like we were serious and headed toward a lasting future together. Considering I hadn't dated anyone since I was seventeen, it did something to me. Filled me with excitement and hope.

"Well, I'm just sorry I can't be there for you tonight. The traffic is clearing up and I'm finally able to drive with my cruise control set, but I doubt I'll make it there before it's over. Especially with the way you're talking like it'll only last a few minutes. I'm interested to see how this bidding war happens."

A smile hugged his voice when he said, "That all happens after it's over. It's done in private. The fighter won't know until way later which ring he's in, or if he's picked at all. Half the time, no one will take him."

"How did you do it? Did they bid on you?"

"Nah. I met Dalton in the gym. He told me about his ring, so I went one night to check it out. It was right after he'd started his own team. The place was crowded—people exchanging money left and right, the air stagnant, the smell of sweat permeating the muggy room. It was like I found where I belonged. I started asking him questions, and before I knew it, he'd signed me on his team."

"But isn't it better to go for a bid? To make more money?"

"It can be. Most of the time it is. But for me, I knew I'd go farther with Dalton than I would if I took my chances with anyone else. He was smart…didn't bid high, and only took the best. Which means come tournament time, his share of the stakes is higher. The more champs he has in his ring, the higher the price tag for winnings. So on top of my personal share for my individual fights, I also get a team cut. Everyone does. You want to be on the winning team, Lee. That's where you'll make your money. Not the starting payout."

"I think I get it now." The more he talked about it and the more I watched him fight, I'd eventually understand how it all worked. As long as I could wrap my mind around beating someone up for money.

"Listen, babe, I have to go. Dalton wants to talk to me first. Call me when you make it into town and I'll tell you where I'm at. I want to see you. I've missed you."

It put a smile on my lips. "I've missed you, too. I'll see you in less than two hours."

The call ended, leaving me with the silence in the car and the hum from my tires on the road. I took the time to think about everything my parents said while I visited them over the weekend. They wanted me to move back to Tennessee. It had always been the plan. Finish college, get my degree, and come home.

But I couldn't.

Even being there this weekend shook my foundation to the core. Smithsville was nothing but a reminder of the things I'd lost. Even though Elise didn't live next door anymore, hadn't in years, it didn't stop me from thinking of him. I'd spent five years wondering where he went, what he was doing, and why he never came back for me. Instead of leaving right after high school, I'd waited around all summer, hoping he'd return. It'd been our plan since we were kids. But he never surfaced.

It'd taken me years to finally open up to someone else. It wasn't like I'd kept myself available for Killian all that time. The ache he left me with was so wide, so deep, so unrepairable, it took that long for me to heal enough to move on. I knew he wasn't coming back—hell, I knew that before I left for Baltimore in the first place. So my reasons for holding back had nothing to do with him and everything to do with me.

Then one day, I ran into Josh. Literally. The traffic light had turned green and the car in front of me had started to go. I glanced down for a split second to change the radio station, and when I looked back up, I saw brake lights. Closer than they were before. It was a slight fender bender, but it'd shaken me up. I couldn't stop the quakes that'd taken over my body as I pulled myself from the car and met the driver between his trunk and my hood. I hadn't even looked at him, couldn't, my attention glued to the cracked plastic bumper.

His arm wound around my shoulder and I fell against his hard, ripped, brick wall of a chest. "It's okay. Don't worry about my car. It can be fixed. How are you? Are you hurt?" His soothing voice blanketed the sounds of the road around us, muffling them, and effectively calmed me down some. "C'mon, you don't need to be in the middle of the road. It's too dangerous. Let's pull into that parking lot over there."

I'd nodded and then got back into my car before nervously following him to an empty building on the side of the road. That was when I finally looked at him, took him all in. He was beautiful in a rugged sort of way. His hair was short, which reminded me of a businessman, yet nothing else about him did. The sleeves of his T-shirt had been cut off and his workout shorts hung below his knees. He had a fading bruise to the side of one eye and a jagged scar along the bridge of his nose that hadn't healed flush with his skin.

Beautiful and rugged.

Thoughts of that day and the ones that followed kept me busy on my drive back. Really, Josh was the only reason I hadn't moved home after I graduated a month ago. We weren't serious enough for me to stay in Baltimore permanently, but we were still too new for me to up and move eight hours away. The new plan was to give it a few more months to see what kind of future we could have before making a final decision. In the meantime, I'd stay in my tiny apartment and keep my job at the children's home.

When I arrived, I pressed his name on my phone and listened as it rang through the car. When it hit the third ring, I figured he was busy and wouldn't answer. Then someone picked up. Not Josh, though. "Lee? Where are you?" There were only two people who called me that: Josh and Dalton. I knew which one it was by the scratchy, smoker's voice.

"I just got into town. Where's Josh? Is everything okay?"

"He won't leave the back room. He's been in there for ten minutes. Already broke a table and punched a hole in the door."

"That doesn't sound good. What happened?"

"Happy happened."

I waited for more, but he didn't give me anything. "I don't even know what that means."

"The kid he fought tonight, his name's Happy. Josh wasn't prepared for him. Hell, I wasn't prepared for him. He's fucking sick...like in the head. Looked like he was ready to tear into Josh and leave him for dead. Size wise, they were evenly matched, but...damn, Lee, I don't know. I don't know where it went wrong. Josh didn't stand a chance."

"Is he hurt?"

"Yeah, he's pretty banged up. But more than that, he's pissed. He's only gone down once in the two years he's been doing this, and that was at the beginning. Granted, he didn't go down without a fight, but it wasn't pretty. I don't think this Happy kid bled at all. How long till you get here?"

"Ten minutes, at the most. I'm on my way. Tell him I'm coming."

"Will do." And then the line went dead.

I pushed the speed limit, keeping my eyes out for cops while my mind twisted with thoughts of Josh hurt. Other than practices and training, he'd only been in six fights since we'd started dating—well, since he told me about what he did for a living. I'd seen him cut, bleeding, and bruised a few times, but never had I seen him *hurt*.

I had no idea what I was about to walk into.

I opened the heavily tinted door to a dark and quiet gym. I could see the boxing ring beneath the spotlights, but other than that, everything seemed empty. The back room where Josh had holed himself up in was on the far side, and I had my sights trained on the hallway while I made my way through the empty space.

As I stepped closer to the ring, more into the light, someone stood up from the pullout, bleacher-type seating. The large man, tall and wide, muscles twined with more muscles escaping the cut-off sleeves of his shirt, caught my attention when I glanced over. His chest was broad, the shirt pulled tight, highlighting every line of his form. My pace slowed and he stood completely still, which offered me a chance to take him all in.

With him standing in the shadows, I couldn't decipher the color of his hair, but I could tell it was pulled back into a sloppy bun and his face was lined with hair the same shade. His brows were pulled together so tight I could barely see his eyes. They squinted as he stared at me. I'd never seen him before, but with the unadulterated hatred embedded in his every feature, I assumed he had to be Happy.

I turned away and quickened my pace toward the hallway. I didn't want to be alone with him. He didn't look like someone you'd want to hold a conversation with. When I reached the door to the back room, I peered over my shoulder one last time. Other than his head, now turned toward me, he hadn't budged an inch.

I wrapped my hand around the door handle and twisted it a quarter of a turn, but then stopped. My sight remained locked on the angry man in the shadows, and my heart practically stopped. The fear that had kick-started my anxiety evaporated, and the backs of my eyes burned with the uncontrollable need to cry.

It couldn't be.

It was impossible.

His head tilted slightly to the side.

And I knew.

My grip on the handle loosened and my knees grew weak. I angled my body toward him, but before I could move, the door swung open, catching my attention. With wide eyes, I stared into the opening, finding Dalton standing in front of me.

"He needs you," he said, and took a step back.

I glanced behind me to the bleachers again, but they were empty. He wasn't there. It had to have been my imagination. I scoured the open space, but found no one. Finally, Dalton cleared his throat and grabbed my attention once again.

Behind him, on the padded table lined with paper—usually clean, but now covered in blood—was Josh. My feet carried me to him, although my heart stayed in the hallway. Lingered with the silent man in the shadows. The man who couldn't have been there. Shouldn't have been there.

"Oh my God," I said with a gasp as I covered my gaping mouth with my fingers. "Are you okay? What happened?"

Josh took hold of my hips and dragged me closer to his battered body. His forehead fell to my chest; he didn't care at all that my shirt would now be stained with his blood. "Just make me feel better. Calm me down, Lee."

He appeared broken and weak, but his tone was harsh and angry. His hold on me grew tighter the longer I stood between his legs, almost to the point of causing me pain. In an effort to settle him down, I ran my fingers through his damp hair and waited for him to lift his head.

Despite the patched cuts, dried and fresh blood, and the discoloration I knew would be bruises by morning, his eyes shone bright like a midday sky, like the shallow waters in the Caribbean. They were stunning enough to lose myself in them, to forget all about the ghost in the gym.

"I'm here, Josh."

FIFTEEN

Killian

I SAT OUTSIDE FOR almost an hour, watching, waiting.

Time stood still. It meant nothing. The numbers on the clock changed, morphed into the next, but it was nothing more than a digit to me. I'd somehow gone back in time while slowly drifting through empty space. I recognized her the second she'd walked in, even without proper lighting, even with the changes in her appearance.

It didn't matter how long it'd been, I knew her.

My *heart* knew her.

I could've been deaf, dumb, and blind, and I still would've recognized her.

Finally, the agonizing wait came to an end. The door opened and she marched out. She appeared to be mad. Her head was down, and from what I could see, she wiped her cheek with the back of her hand. The thought of her in tears made me murderous. She'd gone back to the room to see *him*. And now…she was crying.

I wanted to kick his ass all over again.

Make him bleed more.

And not stop when I was told to.

Seeing her walk through the gym fucked with my head. I hadn't expected her to be there. She *shouldn't* have been there. For a moment, I didn't think she'd recognized me. But then she turned around, and even from across the room, I could see the awareness in her eyes. See it in her shoulders, her mouth…those lips. She knew.

But the gym was no place to reconnect.

So I waited for her to leave. To follow her.

It may not have been the right time, the right place, under the right circumstances, but I didn't care. I may have kept my distance, but it wasn't by choice. I'd stayed away out of determination. Hatred. The need to find my peace. I had to fight against going back every single day since I ran away. Not one day passed without her crossing my mind. I thought of her with every breath I took, every dream I'd woken up from in a pool of my own sweat. Every ounce of come milked from my dick was done with her on my brain.

Her.

It had *always* been her.

I stayed a safe distance behind her car as she unknowingly led me to her house. I had no idea what I was about to get myself into, but I didn't really care. I couldn't exactly turn my back on her after seeing her for the first time in five years. It was sooner than I anticipated, and her seeing me at the gym fucked everything up. But again, I lacked the ability to ignore her.

I'd walked away once before.

I'd never be able to do it again.

After she parked along the side of the one-way street, I found a space several cars away and waited. I saw which building she entered, but I couldn't pull myself together just yet. I needed an extra minute. Needed to figure out how I'd approach her. One minute had turned into fifteen, and before I knew it, I was practically beating down her door. What I'd meant to be a normal knock turned into an impatient, thundering pound with my fist.

It opened slowly, and as if time stood still, there she was.

Rylee Anderson.

Her brown eyes—darker than I remembered—were wide, her mouth agape. Her hair draped over her shoulders, silky and shiny. Straight. None of the curl I'd spent years twisting around my finger. Her white tank top hugged her body and more than alluded to the fact she wasn't wearing a bra. Pert, beaded nipples peaked the ribbed fabric over her heaving chest. Black cotton shorts fit her new curves like a glove, and I wanted nothing more than to see her bare.

Naked.

Sprawled out beneath me.

"W—what are you doing here?" Her breathy words pulled my attention from her hips to her face. The same face I'd sketched thousands of times since I left her all those years ago. Except, none of my depictions of her matched the beauty that stood before me now.

Time had been good to her, and I questioned myself as to why I'd refrained from looking for her. She'd put on at least fifteen pounds. I'd always thought she was perfect, gorgeous. Flawless. But seeing her now, it'd take nothing short of a riptide to keep me away from her.

I stepped over the threshold and grabbed the sides of her face, pressing my body flush with hers. I had so much to say, so much to tell her, but it was too early for that. I had nothing prepared other than what I knew I'd say when I eventually showed my face again. However, I couldn't repeat any of it. I hadn't anticipated how much it would stun me—silence me—to see her again.

"Is it really you?" Her words were filled with tears, the same ones streaking her face.

I leaned down and blew her name across her lips. "Rylee…"

It must've been just enough for her to reclaim her senses. She shoved at my chest, adding space between our bodies, and then twisted her head out from my hold. I matched her step for step—she took one back and I moved forward.

"No!" Her voice deepened, stern and unrelenting. "You can't just waltz back in after five years. You can't just show up at my house and expect me to fall into your arms like you never left. Not now. Not after all you've put me through."

She skirted around me, held the door open, and pointed outside in a silent command to leave. Little did she know, that wouldn't happen. I wasn't about to walk away. I couldn't over an hour ago when I saw her in the gym. I couldn't fifteen minutes ago while I sat outside in my car. And I couldn't now that I'd touched her, smelled her, heard her.

I grabbed her upper arm with one hand, pulled her away, and slammed the door closed. As soon as the latch clicked in place, I moved into her space until her back was against the door and my chest was flush with hers. I twisted a lock of her hair around my finger before setting my attention on the flaring golden flecks in her eyes.

"I'm not going anywhere."

Her whole body shook against mine, and it forced me to back away an inch or two, just enough to assess her. I had no idea why she reacted this way to me. Like I'd scared her. She'd never done it before. The only times I'd ever seen her tremble were after I'd gotten her off. Never out of fear. But by the look in her eyes, I could tell this was different.

"I can't do this with you," she whispered.

My heart cracked open, releasing the emotions I'd locked away for so long. "Why not?"

"I already told you. Too much time has passed, too much has happened between us. You hurt me too much. There's no going back." Her face scrunched with a silent sob and her head hung forward slightly. "Maybe had you come back a year ago…two, three years ago. But you didn't. It's too late now."

I lifted her chin and wiped away a tear with my thumb.

Her body stiffened. "You always said you wanted to steal the moon from the sky to freeze time so it was just me and you. You said you never wanted the next day to come. Well…congratulations, Killian. You stole the moon. You took it with you and left me with nothing but endless days without you. Time stood still, just like you wanted. Except instead of trapping us together, you left me alone."

"I wanted to come back for you."

"Then why didn't you?" Desperation scratched her words. "I couldn't…"

She slapped my chest. Once, twice. Three times. "That's not good enough!"

"That's all I can give you right now."

"Then leave! And don't come back!"

I grabbed her wrists to keep her from hitting me again, and then forced her against the door once more. "That's not going to happen, and you know it. I barely survived when I left you. I can't do it again."

Her gaze fell to my chest and she sneered. "Barely survived? You look like you haven't suffered for a second. Is this what you did with your time away?" She twisted her arms out of my hold and waved her hands over my chest. "What'd you do? Spend every day working out? Bulking up? *Fighting*?"

Her words slapped my face, bringing me back to the present. "Why were you at the gym tonight? Why were you with *him*?"

She blinked rapidly at me while forcing air in and out of her lungs at a hurried pace.

"Why?" My plea sounded as if it were wrapped in air.

Instead of answering me, she shook her head and tried to look away. Her avoidance birthed my frustration until unrestrained heat licked up my skin, my face flaming with the temper I'd released from its cage five years ago.

"Why, Rylee? Tell me!" My patience had started to run out. I didn't want to yell at her, scare her even more than I already had. But I needed the answers. I needed to hear her tell me. Because I couldn't believe it without her confirmation.

Refused to believe it.

"That's none of your business, Killian. You left me…in case you've forgotten."

"I told you I was leaving. I asked you to come with me. *Begged* you. It was your decision to stay. Don't act like I just disappeared without telling you anything."

She scoffed and rolled her eyes, the fear in her seeming to dissipate some. "You're such a jackass," she whispered, almost to herself. Before I had the chance to ask her to repeat it, she shoved me again. "You left me standing in my back yard, all alone, with your come dripping down my leg. You left me there to deal with the fallout all on my own." Her voice raised with each word she gritted out.

"You told me to go!" I slammed my hands against the door on either side of her head, leaning into her space. "You pushed me away and told me to go!"

"I was protecting you!" A rush of tears cascaded down her face and flooded me with unbearable pain. Regret. Her anger was nothing but a front for her grief. "Who was there to protect *me*, Killian? Huh? No one. I had to deal with it all by myself. My dad found me outside at eleven o'clock at night, my underwear on the ground, half naked. *Where were you* when they questioned me? When they looked at me with enough disappointment and disgust to suffocate me? *Where were you* the next day when my mom took me to take the morning-after pill because you came inside me? Or every day that followed when my heart broke more and more? Where *were* you?" She punctuated her last question with her fist against my chest.

"I'm sorry—"

"Don't." Rylee pointed a manicured finger in my face. "Don't you dare apologize to me like one word could possibly make up for the years I had to face without you. I finally got to a point where I wasn't dying, where I no longer felt like I was drowning in the pain of your absence. And here you are, bringing everything back. Bringing all the hurt to my front door. Well, no more, Killian. I won't let you destroy me again."

I wanted to tell her everything, just get it all out so she would know why I was gone. Why I couldn't come back. Why I had to leave then instead of waiting a year. But nothing came out. Everything that came to mind would be excuses, things she'd never understand. Reasons she wouldn't accept. So rather than waste my breath, I stepped back.

I gave her about ten feet of space.

But until she answered my question, that was all I'd give her.

"Why were you there tonight?" I gritted out through clenched teeth.

"I don't know, Killian…why were *you* there?"

"Just answer my fucking question." I'd spent five years without her softness. Five years without her ability to calm my soul, soothe my pain, deplete my anger. A lot of rage can be built up in that amount of time, and it all seemed to be pouring out of me right now.

"I'm not answering anything." She pulled the door open again and stood to the side. "You need to leave. My neighbors will be in the hallway soon, and something tells me you wouldn't appreciate the cops showing up."

Her calm demeanor set me on edge. I took one step toward her but stopped. "Just answer me, please. And then I'll leave you alone."

Her gaze fell away for a second before finding mine again. Something flashed in her golden orbs, but it was so fast, so brief, I almost missed it. I couldn't discern what it was.

Whatever emotion I saw knotted my stomach and nearly knocked the wind out of me.

She cleared her throat and straightened her posture. "I was there for Josh."

I took one more step. My foot was heavy, as heavy as my head and heart, but I pressed forward until I closed in more of the space between us. "Why?"

"He needed me after his fight." She glanced at my hands, probably noticing the small cuts and traces of dried blood on my knuckles. "I guess it's safe to assume you're Happy?"

"Am I happy? No. Not at all, Rylee. In fact, I'm furious."

"No. I mean the fighter. Happy."

Another step and we were now less than a foot apart. I lowered my voice, fully aware the front door still stood wide open, and at any point, someone could've walked down the hall. Someone could've heard me. "Why were you there for him? Why did he need you?"

"Maybe because you beat the shit out of him."

I closed my eyes and shook my head. She knew the meaning of my question, and the more I had to ask it, the angrier I got. "Stop playing games. Stop talking in circles and answer my fucking question. Why. Did. He. Need. You?"

The musical ring from a cell phone sounded from across the room, pulling her attention toward it. I grabbed her by the chin and forced her to look at me instead of the offending noise. Again, she didn't speak. When the song ended, I expected her to give me an answer. Instead, the music started again, barely taking a break before the end and the beginning. She glanced to the side and then back at me. "That's him. If I don't answer, he'll come over. I don't think you want that to happen."

"Then answer me."

"You want to hear me say it? Fine. Because we're together. He's my boyfriend. We're dating. Me and Josh." Each sentence, each clarification, felt like another punch to my chest with a steel fist.

"You can't be with him, Rylee."

"Why not?"

I clenched my teeth with enough force it caused my jaw to ache. The answer sat on the tip of my tongue, but I had to swallow it back down. Instead, I chose a response she'd understand better. "Because you're *mine*."

SIXTEEN

Rylee

MINE. That's all I heard. It replayed in my mind over and over again. He'd bared his teeth and gritted it out in such a deep, raspy voice it sounded like he gargled with shards of broken glass. His eyes had trapped mine.

And then he left.

Left me standing there in the open, empty doorway. A cold chill wrapped around me, but I didn't know where it had come from—other than his absence. My phone continued to ring, and it finally broke the spell I'd been under ever since Killian proclaimed his possession over me and stormed out.

I slammed the door, crossed the room, and snatched up my phone, already knowing the caller. "Hello?" I tried to remove the emotion from my voice, though it still came out shaky and breathless.

"Where were you? I've called like four times."

"I know. I'm sorry. I was getting changed and washing my face."

Josh's sigh drifted through the earpiece, and I wish I could've said it calmed me. It didn't. "I was about to drive over there. I worried something might've happened to you. You left in such a hurry…"

He knew why I ran out of the gym so fast.

Thinking of how he'd treated me—with Dalton in the room—made my stomach turn inside out and push bile up my throat. He'd said he needed me, so I was there. I had no idea his way of needing me was forcing my hand into his pants to stroke his limp dick.

"Listen, Lee...I'm really sorry about earlier. I didn't mean it. I was fucked up six ways to Sunday. I know that's not an excuse, and I'm not meaning it to be. I just want you to understand that's not who I am. It's not what I do. I was just pissed and I lost my mind there for a minute."

"It's fine." That was a lie, because it wasn't fine. Nothing about it was okay. But ever since Killian showed up at my front door, filled my apartment with his presence, claimed me, and then walked away, I couldn't give too much thought to what Josh had done back at the gym. "Just don't do it again. Please. It made me really uncomfortable, especially with Dalton standing right there. I'm not that kinda girl."

"I know you're not. That's why you're special. And trust me, that won't happen again. I won't lose again. Whoever takes that 'roid motherfucker better be prepared to lose a fighter and a lot of money because next time, I'll leave him six feet under."

"Dalton didn't want him?" I held my breath until he answered, worried what would happen if he and Killian were on the same team. I also worried what would happen if they ended up in the ring together again.

"He's not supposed to tell me anything, but he did say the price tag was too high for him. No one has ever bid that high on anyone before. Dalton turned the deal down because it was more than he was willing to pay."

"If he's a good fighter, why is it too much to pay?"

"It all comes down to how many wins you'll have to get in order to pay it back. Dalton never bids higher than what he calls a five-win reimbursement. And with the big tournament coming up, he doesn't want to take the chance on not having enough time to train him properly."

"Oh. That makes sense."

He sighed again, followed by a short, restrained growl. "I don't want to talk about the ring any more tonight. I've missed you. I had to go four days without you, and then you come back to me being a fucking dick. Tell me something good. How did your visit with your parents go?"

I shrugged, even though I knew he couldn't see me. "It was fine. They spent most of the time trying to get me to move back home."

Laughter filled his voice when he said, "I hope you told them to fuck off."

"No, Josh. I didn't tell them that."

"You're not moving back are you?" It was a question, but the way he said it sounded more like a threat. Josh wasn't abusive to me—he'd never hit me. But the way he sounded just now, coupled with his actions in the back room earlier, left me uneasy.

"I don't know."

Silence met me, followed by a loud thud on the other end, probably him hitting something. "You don't know? You're seriously contemplating leaving me?"

"Josh, can we please not do this now?"

"No. We're doing this right now. I need to hear it from you."

"I said I don't know. Meaning, I don't know if I'm staying *or* leaving. Truth be told, you're the only reason I'm still here, and our relationship is still new. I want to see where things go, see how we work out before I make a decision."

His labored breathing calmed some, which meant what I said offered him some semblance of peace. "What do I have to do to prove it to you? You're it for me, Lee. I knew it the moment you crashed into me. The very first time I looked into your eyes, kissed your lips…I knew. So tell me, what do I have to do so you know it's me?"

"You shouldn't have to convince me, Josh. That's not how this works."

"It's him, isn't it? The boy who broke your heart?"

All the air in my apartment vanished and the walls began to close in. The lights dimmed—or maybe that was just my vision darkening. "W–what?"

"The reason you're scared to move forward with me. It's him, isn't it? Listen, babe, I'm not going to run out on you. I'm not going to leave you without an explanation—no, I'm not going to leave you *period*. When will you trust me about that? What more do I have to do to prove it to you?"

He was right. He'd been good to me, patient and attentive. "You don't have to do anything, Josh. I just need a little more time before making such a drastic decision."

"*Drastic*? You already live here."

"The plan has always been to get my degree and then go back to Tennessee. So yes, staying here would be a drastic move for me." I dug my thumb into my temple and closed my eyes. "Can we please not argue about this? I've had a long day and my head is starting to hurt."

"Can I come over?" His tone had dropped a few octaves, sounding deeper than normal. "Or you can come over here. I don't care. I just want to see you, hold you, touch you, kiss you. I've gone four days without you and fucking blew it earlier. I want to make up for that."

"I'm really tired. Maybe tomorrow night. Honestly, Josh, I just want to climb into bed and go to sleep. I might even do it without the TV on tonight. That should tell you how tired I am," I said with an airy laugh. He always teased me about falling asleep with the television on.

There was rustling on the other end of the line, taps and moving around like he was doing something on his phone. "Shit," he hissed. "Cal picked up the fucker."

"What?"

"Dalton just sent me a text letting me know that Happy motherfucker is on Cal's team."

"*Okay…*" I drew out the word, letting my confusion be known in two, elongated syllables. "I have absolutely no idea what that means. Is it bad? And who's Cal?"

"Cal is the owner of the ring Dalton used to fight for before he walked away and started his own. There's bad blood between them. Ever since Dalton left, Cal's been trying to find anyone who can take down the guys in Dalton's circle. No one's been able to take me out, so I bet he's salivating over this new motherfucker."

"Where did he come from? This Happy guy, I mean. Have you ever seen him around before? Has anyone ever heard of him?" I couldn't let Josh know I was aware who Happy was. Couldn't let him know he was Killian. It would only end horribly.

"No one knows. He just appeared out of thin air. But I wouldn't be surprised if he came from another ring. It's not like this is organized nationally. There are rings all over the United States, and no roster for every fighter. We only know of the ones who fight locally. If he came from another state, there's really no way to know. I'd be willing to bet he was kicked out of another team and moved here to rejoin."

"Why would he have been kicked out? I didn't know that was possible."

"If you don't follow the rules, they won't keep you. You're a liability that way."

"Like what kind of rules?" I knew Josh would think I was simply interested in what he did for a living, when in reality, my curiosity was piqued because of Killian, wondering where he'd come from and where he might've been over the last five years.

"It's bare-knuckle fighting, babe. There are lots of rules. Things get bad when someone dies, so they do everything they can to make sure that doesn't happen."

"Has it ever happened before?"

"I'm sure it has, but not around here. At least, not since I've been in the ring." Either he took a break from explaining, or I zoned out, thinking of people being killed while fighting, and it all could've possibly been legal. But then he spoke again and caught my attention. "Don't worry, Lee. Nothing's going to happen to me. I went into the fight tonight a little cocky and unprepared. That won't happen again."

"Will you fight him again?"

"More than likely. If he makes it to the tourney, there's a good chance I'll see him in the ring then. I hope it's for the champ, too. I'd love another chance to make him tap out like the fucking pussy he is."

I yawned, more exaggerated than necessary, but I was ready to get off the phone. "Hey, Josh? Can we talk tomorrow? I'm so tired after my drive, and all I want to do is climb into bed and pass out."

"Why don't you get under the covers and let me hear you come on your fingers?"

Normally, that would've turned me on, but not tonight. Not after seeing Killian. I was rattled, my nerves fried and on edge. Touching myself would've only left me more confused than before, knowing the man I'd be thinking of while doing it wouldn't be the same one I was on the phone with. "Sorry, but not tonight. I can barely keep my eyes open as it is."

"You don't have to keep your eyes open while you do it."

His insistence added fuel to my irritation, and I was ready to just hang up the phone. "Josh…" I said with a sigh, clueing him in on my exasperation.

"I know. I know. Sorry I mentioned it. Goodnight, Lee. Talk to you tomorrow."

He hung up, making his aggravation apparent.

I climbed into bed, but instead of falling to sleep like I'd told Josh, I spent hours tossing and turning with one man on the brain. Killian Foster. It was hard to picture him, my mind going back and forth between the boy who'd held my heart and the man who'd broken it.

He'd always been attractive, but now he was…more. Way more. Sexy. Hard. Angry. Everything the boy from my dreams wasn't. When he was younger, he had moments when he was upset or pissed off at something, but it never lasted long around me. I calmed him. However, tonight, as he stood in front of me, it didn't seem like I still possessed that power. He was enraged, and there was nothing I could've done to soothe him. It also didn't help that I, too, was madder than hell.

Eventually, I fell asleep to thoughts of a larger, stronger Killian, doing to me—my body—what his younger self used to.

• • •

MY HEART WAS IN my throat when I pulled into the parking lot. Truth be told, it was on its way there long before I even left work. It'd been four days since Killian had come back into my life—and four days since he vanished again. I hadn't seen him, though I'd heard enough about him to know he hadn't left town.

In a vain attempt to find out more about him, I'd asked Josh random questions about fighting and how the rings worked. Where they worked out and what the schedules were like on other teams. He was easily fooled by my feigned interest. In all actuality, I simply wanted more information on where I could find Killian…in the event I ever needed to.

I pulled into an empty parking space around the back of the building. My stomach was in so many knots I wasn't sure how I'd made it to Cal's gym without having to pull over and vomit on the side of the road. There was no guarantee Killian would even be here. I had to constantly reassure myself of that fact, reminding myself I could very well walk in and the place be empty. Although, it didn't help to calm my nerves at all.

Needing an extra moment to compose myself and garner enough strength to confront the ghost of my past again, I covered my face with my hands and leaned my forehead against the steering wheel. A moment was all I had—well, more like a split second—before my door was thrown open. A half gasp, half scream, breathless and filled with panic, escaped as I pulled back to see who was there. The only thing in my line of sight was hard muscles wrapped in a ribbed tank top. I followed the lines from the wide, bare shoulder down a large arm corded with so much strength it looked like thick rope colored in vibrant ink. When I made it to his forearm, the entire world ceased to exist. I felt like I was in a vacuum, all the air gone, and I couldn't breathe.

SEVENTEEN

Killian

I WASN'T SURPRISED TO see Rylee at the gym. What did surprise me was how long it'd taken her to come after me. It needed to be on her terms. Her time. I'd followed her, cornered her, and now it was her turn to seek me out. I honestly thought my claim on her would've left her chasing after me, but I was wrong.

Coming out of the gym, I didn't expect to see her sitting in her car. Not here. She didn't belong in a tiny parking lot behind Cal's, where men came to train. Train to fight. To take down other men and make them bleed. She shouldn't have been here.

Yet here she was.

Huddled in her car with her face buried in her hands, pressed against the steering wheel, I knew she'd come for me. I knew instantly her piece-of-shit boyfriend didn't know where she was. No way in hell would he allow her to come here.

When I yanked her door open, I had to control my impulses. I wanted to rip it off its hinges. I wanted to tear away every piece of metal keeping me from Rylee. I hadn't thought about the prospect of scaring her until she screamed and turned wide, fearful brown eyes in my direction.

But then something else happened.

Those eyes fell to my forearm. The brown turned to gold as they glistened with a sheen of unshed tears and studied my tattoo. I don't know how she hadn't seen it the other night; it covered my entire forearm. The trees—in varying stages of seasons—making up her name. The top of the R created from a crescent moon. I'd designed it myself. It was one of the first things I did after leaving Smithsville. And now she finally saw it. Maybe she'd stop questioning me, stop fighting, and give in to what I knew we could have.

Together.

I leaned down and jutted my chin, pointing to the passenger seat. Without question or argument, she climbed over the center console and settled into the other side, leaving room for me to get in. After tossing my gym bag into the back seat, I squeezed behind the steering wheel.

I backed out of the parking lot…in silence.

Circled the block to navigate through the one-way streets…in silence.

Parked in front of the house I stayed at. Still no words spoken.

Leaving her with her mouth agape and her eyes wide with question, I turned off the engine and exited the car. I had her keys, so I knew she'd follow me as I climbed the five steps to the front door and walked in.

Twenty-one seconds.

That's how long it took for her to come inside.

As soon as she crossed the threshold, I grabbed her by the arm and closed the door behind her. I pressed her body against the adjacent wall and covered her lips with mine. I couldn't wait a second longer. Seeing her the other night and not feeling her lips was pure torture, and I refused to make that same mistake again.

Her nails clawed at my bare neck, her palms pushed against me. She kept her lips tight, resisting me as best as she could. But the second my hands landed on her hips and our bodies molded together, her fight waned. I sought entrance into her mouth, which she gave me with a sharp inhale through her nose. But it wasn't soft. It wasn't sweet or loving like her kisses used to be. It was hard and punishing. Full of anger. Full of resentment. She nipped my bottom lip and fisted her hands in my hair, tugging strands out from the knot and leaving my scalp burning with each tug.

A throat cleared from behind us. It couldn't be Cal. I'd left him at the gym, where he'd be for a while. It would've been easy to ignore the interruption, but Rylee gasped and pulled her lips away, her body turning rigid as it trembled against mine.

"I didn't know you were bringing home a guest." Her soft voice filtered over my shoulder, and with the way Rylee peered around me in shock, I knew she'd seen her.

I grabbed Rylee's hand and turned around to find Sophia with a wicked grin on her lips. She more than likely wanted to wag her brows at me, but probably refrained, knowing it'd only make everything worse. Without answering her or giving her anything to go on, I led Rylee through the living room and into my bedroom, and closed the door.

My lips found hers again, but this time, she put up more of a fight. With my body against hers, I walked her backward, only stopping when the edge of the bed hit the backs of her legs. Then I leaned into her, knocking her back onto the mattress, and following on top of her.

"Killian…" she breathed out. "Stop. Wait. Please slow down."

I moved away from her face, but I didn't relent. She wanted time to process why this shouldn't feel so right, why she still wanted to hold on to the anger I left her with. I refused to give her time to question what was always meant to be. Instead, I trailed my tongue down her neck and back up again until I reached her earlobe, where I sucked it into my mouth and gently clamped it with my teeth. She hissed and bucked into me, surely feeling my desire for her through my loose gym shorts.

"Who was that? That woman out there…who is she?"

With my arms wrapped around her, I moved her up the bed more to allow room for me to settle between her legs. I rolled my hips into hers, eliciting a strained whimper from her chest, but she made no move to escape. "Cal's wife. Don't worry about her," I growled into her ear without letting up on my intention.

"Wait." She pressed against my chest, pushing me back. I needed to see her face, and she apparently needed to talk. So I eased up to allow that. "Why's Cal's wife here?"

"This is his house."

Her brow furrowed when she asked, "Why are we in your coach's home?"

My hand trailed up her side while she spoke, keeping her nerve endings sensitive. I palmed her breast and rocked into her again. "Enough questions, Rylee." My fingers skimmed down her stomach and snaked beneath her skirt where I trailed the tips of my nails lightly down her inner thigh, like I'd done so many times in the past. "If I touch you, will I find you wet for me? Dripping with need?"

Somehow, she managed to pull herself from her lust-filled haze and exert more effort against my pecs. But I didn't budge. It only made her resolve stronger, her touch harder, her round eyes now squinted in determination. "We can't do this, Killian. You can't touch me. I have a boyfriend." She fought an internal war—good versus evil, right versus wrong. It was apparent Rylee wanted me the way I did her, but she struggled to accept who she would actually be cheating on—Josh or *me*. There was no doubt in her mind she belonged in my arms, but she had some false sense of commitment to this boyfriend.

Boyfriend.

Josh.

It was enough to send me into a blind rage. "I told you…you're mine. Not his. You do not belong to Josh motherfucking Disick." As I gritted out every word, I proceeded toward her pussy. I didn't need to touch her to know her words didn't match her desires—I could smell her arousal around me. Filling the room. Consuming me. Fueling my craving. I knew beyond a shadow of a doubt her loyalty to Josh had less to do with him and more to do with her need to punish me for leaving her.

"Not anymore. You may have my name branded on your body, but I've washed my hands of you. You don't own me. I don't belong to anyone. You made that decision when you left me five years ago. When you chose to walk away from me. I'm not yours," she ranted desperately, her words shaking as much as her legs around me. But, she didn't let me go; her thighs kept me encased in her grasp.

I curled my fingers beneath the band of her underwear, feeling her heat immediately. The lace barely covered her, and it only took one swift tug to hear the fabric rip between us. Her gasp followed. And just as quickly as I rid her of the barrier between me and her drenched cunt, tears filled her eyes and leaked out the sides.

"Don't cry." I licked the trail of salt leading from the corner of her eye to her temple while circling her hardened clit with the tips of my fingers. Her body was at odds with itself—she cried, her face scrunched in distress, while her hips rolled ever so slightly against my hand. Small whimpers passed her throat in labored chords of my favorite song. Her body wanted more, but her mind struggled to hold her back.

She threaded her fingers into my hair, but it seemed she intended to hold me at bay instead of pulling me closer. Her eyes were shut as the tears continued to streak down her cheeks. The delicate lines on her forehead had deepened and her dark eyebrows drew together tightly, the space between nearly translucent with strain. Her lips formed a tight line that stretched back, almost mirroring a smile, but one full of pain and conflict.

Continuing the attention on her clit, my body softened over hers. I found myself facing my own battle. Wanting her. *Needing* her. Unable to walk away again. While at the same time, completely broken by her tears. Gutted and empty by the expression marring her beautiful face. I wanted to calm her fears, soothe her pain. I needed her to believe everything would be all right. But I didn't know how to fulfill those promises. Didn't know how to make her believe something I couldn't tell her. I could only show her what my words failed to deliver, but the thought of breaking her any more suffocated me.

My forehead fell to hers. I kept my eyes open while hers remained closed, our breaths mingling between our mouths in a plume of muggy desperation. The second her breathing halted and her eyes squeezed tight, I knew she was on the edge of an orgasm. I quickly removed my hand, earning me glistening, wide brown eyes and a desperate gasp.

It took no time at all to lower my shorts down my hips and free my throbbing hard-on. With her legs bent, her skirt shielding her view of me—her eyes locked directly on mine without retreating—I didn't once think about her not knowing what I was doing. Her heels encouraged me closer. Even as I stroked myself, using her arousal to lubricate my dick, it never crossed my mind that she wasn't aware of what would come next. There were no words of discouragement, no actions to show me she didn't want me the way I needed her.

It wasn't until I'd pushed in halfway, that realization hit. Her hands in my hair tightened and pulled, her fingernails practically slicing into my scalp. Her eyes turned to liquid gold as a deluge of tears cascaded to her hairline.

I thrust in the rest of the way, until my skin was flush with hers, and then I stilled my movements. Her heat was almost unbearable, threatening to end it all. My breathing became harder as I tried to will myself to hold back. I kissed and licked the briny evidence of her torment away before burying my face in the curve of her neck. "Don't cry. Please don't cry," I whispered against her silky skin.

Her head tilted forward, fitting in the space between my neck and shoulder, and her body shook with her hearty sob. I'd never felt pain like this before. My heart had taken a beating when I'd left Rylee behind the last time. But nothing compared to the crippling agony of being inside her, feeling her body convulse with turmoil, her tears wetting my face.

I did this.

I caused this.

And yet…I couldn't walk away.

I couldn't withdraw from her and offer her the distance she claimed she needed. I didn't have the strength. Because I knew she was wrong. Her tears weren't because she didn't want me, or because she loved Josh—she was releasing five years of abandonment and heartache. Leaving her, putting time and space between us, wouldn't help. It wouldn't do any good. It would only add to the crushing emotion she already felt. My heart needed her, and hers needed me. She was the air I required to breathe, the nourishment my body demanded to keep going, the strength that kept me alive. She was the reason for everything I did. Whether she ever believed that or not didn't change the truth.

I undulated my hips, slowly and carefully while she adjusted to my size. Her panting breaths echoed in my ears and enticed me to keep going. In and out. Slow. Methodical. My pelvis rolled into hers with every subtle thrust, and each time I grazed her clit, she gave in that much more. Her soul relenting to her destiny.

"I'm sorry, Rylee. So sorry. Don't cry. I never want to make you cry."

"That's all you've done for the last five years." Her confession was ground out, hoarse and strangled by the reluctant emotion clogging her throat.

I snaked my arms up between her back and the bed, and hooked my hands over her shoulders to pull her into me more. Her legs curled against my sides with her heels digging into the clenched muscles in my ass. Her feet tugged me into her, pressing our connection deeper.

"I'm not leaving you, Rylee. Never again." I lifted my head for a moment to stare into her glassy gaze, needing her to see the truth behind my every word. The honesty in my proclamation. "You're mine." I punctuated my claim with a slow, deep thrust. "Always were, and always will be."

Her lids grew heavy once more, visually shielding herself from my promise. Or possibly, shielding me from her rejection. Her head shook from side to side on the comforter below her, hard and fast as if trying to convince me of her resolve. Or...convince herself. She released her grip on my hair and blindly found my shoulders. Her nails dug into my skin as she silently pleaded with me to slow down.

"Rylee..." I stopped my movements, still seated deep inside her.

"No, Killian. We can't do this. *I* can't do this." Her eyes flew open and locked onto mine. "I can't survive this—I *won't* survive it again," she cried, her words garbled with tears and tense with her grimace. The demons were launching an all-out attack on her psyche and she allowed them to breech the boundary. Her legs never released me. She needed me to win the battle for her—to slay her inner dragon.

One by one, I took her hands in mine and moved them to the bed on either side of her head, pressing them into the mattress. She didn't struggle, didn't resist being consumed by my restraint. When I slowly pulled away from her core before I rolled back in, meeting her flesh to flesh, she didn't deny me. Instead, she tightened her legs around me and clenched her pussy around my cock. Inviting me to stay. Begging me to make good on my promises.

I pulled almost all the way out. "I'm not…" Then I thrust back into her with committed drive. "Leaving you." I drew my hips back again as I said, "Ever. Believe me…" My pelvis ground into hers. "When I say that." And back out again. "Believe me when I tell you"—I slid my knees closer to her body, keeping my back arched while hovering over her— "you're mine." With her ass practically on my lap, lifted off the mattress, and my face inches from hers, I had more leverage to illustrate my intensity. Which I did as I gritted out, "Believe me when I say…" Instead of the fervent aggression, I tamed my actions, slowed it down and carefully dragged my dick along her inner walls until only the head remained consumed by her warmth. Then, as if the clock had stopped and we had all the time in the world, I slid back into her until my tightening balls met her bare ass. "I love you, Rylee." I stilled, unmoving, and grazed her lips with mine while whispering, "I'm not leaving. Ever."

More tears came, followed by a hiccupping sob. I closed my mouth over hers, attempting to coax her into returning the affection. I held my lips firmly against hers while my hips pressed eagerly into her as though I tried to meld our bodies into one unit.

Leaning back on my haunches, I released her hands and gripped her hips, fully aware she'd be marked with bruises where my fingers sunk into her skin. My pace quickened until I rocked into her with such great intention it left her extending her arms above her to brace her body with the headboard in an attempt to keep still. Giving her the freedom to push into every thrust, intensifying the impact.

Her sharp inhale, followed by the lack of exhale, coupled with the way her pussy gripped my cock, eluded to her impending orgasm. I kept up the pace, pummeling her, until I ripped garbled moans and impassioned whimpers from her. Her head tilted back, her chest lifted, showcasing her hard nipples through her thin shirt. I couldn't stop myself, and leaned forward just enough to take one of the peaks between my teeth, pinching it through the thin fabric barrier. A deep roar accompanied her tight cunt as she fell over the cliff of ecstasy. I'd be right behind her, but I wasn't ready for this to end.

As soon as her back met the mattress again, her body going soft beneath me, I released her hips and slid my knees apart enough to close the gap between us. I roughly gripped the back of one thigh and pushed her leg against her heaving chest, opening her so I could go deeper.

"One more, Rylee," I panted against her face once I settled into position. I supported my weight by one side—an arm and a knee—and despite my strength, I worried I wouldn't be able to hold myself up much longer.

Being with her again left me weak.

Desperate.

Frantic.

"Come for me one more time," I ordered in a biting tone, baring my teeth like some kind of wild animal. But that's what she did to me. Not only did she possess the ability to call to the child within me, she also brought out the beast—the one I'd discovered in her absence. The one I never wanted her to see. But here I was, fucking her like we had a camera on our every move as she unleashed the villain from inside.

"Killian…"

"That's right. Say my name. *My* name."

"Killian…" she repeated once more, forced out through a labored exhale.

I tucked my face in the crook of her neck as I continued my assault. Our breaths were frantic—hers causing her chest to rise and fall unnaturally, and mine billowing against my face in plumes of humidity, clammy and suffocating. I dug my fingers into her meaty thighs, harder, claiming her.

Possessing her.

Taking her.

She grabbed my back and held me closer. Nothing had ever felt that amazing. She could say she didn't want me or that we couldn't be together until she was blue in the face, but her body spoke a different truth. Her actions proved her words wrong as she clung to me, biting into my skin through my shirt. Leaving her mark on me. Claiming me as her own.

Her body arched into mine until we were chest to chest, and her pussy gripped me so tightly I couldn't hold back any longer. When she fell, I fell. When she groaned, I groaned. We were in sync, united, coming apart and coming together as one.

I pumped into her until her tight cunt milked every last drop, emptying myself into her core. I wanted her filled with me. Overflowing. I wanted to drip from her pussy for days so she couldn't deny what I'd always known. So her lowlife, piece-of-shit boyfriend would know.

She was mine.

Once we caught our breaths again, she carefully rolled me off her. My dick slid out of her, causing her to wince. I fell to the bed next to her on my back and stared at the ceiling. A chill flitted up my body, reminding me of the absence of her warmth. I couldn't do anything other than concentrate on getting hard again so I could be buried inside her, needing to never be apart from her.

"Dammit, Killian!" Her anger tore me from the thoughts of making her come again. She slid off the bed and turned in a circle, searching for something in my room. "You fucking came in me. I can't believe I let this happen again. I can't believe I'd be so stupid." She covered her face with her hands, but it didn't hide the fresh wave of tears and pain.

I pulled my shorts up and moved to stand in front of her.

Before I could utter a single word, she began a physical assault on me, slapping and punching my chest. Even though I could barely feel her attack on the outside, it tore me apart inside. I always thought the term "breaking my heart" was weak and made no sense, but watching Rylee shut down and push me away truly cracked, fissured, and splintered the essence of my being. My lifeline was tied to her—always had been—and she threatened to take it all away.

"I can't believe you'd put me in jeopardy like that. No concern for my health or safety. You're an asshole. A selfish piece of shit." Her shoulders dropped and her back hunched forward, quivering with the torment taking hold of her. "And I'm the idiot who let you. The weak girl who didn't stop you."

When her knees gave out, I wrapped my arms around her and lowered us both to the floor. "What do you mean I put you in danger? Does he hurt you? Has he ever laid a hand on you? I'll fucking end him. He won't take another breath. I'll protect you, Rylee. I'll keep you safe."

"No." She pulled back and locked her dark-brown, glistening eyes on mine. "Not against him. Against the time you were away. I don't know where you've been, who you've been with. And given your penchant for going bareback, I don't even want to think about what you could've passed on to me."

The thought never entered my mind. Not once. But hearing her accuse me of being unsafe with other women and infecting her in the process gutted me. "You know where I've been, Rylee. I didn't put you in any danger. I swear."

"You can't promise me that."

"Unless I contracted something from you, I can."

Her eyes widened and her mouth hung open. She didn't even bother to cover her shock. It painted her face in red and pink hues, lined her features with creases. Her eyebrows raised into perfect arches, like two inky brushstrokes on creamy paper. "You…haven't…?"

"No, Rylee. I haven't. It's only ever been you. And it'll only ever *be* you." I couldn't even allow myself to think of where she'd been. Couldn't entertain the thought of her and Josh. The possibility made me sick to my stomach and left me seeing red, desperate to rip him apart limb by limb.

"Where the hell have you been for five years?" Her need for answers lilted her question into a high-pitched squeal. "What have you been doing? I don't understand. Did you leave so you could turn into some angry fighter? It doesn't make sense, Killian. You've never been a violent person. Why do this? Why morph into this alternate persona?"

So many questions had been launched at me, I wasn't sure which one to tackle first…or how. There was only so much information I could give. "You knew I needed to go home. I needed to be where my parents were, needed to see it all with my own eyes."

"So you went back to Pennsylvania? This whole time you've been in New Hope, hours away from here?"

"Not the whole time."

Rylee opened her mouth to say something else, but must've thought better of it because she shut it and quickly stoned her expression. Her posture stiffened moments before she launched herself to her feet, abruptly standing and leaving me on the floor.

"I can't do this, Killian. I can't go 'round and 'round with you over where you've been. It doesn't matter. The only thing that matters is you left. You walked away and left me alone. For. Five. Years. The where and why and hows don't change it. It doesn't fix it or make anything better."

I stood and reached for her hand, but she yanked her arm behind her to prevent me from touching her. "Rylee...don't leave."

Her eyes softened, as well as her shoulders and lips. But just as I'd allowed my hopes to take root, she said, "I can't stay. I can't do this with you...now or ever. This was a mistake, and it can't happen again. You chose to leave, remember? I asked you not to. I begged you to wait. And now, as you're asking me to stay, *I'm* choosing to leave."

EIGHTEEN

Rylee

I WALKED AROUND HIS statuesque body and found my shoes on the floor at the end of his bed where they'd fallen from my feet during his attack on me. My keys lay next to them—not sure how they ended up there, but thankful they did so I didn't have to ask for them.

Silence came from him as I left his room. No padded steps behind me, no pleading requests for me to give him another chance or stay and hear him out. Nothing to indicate any effort on his part to come after me. It was what I wanted, but at the same time, it pushed the knife in that much deeper. My chest couldn't take any more. My heart couldn't handle it.

Thankfully, the woman we encountered earlier was nowhere in sight while I quickly made my way to the front door. I made sure to open and close it as softly as I could, not wanting to garner her attention. It was bad enough I'd been in Cal's house with Killian, but having a witness made it that much worse. If Josh ever found out…I didn't know what he'd do.

Tears leaked from my eyes during the entire fifteen-minute drive home. I was filled with anger and grief, elation and sorrow, all warring with each other. I had no idea how to feel or what to think. My body remembered his as if not a day had gone by without his touch. But it had. More than a day. More than a hundred, five hundred, a thousand days. Too many to count. And none of them could've been given back.

However, I couldn't stop dwelling on one piece of information: his confession of never being with anyone else. Only me. It didn't make sense no matter how I looked at it or how much I picked it apart. When we were younger, he was sexually driven. The amount of porn he watched could attest to that. Not to mention, how obsessed he was with touching my body at each stage of our relationship. From the moment I'd given him the green light to have sex, he wanted it all the time—which was fine by me, because I felt the same way. Whenever we had a chance, a free moment, he was in me, dragging out as many orgasms as he could. So the idea of him refraining from sex for so long astonished me.

When I pulled up to my building and found a spot along the curb, I was surprised to find Josh waiting on the front stoop. He never showed up without calling first, and not normally this early in the evening. He took his training seriously, and with a tournament approaching, he should've been in the gym. Instead, he sat on the top step with his phone in his hands.

He glanced up when I approached, but his face was void of any happiness. No smile curled the corners of his lips and his blue eyes seemed dull. "Where were you?"

Stunned by his harsh tone, I stopped a foot away from the concrete steps. "I was working, Josh. It's a Wednesday. When haven't I worked on a Wednesday?"

"You weren't at the office. I tried there when you didn't answer any of my calls. They said you left early. That was over an hour ago. Where were you?" The way he demanded an answer left me with a sick feeling in the pit of my stomach that he somehow knew I was with Killian.

Thinking quickly on my feet, I said, "I left early because I had to meet with a family to close a case. I came straight home after it was over. Why are you so mad?"

He hung his head, seemingly in defeat. "I'm sorry. I was just worried about you. I didn't know where you were and you didn't answer my calls." When he lifted his head, he regarded me with utter heartache. The cuts on his face had started to heal and scab over. Some were still taped with butterfly strips, and the bruises had turned a lighter shade of green. Ever since the fight with Killian, he'd been a different person. Aggressive at times, argumentative, and like the flick of a switch, he'd become calm, apologetic, caring, and attentive.

I opened my purse and pulled out my phone, remembering I hadn't had it on me while I was with Killian. Sure enough, on the screen displayed numerous missed calls and unread texts from Josh over the last hour. As I scrolled through them, I could practically feel his growing anger through his later messages.

"Josh…I'm sorry. I had my phone on vibrate and in my purse. I didn't bother to check it when I left my meeting. I was too focused on getting home. I feel like crap…maybe I'm coming down with something." I feigned fatigue with my hand wrapped around the back of my neck.

He stood and reached out to help me up the stairs and into the building. "Come on, let's get you inside. I'm sure it's nothing a hot bath, a bowl of soup, and a movie won't cure. We can take it easy tonight and just curl up on the couch together."

His kindness twisted the guilt rooted in my chest. Tears sprang to my eyes at the mere thought of what I did with Killian behind Josh's back. It gutted me, shredded me, left me hollowed and covered in filth. Not that Killian made me feel dirty, but knowing I'd been with him behind the back of my boyfriend, and he'd come inside me…it left me feeling cheap. Soiled. No good and a worthless piece of shit.

But Josh could never know.

He could never find out.

It'd be something I'd have to live with.

Josh helped me into my apartment and immediately went to the fridge to grab a bottle of water. I preferred soda or tea, but always kept bottles of water stocked for him, knowing it was the only thing he drank. In the four months we'd been dating, I'd never seen him so much as touch a drop of alcohol. I assumed it was because of training, but never bothered to ask.

I hurried into my room and closed the door. I needed to clean myself off, grab a pair of panties, and change my clothes before Josh came in. I knew if I locked the door and he tried to open it, it'd only piss him off to know I'd purposely kept him out.

Luckily, he didn't come in until after I was halfway dressed. I'd already pulled on a pair of panties and a plain T-shirt after cleaning Killian off my thighs and swollen sex. Josh crossed the room with hooded eyes until he met me on the other side of my bed. He took my cotton shorts from my hand and knelt down on one knee to help me into them.

The guilt burned brighter as I held onto his hard shoulders and stepped into the leg holes of my shorts. His fingers skimmed my bare legs on his way up, pulling the elastic band over my hips and backside while he raised to his feet in front of me. He caressed my cheek with the backs of his fingers and held his lips to my forehead.

"You don't seem to have a fever, so I don't think you need any medicine. I have soup heating on the stove—your favorite: chicken and broccoli—and I grabbed that soft blanket from the closet and put it on the couch for you." He reached behind me and took my pillow off the bed before lacing his fingers through mine and leading me to the living room.

After he situated me on the couch, he found the remote and handed it to me. "Pick whatever you want to watch. Your choice. The girliest movie you can find if that's what'll make you feel better." He walked away.

I turned on the TV and then scrolled through the guide without once looking at the words on the screen. My vision blurred with tears, proving they hadn't dried up yet. I tried to sniffle as quietly as I could, not wanting him to hear me. He'd know something was up and would pull it out of me—and I didn't want to outright lie to his face. What I did was bad enough. I didn't care to add lying on top of my deceptions for the day.

By the time he came back with a bowl of soup and piece of toasted bread, I'd successfully wiped away the evidence, although I continued to hide from him. I had no idea what movie I'd settled on, if it was even a movie and not a TV show, and spooned as much of the chicken and broccoli into my mouth as I could. Truly, my stomach was upset. But not because of a bug. It was twisted and knotted, and it wouldn't surprise me if every last bite came back up later.

Seeing my discomfort, he urges me to lie down and tucks himself between my back and the couch with his arm slung over my waist. I wanted to relax into him like I'd done so many times before, but I couldn't seem to get my body to soften.

Regret coiled tight in every muscle, panic and fear burned in every joint.

"You're tense, babe. What's wrong?"

"I just don't feel good."

He pressed his lips to my neck and slowly kissed his way to my shoulder. Just as slowly, he moved his hand beneath my shirt and pressed his heated palm to my bare stomach. It was a simple gesture, one of consideration and comfort. But he didn't stop there. He splayed his fingers across the smooth skin of my belly until the tips reached beneath the waistband on my shorts.

I gently grabbed his wrist to offer a subtle hint that I wasn't in the mood, but it went ignored when he ground his hips against me from behind. His erection pressed into the curve of my ass and caused me to jolt forward, almost falling off the couch.

"C'mon, baby…just calm down. Let me make you feel better."

"No, Josh." It was meant to be strong and affirmative, but instead, it came out meek and airy. As soon as he pulled my shoulders flush with his chest, I knew he'd mistaken my tone as being desperate and turned on. Which wasn't the case. After what Killian had done to my body, and the uneasiness he'd left me with, the last thing I wanted was to be touched. "Please, Josh. I'm not in the mood. I told you…I don't feel good."

He stilled for a moment, and just as I thought he'd settle behind me and watch TV like he said he would, he bolted into a sitting position, taking the blanket with him. "What the hell, Lee? Ever since you came back from that Podunk town of yours, you've barely let me touch you. You push me away every time I try." His piercing blue eyes darkened like a storm cloud covering their shining pools. His eyelids lowered more than usual while he trapped me in place with his stare. "Did you see him?"

"W–what?" I gasped, praying I'd misunderstood him.

"That kid you grew up with. Was he there? Is that why you've been acting like this? Is that why you've been pushing me away, being all quiet and down and shit?" He backed away even more until he sat on the edge of the couch, the blanket now completely off my bent legs. "Don't fucking lie to me, Lee. Was he there? Did you see him?"

"No, Josh," I said with a sigh while trying to sit up as well. "He wasn't there. I didn't see him. I swear." It technically wasn't a lie, enabling me to say those words to him with confidence. The fire in his eyes worried me, but upon my declaration, it seemed to settle him a bit.

"Then why won't you let me touch you?"

Because I'm filled with Killian's come.

Because not even an hour ago, Killian's dick was deep inside me.

Because you're not Killian.

But I couldn't say any of that. I hated to even think it. "How many times do I have to tell you I don't feel well? My stomach hurts and I'm tired. I'm not in the mood to mess around today. Saturday, after I came back, you were hurt—not to mention, we'd gotten into a fight. You were busy most of the day on Sunday, and then I've been at work since Monday. You act like I've shunned you or ignored you. I've done neither of those things. In fact, I've seen you every night since I came back."

"I just want to make you feel better," he whispered while trailing his hand up my soft shin, stopping with his bear-like paw covering my bent knee. He glanced to where he touched me, and the moment his brow creased and his eyes narrowed, I knew things were about to go from bad to worse. "What the fuck is that?"

My heart stilled at his thunderous roar. I turned my attention to what held his focus. He pushed my legs apart and ran his thumb over a fresh bruise that seemed to form and darken before my eyes. Without looking at me, he manipulated my leg in the other direction, observing the other side of my thigh. I didn't need to see it to know what he'd find there—four more bruises. I could still feel Killian's grip on me from when he took everything I had and gave me everything he was.

"Lee…" My name rolled off his tongue in a threatening tone while he trapped me with his unrelenting stare. "What the fuck is this?"

Excuses and lies swarmed my mind, but I knew none of them would go over well. It was obvious they were caused by a hand, and not those of the children I dealt with at work.

Knowing if I stalled, it'd only anger him more, I blurted out the first thing I could think of. "I have no idea. I didn't even know they were there. I noticed them this morning and figured they were from you."

"From me?" he asked, his tone showing no hint of him buying anything I said.

"Well, who else would they be from, Josh?" I tried to sound nonchalant, leaving no reason for him to question it. "We wrestled around on the floor last night. Remember? You were teaching me how to get out of a hold. I just assumed I got it then."

It wasn't a lie…we had wrestled. Although, it wasn't rough. He remained gentle the entire time he showed me different moves and techniques. If he thought about it hard enough, he'd probably see the lie through the thin veil of truth.

I only prayed he wouldn't.

He caressed the forming bruises with the lightest touch of his fingertips. "I'm sorry, Lee. I'll have to make sure I'm more careful with you. I didn't mean to hurt you." The underlying remorse in his tone deepened the ache in my chest until I thought I'd physically explode with grief.

Needing to move forward instead of obsessing over my failures, I leaned back and rested my head on the pillow. "You're more than welcome to cuddle with me while watching TV, as long as you don't try to press the issue. I want you here." The words scorched my tongue as I uttered them. "But I honestly just want to take it easy and relax."

With a smile, he moved behind me and folded me against him.

"I could get used to this," he said with a soft kiss to my shoulder.

"I could, too."

It was official…I hated myself.

NINETEEN

Killian

I PULLED MY CHIN to the bar and slowly let myself back down again, keeping my legs crossed in front of me. Chains clanked in the distance, as well as the thundering echoes of the speed bag not even thirty feet from me. There wasn't much talking, but with the bustling in the gym, no words needed to be uttered. The room smelled of sweat and determination. It wasn't something I found intoxicating, but it drove me forward.

It was what I needed to push me.

Center me.

Remind me of why I was here in the first place.

"Ten more, Happy," Cal called out while watching my form.

Silently, I obeyed. I didn't need to nod, because everyone knew there was no questioning what the coach said. I continued to pull my chin to the bar before lowering myself again, never touching the floor. My back and core burned from the countless chin-ups I'd already done, but I wouldn't call it quits until Cal did.

However, out of the ten remaining, I only reached eight.

With two left, I stilled at the sight before me. Her silky hair, darker and shinier than before, framed her face as she moved toward me. Her eyes were lined in coal, making them appear smaller than usual. Pale pink gloss covered her lips, and it made me crave them—yearn to feel them on me. Everywhere. Leaving behind the sticky residue of the artificial color.

"Happy..." Cal threatened, but once he realized I wouldn't look his way, he turned to see what had caught my attention.

He sighed and shook his head. "Sorry, doll, but this is a closed area. The main gym is up front."

Rylee stepped up to him, never taking her hardened stare off me, and dropped my gym bag at my feet. I'd left it in her car, forgetting all about it by the time I'd gotten her back to Cal's house two days ago. I'd decided to let her keep it, hoping Josh would find it. It gave me pleasure knowing she had something of mine with her, and at any moment, he could realize who she truly belonged to.

"Figured you might need this." Her tone was just as harsh as her glare.

"Sweetheart, he doesn't speak. There's no point in trying to have a conversation with him. Thank you for returning his bag, but he really needs to get back to training."

I pushed Cal aside without once glancing at him, and stepped forward, closer to Rylee. I stood so close she had to tilt her head back to look at me, but neither of us spoke. Only stared. Saying everything we needed to with our eyes. I could see in hers that she was angry, livid with me for leaving my bag behind. And I hoped she could see the satisfaction in mine, letting her know I didn't give a flying fuck about whether or not her boyfriend could've found it.

"That's all. I have nothing else to say." And then she turned her back to me to leave.

As soon as she was far enough away, Cal spoke up. In as quiet of a voice as he could muster, he asked, "What the fuck was that about?" When I met his stare, I realized he knew more than he'd let on while in Rylee's presence. "Who is she to you? How the hell do you know her?"

Answering him, I extended my arm, showing him the tattoo he'd made mention of countless times since we met. He'd given me shit for putting a woman's name on my body permanently, and how that was nothing but asking for trouble.

He exhaled loudly and dropped his head into his hand. "You've gotta be shittin' me, Happy. Are you for real? Do you know who she is? Do you know she's—" He shook his head with a mirthless chuckle. "Of course you do. Is that why you paid your own way in? Why you said you wanted the toughest, hardest fighter for your bid? Is she the reason you want into the ring with him?"

I didn't move, didn't offer an explanation—not that he'd truly expected one, considering he knew I wouldn't speak to him. But he more than likely took my silence as confirmation. Honestly, I didn't care what he thought or assumed. It didn't matter to me. Didn't mean a damn thing in the end.

"Jesus Christ, Happy…" he muttered with his hands fisted at his sides, his words grinding out through clenched teeth. "You're playing with fire. You know that? Do you even have a clue what you're doing? I don't care what you two had when you were younger…she's with him now. And after you laid him out last week, he's gonna be gunning for you. I can train you, and make sure you're prepared, but I can't save you. If he finds out you're chasing his skirt, there won't be a prayer's chance in hell for you."

I turned my attention to where Rylee retreated, and instantly, my blood boiled. One of the other fighters from Cal's ring had her cornered. Her stiff posture showed she was uneasy and not interested, but he didn't seem to get the hint. I didn't even know his name, never had any interaction with the kid before, but I was about to change that. I stalked toward him, coming up behind Rylee. He didn't even notice my approach until I had my hand wrapped around his throat, his back pinned to the wall. A resounding thud rented the air as his skull connected with the concrete. His eyes grew wide and his mouth hung open while he unsuccessfully fought for air.

My gaze found Rylee's, wordlessly asking if she was okay. She had her arms hugged tightly around her midsection, fear embedded into her features, but she nodded anyway. And with her chin trembling, dimpling as she fought against the onslaught of emotions racking her body, she whirled around and fled.

I waited until she disappeared through the back door before releasing the piece of shit I had pinned to the wall. It wasn't until I let go that I realized in my haste to protect Rylee, I'd held him off his feet. He clawed at his neck and gulped in air while I stood back and watched him. Taking pleasure in another person's pain had never been my thing. There were only ever three men I wanted to see suffer, and this twig wasn't one of them. But for some reason, the thought of him making Rylee uncomfortable blinded me against logic. In that moment,

I wanted to hurt him. I wanted him to fucking fear me with every breath he took until he learned from his mistake and never set his eyes on her again.

"Break it up, you two." Cal stormed over to us and poked me in the chest. "For that stunt, you can add twenty more to the two you didn't finish, and when you're done, you can hit up the speed bag until I tell you to stop. Save your anger for the ring—preferably not against my men."

I left him tending to the fucker on the floor, gasping for air.

• • •

THIS WHOLE bare-knuckle fighting organization still confused me. But I took it as I went and stuck to the rules laid out for me. It was Saturday night, two weeks since I'd taken down Josh the Jaguar Disick, and we were officially in the preliminary rounds for the tournament. This would settle who would move forward and who would have to sit back and watch everyone else battle for the title.

None if it made sense to me. Cal did his best to teach me how it worked, but really, it didn't matter. After I fuck up Josh and have Rylee back in my arms, in my bed, I wouldn't be around any longer.

"You solid?" Cal asked and handed me a bottle of water. We were waiting along the far wall in a different gym, one I'd never been to before. There was a fight currently taking place in the ring, and the clamor of the crowd eliminated almost any chance of holding a decent conversation.

I nodded and drank enough of the cold water to wet my tongue. I didn't want a belly full of liquid, but needed to remain hydrated. It was the first thing Cal had taught me after I came to him with my proposal.

Some scrawny kid everyone called Brawny was minutes away from winning the fight against someone twice his size. It just proved strength wasn't everything. Sometimes, the smaller ones were faster. And by that point, it didn't matter how much power your punch packed. If the other person could dodge it faster than you could swing, it didn't do much good.

Cal droned on, but I didn't pay him any attention. Not only did the people in the crowd become more boisterous, but something just around the corner of the stage caught my eye. *Someone*. A built motherfucker with his arm around my girl. If I hadn't already made a vow to take him out, I'd do it right now.

Josh and Rylee stood a few feet away from the action, both had their eyes glued to the fight in front of them as it came to a close. Brawny was in the same circle as Josh, so him being there made sense, taking it all in, smiling from ear to ear as if he had some kind of stake in the match. What I didn't understand was why Rylee was there, standing alongside Josh, tucked into his side.

If I wasn't next, I would've stormed over there and taken her away.

"Hap!" Cal screamed into my ear, garnering my attention. He glanced to the side, catching what I'd been staring at, and glared at me. "Get your fucking head in the game, son." Him calling me "son" fueled my rage.

I wasn't his son.

He wasn't my father.

My dad was gone.

One last time, I turned my head toward Josh, my fists balled so tightly I lacked blood flow to my fingers. But then Rylee glanced my way and an eerie calmness began to settle in my veins. Giving Cal my attention once more, I nodded and stoned myself for the ring.

The officiant held Brawny's arm in the air as a crashing wave of mixed responses overtook the small, dark gym. The only lights in the place were set on the stage, highlighting the events that held everyone's attention.

The skinny twig slipped through the ropes lining the ring and shook hands with Josh while Rylee stood off to the side. Had it not been for Cal slapping me on the back, I would've missed my introduction, too absorbed with the sight before me.

I climbed onto the stage and took my side, staring down a guy who probably had five years on me. His mangled face proved he was no stranger to fighting, although it also told me he was hit more than he dodged.

The expression on his face was that of a man who didn't want to be here. Maybe he wasn't interested in the fight, or maybe he wasn't thrilled about standing in front of me. Whatever it was, the determination in his eyes wasn't there. He wasn't amped up or bouncing around like I'd witnessed from others. He remained still and calm as I stared him down.

"Happy, ready?" the officiant roared in a hoarse voice. I nodded. "Cain...you ready?" The man opposite me nodded, never taking his eyes off me. Suddenly, the fierceness took hold of him and he readied himself. It was like night and day.

Gritting his teeth and flaring his nostrils, this was a man who came for a fight.

And a fight is what he'd get.

The officiant stepped back and Cain moved forward. I remained where I was and allowed the old man to come to me. Like a bear in a trap, he lunged forward, arm cocked to the side, ready to strike, but before he could swing, I rammed my fist into his side, just below his ribs. He stumbled back, bent at the hips, and clutched his hand over the spot I'd punched.

I didn't move.

Cal screamed at me from beyond the ropes, ordering me to go after him, but I didn't. Instead, I stood with my legs parted, my arms at my sides, and waited for Cain to regain momentum. When he straightened, he blindly charged at me. This time, I didn't deflect his attack. His knuckles rained down on my jaw, barely meeting it, but it was enough force to toss my head to the side. Briefly. Nothing I couldn't recover from in half a second.

I blocked out Cal's murderous rants from over my shoulder and straightened myself. Cain didn't pause in his assault, using his left hand to come at me from below. It was at the perfect angle to take hold of his wrist and twist his arm until I locked it behind his back. From there, the ball was in my court. Not even breaking a sweat, I kicked his leg out from under him and pushed him flat on the ground.

He broke free and flipped over, but I didn't take a breather this time. I struck him twice in the face. Blood pooled beneath him. He hadn't tapped out and the officiant hadn't called time. Cal's demanding voice drifted through the barrage of excitement on the other side of the ropes, telling me to take him out. But I didn't have it in me to do so.

Rather than continue to attack him while he was down, I remained on my knees next to him and studied his body language. Cal may have been a proficient fighter and knowledgeable coach, but he didn't know how to read people like I did. Take away a person's ability to communicate, and they'll learn ways around the verbal language.

When I looked at Cain, I saw a man on the verge of giving up. The fight drained from his eyes and his body went slack. He didn't lose consciousness, but he did lose his will to keep going. With blood seeping from his nostrils and mouth—more than likely a broken nose and, at the very least, a loose tooth—he patted the springboard beneath him, indicating his concession.

The officiant called the fight, but I didn't move. I took Cain's hand in mine and assisted him in sitting up, then looked him in the eye to make sure he was all right. Graciousness stared back at me. It was enough to get up and help him stand. We shook hands as he muttered, "You got this, man. You got this."

Commotion filled the room as the referee lifted my arm into the air, but none of it really registered with me. On my quest to find Rylee through the crowd, Cal caught my attention. He handed me a bottle of water in lieu of a towel, considering I hadn't perspired enough or bled at all to need the rag.

"What was that?" he asked with his mouth close to my ear, shouting above the ruckus.

I furrowed my brow, not having a clue as to what he meant.

He pointed to the ring, where I'd stepped away from seconds ago, and said, "You just stood there. You could've taken him out in half that time. You let him get a hit on you. What the hell was that?" His eyes grew large. "And then you showed him mercy. This isn't the playground, kid. This is the ring. This is fighting. Winner take all. I don't wanna see that shit from you again."

I shrugged and quirked a brow at him, which translated into, "I don't give a fuck what you say, because I'll do what I want." Of course, he probably didn't quite get all that, but at least it was the message I'd given him.

"Go to the locker room and clean up. When you're done, come back out here and watch the rest of the matches...see how it's done in this part of town. It doesn't matter where you've fought before or what your reason is for being here. Showing compassion on the other side of those ropes is weakness, and they'll eat you alive at the first sign of it."

Without acknowledging him, I turned on my heel and headed toward the hallway. There were three doors on each side, each team taking one. Our room was the last one on the left, so I had to pass the others on my way there. Halfway down the hall, I heard, "They call him Happy because the fucker never smiles. Seriously, he looks like his parents just died. Pissed off at the world."

If only they knew.

The room was empty when I walked in. Towels hung on hooks lining the wall, a medical table sat in the middle, and beyond that was a small alcove with one shower stall. I didn't need to wash up, but I went back there anyway to change my clothes. I'd just taken my shorts off, leaving me in nothing but my birthday suit, when the door creaked open.

Peeking around the tiled wall, I spotted the intruder.

And those round, brown eyes brought my dick to life.

TWENTY

Rylee

"THIS IS FUCKING pathetic," Josh roared over the noise around us. "Motherfucker can't even throw a punch when the other guy's practically begging for it. I can't watch this shit anymore. Seeing him advance pisses me off."

He kissed me, hard, staking his claim around the other fighters, and then stormed off. I wasn't sure where he was going, so I stood in the same place, waiting for him to come back. Killian won and then exited the ring while I watched from the sidelines. There was something about watching him fight that called to me, and when he began his trudge to the back room, I found myself following him, all while glancing over my shoulder for Josh.

After waiting for Josh for several minutes, I made the decision to corner Killian, praying he was alone. I knew he wouldn't talk to me around other people, but considering he didn't need medical attention and he'd left his coach behind, I figured it was safe to assume he wouldn't have company. I only wanted to talk to him, to find out why he was doing this. It wasn't him. Not the same Killian Foster I'd known. The same boy I'd cried myself to sleep thinking about almost every night for years on end.

I rushed through the door and quickly closed it behind me. After I realized no one else was in the room, I engaged the lock. A man peered out with sandy blond hair drawn back to reveal the shaved parts underneath. My heart skipped a beat against my wishes. No matter how angry I was with him, how many times I told myself I wanted nothing to do with him, he still managed to ignite my body in flames of heated passion and desire. Still held the ability to affect the natural rhythm of my heart.

He may have stepped out of that ring as Happy, but standing here now, he was the boy who wanted to steal the moon for me. The boy who drew colorful flowers on my hands and signed his name on various hidden parts of my body.

The one who'd held my heart since I was ten years old.

"Who are you?" I asked quietly, not because I was afraid of being heard, but because my voice refused to work. He literally stole my breath away.

Killian stepped away from the wall, baring his perfectly ripped body. It was a masterpiece. He couldn't have sketched it better had he tried. Each line was precisely cut to accentuate every carved muscle, including the lick-worthy V that brought my attention to his hardening cock between his legs. It'd been ten days since I'd felt him inside me. Eight since I last saw his face.

Rather than greeting me with words, he took his shaft in his hand and began to stroke himself. Slowly. Oh so slowly until my panties were drenched and my nipples painfully erect. As he stalked toward me, his hooded gaze trapped me in place. Cemented my feet to the floor. Ceased my ability to move, breathe, blink.

Somehow, he'd crossed the small room and stood before me. Inches away. His body heat wafting over me in shallow waves of blistering warmth. His heavy breathing scratched the silence cocooned around us. I closed my eyes against the assault his presence had over me and inhaled deeply.

Killian had always had this unique scent. It'd been weaved into the fibers of my life for seven years, and then lingered for a while after he was gone. It was irreplaceable. No matter how much time I spent trying to rediscover it, I never could. It was him…just him. Not from a bottle or bar of soap. It wasn't shampoo or laundry detergent. It was Killian Foster. But now, standing in front of him, breathing him in…it was gone. No hint of the smell I'd been addicted to. No remaining trace of my first love. The aroma that had been tied up in my dreams for so long had disappeared. And in its place was something vaguely familiar—like a relative you knew when you were a small child, your best friend in kindergarten you run into after high school, or an old photo you come across, remembering the faces but can't recall when it'd been taken.

I covered my face with my hands and fought back the need to cry. The emotion came out of nowhere. It attacked me, took me by surprise. Unclear and vicious. Ready to take me down at any moment. But the need to sob fled as soon as he wrapped his fingers around my wrists. Fear took hold of me when I remembered the last time someone had done this. Josh. When he wanted me to touch him. I squeezed my eyes tighter, as if I could close them more than they already were, and lowered my head once he successfully pulled away my mask.

"Rylee..." He whispered my name so softly, so full of air, it almost didn't seem real. It reminded me of the times I'd hear him on the edge of consciousness, seconds before I'd drift off to sleep, only to hear his voice as if he stood before me and sat straight up. But not this time. Hearing him now, I knew he was here. So I kept my eyes shut, my chin tucked toward my chest, and tried with every ounce of fleeting fight I had to pull my arms away.

My resolve came when he didn't move my hands to his groin. Instead, he pulled one to his chest, laying it just over his pectoral muscle. My palm absorbed the heat of his skin when I splayed my fingers, his collarbone just beneath the tips. He took my other hand and pulled it to his face, keeping his hold on me, forcing me to touch him. His facial hair felt soft, nothing like the coarse hair it appeared to be, and I couldn't find it in me to pull away.

I dropped my forehead to the center of his chest and melted into him, allowing him to hold me up. Humidity plumed against my face when I asked again, "Who are you?" This time, the words shook as I embedded them into his skin, making him feel every emotion and bewilderment within them.

"You know who I am, Rylee." Without leaning over, he dropped his head so his mouth was next to my ear, forcing me to hear every word. "You've always been the only person who knew me. That hasn't changed."

"No." I shook my head, kept my hands exactly where they were, and pulled back enough to look into his eyes. The pistachio color calmed the storm raging inside. It reminded me of the first time I ever saw them, the first time I met Killian. The day my life changed forever. "I don't know you, because the person I remember you being wouldn't be in that ring. He wouldn't have beat up some guy he'd never met before—for the hell of it."

"I'm fighting a demon inside. I've been trying to slay it since I left you…since before I left. But I'm doing it. I'm ridding myself of the anger, the hatred, the burning hole in my chest. And this is how I have to do it, Rylee. Please, trust me. Trust that I'm the same person. If anything, I'm a healthier version."

I scoffed, unable to hold in the wave of humorless laughter. "Healthier? You call punching people until they bleed healthy?"

His eyes darkened, but they never left mine. "You don't seem to have a problem when your boyfriend does it. He takes no mercy on his opponents, and you don't seem to care. What's the difference? Why is what I do any different than what he does?"

I dropped my gaze to my fingers, laced through his wiry beard. I scratched his jaw and found a strange comfort in the sound of the hairs beneath my nails. "You're not him, Killian. You're better than that. Always have been."

"Yet you're with him…"

My gaze snapped to his, the desolation in his tone capturing me and refusing to let go. "Because he's nothing like you. Anyone who reminded me of you only brought back the pain of your absence. Reminded me of the heartbreak you left in your wake. I couldn't do that. I need someone completely opposite of you; otherwise, I'd do nothing but exist. I was tired of existing. I wanted to live, to breathe, to laugh and smile. I wanted to feel whole again."

"Do you? Does he make you feel whole?"

I tried to push him away, but he gripped my wrists again and held me still. "I'm not doing this with you. I refuse to let you control my life again."

"Why did you come here?"

With an exasperated sigh, I fell into the door behind me, pressing my back into the thin, cheap wood. "I needed answers. I don't know why I needed them—or even wanted them. The last time I saw you, we were in my back yard in

Smithsville. In Tennessee. Five years later, I find you in a gym in Baltimore. Making money beating the shit out of people you don't know. Nothing makes sense to me anymore."

He dropped his forehead to mine and closed his eyes. In this moment, he was everything I remembered him being. He was the epitome of my dreams, my hopes, my prayers. He was here. I was here. We were together again. Nothing else mattered.

But it did.

Everything else mattered.

And it took conscious effort on my part to keep that in mind.

"You're different, Killian. And I don't know how to take it. It's like when you go back to your childhood home, and it's nothing like you remembered. It's the same, but not. At all. The same walls, the same big oak tree in the front yard. The same front door. But the grass is higher and the tire swing is missing. The front porch is a different color and new drapes hang in the window. Different. That's what you are to me now. An old house, full of memories, but none of it belongs to me anymore."

"Nothing has changed. I'm still me," he argued with a voice so deep it could've been a growl. "I still love you as much as I did the day I walked away to chase my demons. More. I love you so much more. Because now I'm closer to being free. And I want nothing more than to love you freely. Openly."

His confession slammed into me and knocked the wind from my chest. My lungs burned, my head grew light, and I feared my knees would buckle. I knew he'd said it to me before, in bed. But that didn't mean anything to me. He was trying to get what he wanted, and using that term was what every guy knew worked.

But he wasn't every guy.

He was Killian.

"Don't act like that's the first time I've ever told you that."

"It kind of is. Saying it while buried balls deep in me doesn't count. Not to mention, you can't come back after being gone for years upon years and expect me to believe it. It doesn't work that way."

The space between his brows narrowed and the lines creased heavily while he stared into my eyes. The seafoam green had darkened, and I could practically smell the storm brewing inside him. "That wasn't the first time I ever told you."

"What? Of course it was."

"I told you in your back yard, when I had you pinned against the wall. And yes, it still counts even though I had your pussy wrapped around my cock, milking me. It counts. I meant it. And I meant it when I said it again after you pushed me away and told me to go."

My mind drifted back to that night, recalling him saying something. But I never knew what. His mouth had moved, his grunts had filled my ears, but at the time, it never made any sense to me.

Until now.

He'd told me then he loved me.

And I didn't know what to do with that information.

"And don't, for a fucking second, think I didn't mean it the other day. You've been mine since the day you followed me into the woods. And no matter what you say or do, you'll always be mine. I've loved you since the moment I laid eyes on you and I'll never stop. So believe what you want, be shocked, be surprised, but whatever you do...don't *ever* fucking doubt it."

A knock on the door to my back caused us both to freeze. We stood silent, waiting for whoever stood on the other side to say something, or knock again. "Happy, it's Cal. I need you to open up, man."

Killian grabbed a towel hanging from a hook next to us and wrapped it around his waist. He held his finger to his lips, signaling me to be quiet. After I stepped to the side, he opened it a crack to speak to Cal. Only seeing half of this one-sided conversation made it difficult to gather the full scope of it all.

"Hurry up, man. The lineup is almost over and you need to be out here. You'll be up against some of these people, and you need to study them so you'll be prepared." There was a pause and Killian nodded. Before he could close the door, Cal spoke again. "Tell your girl she needs to come with me. Jag is out there and if he catches her in here..."

Killian turned his attention to me, and I could see in his eyes how much he hated the thought of me leaving. But we both knew we didn't have much of a choice. His coach was right. If Josh knew I'd been in here, shit would hit the fan.

I slid between the door and Killian, offering him a sliver of a smile as I exited the room. Once the door was closed, the latch clicking into place, I moved around Cal and started toward the mouth of the hallway.

"Not so fast." Cal gently held my elbow and stopped me. "What you're doing is dumb and dangerous. These men go in there"—he pointed to the stage just beyond the end of the hall—"and fight with barely any safety net. No gloves, no padding. Only one man who stands there and calls the shots. Giving one a reason to beat the other, aside from a win and money, is stupid. And quite possibly, deadly."

"That's not what I'm doing. You don't know—"

"I know enough," he said, interrupting me. "I know you're the girl Happy is after, the name on his arm. I know he came here for a reason, and it's my understanding that reason is you. He has it out for Jag, and he won't stop until he gets you back. But what neither of you understand is Jag won't go down easily. I've seen him fight. He goes for the jugular. He's skilled and has many more fights under his belt than Happy. This won't end well if you switch sides before the tournament is over."

"No one ever said anything about switching sides. I only went to talk to him. To clear the air and get some answers. Maybe a little closure to the way he left things. It's not what you think. I'm with Josh, not Kill–*Happy*." That name burned my tongue, knowing just how false it was. "It wasn't a sweet reunion or fun times."

I turned and began to walk away, but stopped dead in my tracks when he said, "You might want to tell him these walls are thin. Anyone standing on the other side of the door can hear everything that's being said."

Instead of acknowledging him, I resumed my stride and made it to the large room. Josh stood in the center of a small crowd. Once his gaze landed on me, he parted through the bodies and stormed the ten feet between us.

"Where were you?"

I felt his anger before I heard it. "I had to use the restroom. I waited for you, but you never came back. I couldn't hold it any longer."

He nodded, accepting my lie, and grabbed my hand. "You about ready to go? It's pretty much over and I need to get some sleep." Josh had always had a ritual the night before a fight, and I prayed he wouldn't want to keep it tonight. But I knew that was a wasted wish when he said, "I'll drop you off at your car so you can follow me back to my place."

"Josh...I'm tired. Can't you just drop me off at home?"

His eyes lit up like the sea at noon and a wicked grin tugged at his lips. He leaned down and licked the outer edge of my ear before lowering his voice and whispering, "No, babe. You're coming with me. You know I need your pretty lips wrapped around my dick before a fight. The last time, you were gone, and I lost. Being buried in your throat is my good luck charm."

My stomach rolled at the thought.

But I complied anyway.

TWENTY-ONE

Killian

"WHAT'S WITH THE fucking compassion, Happy?" Cal stormed into my room with his hands on his hips, looking more like a pissed-off father than a man who'd taken me under his wing only a month ago.

I dropped my sketchpad to my lap and released the pen from my grip. Irritation bubbled up at the thought of being interrupted before I had her image complete. It was the only time I found peace within the chaos—when I drew the lines of her face, the curve of her lips, the wide arches in her eyes. And now, as Cal stood before me in my private space, the contentment faded away.

He grabbed the whiteboard off the dresser next to him and threw it at me. I glared at him and managed to catch it before it hit me in the face. He wouldn't let up, and we both knew it. He'd demand answers from me until I gave them up.

"You're a fighter, Happy. The name of the game is to fight."

I pulled the cap off the dry erase marker and furiously wrote my reply.

What's your point?

"My *point*?" His voice rose, growing stronger and deeper. "My point is you can't show weakness, Happy. When you hesitate, not taking a shot when you have the chance, you're showing the others when to strike. You're giving them an in when there shouldn't be one."

I wiped off the board and started again. *I refuse to knock someone down who's unprepared. It's dirty and I won't do it.*

165

Cal threw his head back and released a roaring laugh. "Then you're in the wrong game, my man. The *wrong* game. There's a winner and a loser. What side do you want to be on? Because with that mentality, I can promise you'll end up on the wrong one."

I'll win. My way.

"And what way is that? Standing there and not doing a damn thing while your opponent throws a punch? Letting it connect with your face? What would've happened if his aim hadn't been off?"

I would've bled.

"And you would've *lost*!"

I leaned forward, gritting my teeth to refrain from screaming back at him.

"Go ahead, Happy. Yell at me. Scream at me."

I shook my head in warning.

"You think I don't know? That I didn't hear you talking behind that door tonight? I don't know what your endgame is, why you came to me. And to be honest…I don't really care. Whatever you're hiding, that's your deal. But you sought me out. For a reason—whatever it may be—and I can't help you unless you start listening to me."

I grabbed the marker so tight in my hand I could've snapped it in half. The need to retaliate grew stronger until I almost broke the seal of silence and put him in his place. But with a deep breath, I calmed enough to write something down.

I get in the ring because I have to. Not because I enjoy beating the shit out of people.

"Why do you have to?" His tone had lowered, losing some of its bite.

Without taking my eyes off his, I wrote down the three letters of my answer and held it up for him to see.

Jag.

"Because of the girl?"

I nodded, not offering him anything else.

"Come tomorrow night. If for nothing else than to study Jag. If your goal is to get him in the ring, that'll only happen one way—you have to win every fight. And when you get there, you need to be prepared for him."

I am prepared. Don't worry about that.

Cal threw his hands up in defeat. "Whatever. Just come."

I shook my head and wrote out, *Not gonna happen*.

"Why not? How can you possibly expect me to get you ready if you refuse to listen to anything I say outside of daily training...which you only do because, if not, the other guys might catch on."

I can't see her with him. She'll be there to watch him, and I can't handle it.

"Get the fuck over it, man. You're acting like a creeper. You sit in here, drawing her face like some kind of stalker. Is that what this is? Did I get the wrong impression of you?"

I glared at him, biting back my words.

"Listen, I don't care what you and this girl have together or if you end up winning her back. That's none of my business. But if I'm putting her in harm's way by getting you in that ring, by giving you the ultimate chance to take her back...I need to know. I refuse to do that."

She loves me.

"Oh, yeah? Did she tell you that?"

I chucked the whiteboard at him and growled.

"That's what I thought. Don't make me regret taking you on, Hap. If you don't wanna talk, fine. Don't talk to me. I don't need to hear you speak. What I need is to know I'm not being played. I need to know you're in this for solid reasons. And then I need to see you win."

I closed my eyes and pulled in a full inhale. I blew the air past my lips then whispered, "The reasons are solid." I couldn't look at him while I said the words, and truth be told, I wouldn't have even uttered them had I not lost my cool and threw the only thing I had to communicate.

"So I'm just supposed to be okay with that answer?"

I nodded and reclined back until I met the headboard.

"Listen...I let you into my home. I've taken you into my club. I don't do this for just anyone. And to be honest, I don't know what it was about you that made me agree to it. I guess there was something in your story, in the way you sat in my office like a lost fucking boy. Whatever it was, I believed you. I believe you now. Don't make me regret it."

No other words left my lips, nothing spelled out on paper. I stared at him, hoping he could see the sincerity in my eyes.

He wouldn't regret doing this for me. And neither would I. I had one goal when I came to him, one thing on my mind.

Now I had two.

And I wasn't about to lose either one.

When he left the room, I went back to Rylee's face. I grew lost in each shadow, each detail of her likeness. Until I had her back—permanently—I'd continue to sketch her. Hell, I'd probably never stop, even after she was mine again. There was just something soothing, calming, about her. About her features. The love I saw in her eyes every time I looked into them, despite her reluctance to verbalize it. I didn't need to hear the words to know they were true. To know she was mine.

She was.

Mine.

"Knock, knock," a soft, feminine voice came from the barely parted door. "Your gym clothes are clean." Sophia, Cal's wife, walked in with a laundry basket tucked beneath her arm. She dropped it on the bed but didn't make any move to leave.

I offered her a smile and nod. My gentle gesture of appreciation, as well as a subtle way of letting her know she could leave. I wasn't in the mood for company. Not with Cal, especially not with Sophia, and most definitely not in my bedroom while I lay on my bed in nothing but track pants.

"So...that girl you had over here..." She sat down next to me and peered over my arm to the paper in my lap. "She's the girl, right? The reason you came here?"

I flipped to a clean page and began to scribble my response. This was nothing new to her. I'd been here over a month, and she was quite familiar with how I communicated. *Did Cal send you in here?*

Her airy giggle was sweet and gave me a sense of security. "You know him too well. Yes, he asked me to come talk to you. He's worried. You can't blame the guy. How would you feel if you took someone in, had their back, trusted them without reason...only to find out their secrets ran deeper than you imagined?"

I take it he told you.

"That you can talk but choose not to? Yes. He did. But he doesn't know why, and even though he says he doesn't care, I know he does. Not to mention, I care. Would you mind telling me why you live like this?"

Like what? If she wanted answers, she'd have to be more specific.

"You made a deal with Cal—he'd outbid the others, knowing you'd get none of it. In return, he gets to keep your share of every win, including the big team bonus for the outcome of the tournament. Why give up all that money when you could've gone in there and sold yourself without a problem?"

My eyes closed long enough for me to find the right words. When I opened them again, I began to pen my thoughts as quickly as I could. *I don't need the money. It was never about the paycheck. This has always been about taking back what was mine to begin with.*

"Her?" She pointed to the paper, even though Rylee's face was no longer in view.

I nodded, but the silence was too much to bear. *She's the only one I've ever talked to...aside from Cal tonight.*

"So why don't you talk?"

My head snapped up, my gaze finding hers. The mixture of green and brown stared back at me, beckoning me to answer with piqued curiosity. I could tell this wasn't her way of prying—she sincerely cared and wanted to be a friend to me. I hadn't had many of those in my life, so it was hard for me to accept. But being here, in Cal's house, around him and his wife...it felt safe.

I was told not to.

"By who? When?"

I can't say. Please don't ask again.

"Killian," she whispered as she laid her hand on my forearm. "Is it okay if I call you that?"

Sophia and Cal knew my name, but for the purposes of the ring, we'd agreed I'd strictly go by Happy. I nodded. There was something about this woman that reminded me of Elise, and I couldn't tell her no—didn't possess the ability to. Sophia was an unlikely connection to my aunt when I couldn't be around her, and when she spoke to me this way, it left me feeling like the little boy who'd gone to live with her twelve years ago. Afraid she'd kick me out. Petrified of her rejection.

"You remind me of an old-soul type," she continued. "Even though you look tough, carry yourself with an attitude most find scary, you're soft. I can see it. Despite the tattoos, the cut muscles, the permanent scowl on your face, there's a softness about you. It's evident when you smile at the TV—when you think no one is looking. In the way you shuffle around us, even when you're not in our way. I see it in the way you avert your eyes when Cal shows me affection, like watching it would be rude and intrusive, so you turn away."

Her words surrounded me, and left me incapable of thought.

"So it doesn't make much sense why you're doing this. Why you'd give up the money when it's obvious you could take it all. I don't understand why you'd choose to fight, when—from what Cal says—hurting someone else seems to affect you in ways it doesn't the other guys. You're not made for this life, Killian. Sure, you could dominate this sport, take the top seat…but why?"

I glanced at the trees inked on my arm, the trunks forming the letters of Rylee's name. The moon at the top curve of the *R*. My finger traced the black and grey lines like I'd done so many times since it was put there. No matter how many other tattoos decorated my skin, this one would always be my favorite.

"It's always a girl," she said with a soft giggle. "Maybe that's why Cal likes you so much. You must remind him of himself. He left the ring for me, you know. He was at the top of his game, stashing hoards of cash in savings, all to give me the life I've always wanted. But I didn't want the money. I wanted him to come home *whole*—no broken bones, swollen knuckles, bruises, cuts or scrapes. I was tired of kissing his boo-boos and wanted, just one time, for him to hold me. Heal *me* when I was hurt. So he left it all. For me."

My confusion must've been evident, because she laughed and shook her head.

"I didn't care if he owned a team. It wasn't the sport I disliked. No one can understand what it feels like to stand back and watch someone throw punch after punch to the man you love. How bad it hurts to watch him bleed, to see him in pain. That's what I didn't care for, what I couldn't endure any longer. Now, he gets to do what he loves without coming home to me in bandages." She covered my hand with both of hers. "Tell me this…if she asks you to leave, would you?"

Her question didn't warrant any thought. The answer was immediate.

I nodded. Because I would.

In a heartbeat.

As soon as I took Josh Disick down.

In a pool of his own blood.

TWENTY-TWO

Rylee

HIS BARE SHOULDERS flexed, the muscles in his back coiled tight with each punch. Each swing. Each twist of his body as he mercilessly took down his opponent. It was a longer fight than Josh had anticipated; he'd underestimated the drive the other man possessed—the unwillingness to give up.

Until this moment, I never had much of a problem watching Josh fight. The idea of doing it as a sport wasn't something I found appealing, but it never bothered me. Suddenly, standing here, outside the ring, watching it all take place, I was repulsed. A knot formed in the pit of my stomach at the sight of my boyfriend landing punch after punch to a man who clearly had a problem standing on his own. Josh's knuckles were covered in someone else's blood. Perspiration clung to his skin. And anytime he turned my way, the murderous glare in his eyes sickened me.

So much had happened since last night. Seeing Killian take out a fighter on his quest to the top was disheartening. However, it was the compassion he showed at the end that told a different story. It was the grey area between the eighteen-year-old who'd left me behind and the man who stormed back into my life. It left me feeling bewildered toward this "sport." And in turn, brought forth a disconnect with Josh I hadn't ever known existed.

That detachment might've had something to do with the conversation that took place in the back room. Killian's admission—no, his proclamation—of love. Whatever it was, I found myself wracked with guilt. But unlike the last time I was with Killian, I didn't hate myself for sneaking around behind my boyfriend's back. I felt like shit for having Josh's dick in my mouth, as if I wasn't faithful to Killian. It kept me up all night. I'd let Killian get to me—allowed his claim to consume me. And in the end, I gave him ownership of me by permitting him into my thoughts. Into my boyfriend's bedroom while I knelt between Josh's legs.

I refused to let this go on any longer and hoped I'd see Killian tonight. The tight jeans, low-cut top, and ankle boots were meant to make him drool. My perfectly straightened hair and heavy makeup were to serve a purpose—a slap in the face when I told him I no longer belonged to him, and then walked out on Josh's arm.

A lie to pacify my inner turmoil.

I ignored the images filtering through my head of him taking me in the back room while Josh fought in the ring. I pretended to hate the idea of feeling him inside me, his skin pressed against mine, his voice rumbling in my ear. The need to hurt him and walk away in the manner he had was great, but paled in comparison to my need to be with him. The dizzying thoughts battled against each other, leaving me the only loser in the entire situation. Because Killian wasn't here. He hadn't shown up to see the second night's fights. And that's when I succumbed to the realization I'd gotten dressed up *for* him.

It had nothing to do with retaliation.

Josh straddled the man in the ring and threw a few more punches, disregarding the officiant next to him, ordering him to halt. The crazed look in his eyes struck fear into my chest, and I realized I truly had no idea who this man was. I'd seen his sweet side, his caring side. The part of him that made me swoon and give in whenever he asked. And then there was this side. Jaguar. He was vicious and unrelenting. Had this part of him only surfaced while he was in the ring, it'd be one thing. But that wasn't always the case. Jag came out when I turned him down, when I couldn't do as he had asked. He showed up in arguments, when I wouldn't give him his way. Granted, he'd never laid a hand on me, but the relentless attitude and his inability to stop before taking it to a new level was the same—Jag truly was Josh at the core.

I hadn't realized the daze I'd been in until I found myself in the back room with Josh and Dalton. He wiped himself off with a towel while Dalton filled a plastic bag with ice for his hands, which were smeared with blood. I couldn't remember him climbing out of the ring or following him back here.

"We're gonna celebrate tonight, babe. Me and you." His wagging brows didn't go unnoticed. I knew what his words implied, and they made my stomach clench and bile burn the back of my throat.

"I'm really tired, Josh."

"Yeah, and you'll be even more tired when I'm done with you."

I took a step back, closer to the door. "No, I'm serious. I'm just going to head home."

His piercing stare practically stopped my heart. "Where's your head at, Lee? Huh? Last night I had to do all the work, like you were off in space while I fucked that mouth of yours. And now you're—"

"Stop, Josh. Please...just cut it out." I glanced over at Dalton, hating him being in the room to hear this. Although, he didn't seem to mind bearing witness to Josh's insults. "I told you I'm tired. I was tired last night. I just want to go to sleep."

He dropped the towel to the floor and pushed away the offered ice. When he had me cornered against the wall—like Killian had last night, yet not at all like Killian had made me feel—he roughly grabbed the sides of my head and forced me to look into his eyes. "Tell me what's going on. Why are you pushing me away?"

I huffed and let the tension out of my shoulders. Defeat. It was debilitating at times. "It's like you're two different people." Déjà vu consumed me, thinking of the similarities between this conversation and the one I had with my former lover. "When you're Jag, you're mean. You're demanding, and I don't like it. When you're here, in the ring, the club, or a back room, it's like you forget who I am. You treat me like a whore. Like I'm disposable."

His gaze softened a few degrees and his hold on me eased slightly. "Let me make it up to you," he said in a softer tone, lacking the crudeness from moments ago. "Baby, I'm sorry.

Come home with me and let me show you how bad I feel. Let me prove to you you're not disposable."

My eyes closed and a long sigh drifted past my lips. "I'm really tired, Josh. I'm not lying about that. Rain check?" I dared to peek my eyes open to find his. I saw curbed anger reflected at me, and it made me uncomfortable. The idea of him being pissed off lit a fire inside—although I did recognize his restraint.

"Wait for me to clean up and I'll go with you."

"I just want to be alone tonight," I croaked out, fearful of how he'd respond.

Rather than arguing or saying something nasty, he let me go and took a step back. My body deflated, believing I'd survived his anger. That is until he flung the door open and stood in front of me with his shoulders pulled back and his chest puffed out.

"Then fucking go. Get your damn beauty sleep and call me when you've got your head out of your ass."

I hated the way he made me feel.

Hated even more my inability to fight back and defend myself.

But instead, I bit my tongue and left the room with my head hung low.

As I trudged down the hall, I passed Cal. I didn't acknowledge him, and he didn't say anything to me. There was an awareness between us, which was odd considering I didn't really know him. Seeing him in almost the same place we'd had our conversation the night before, brought forth emotions I wasn't ready to deal with.

And they plagued me all the way home.

• • •

THE *ROCKY* THEME song reverberated from my nightstand for the tenth time in what seemed as many minutes. As soon as it'd end, Josh would wait a minute or two and then call again. I couldn't take it, and eventually, covered my head with my pillow. I didn't have the strength to move to turn off the ringer. My body had been depleted of energy after crying for hours ever since I'd left the gym.

This time, however, it didn't ring again. Once it stopped, I was afforded a long span of time filled with nothing but silence. Until the banging on the door started. I couldn't ignore the incessant pounding, knowing it would alarm my neighbors.

"Please, Lee…open up. I'm an idiot. Let me prove to you how sorry I am."

I pressed my forehead to the front door and closed my eyes. More tears leaked out and stained my face with proof of the internal war waging inside me. His remorse was evident in his tone. His sorrow as tangible as the floor beneath my bare feet. But no matter how sorry he was, it didn't take away what he'd said to me. The hurt he'd caused. The horrible things he'd said in front of Dalton.

"Baby. Open up. I can't leave until I know you're okay."

"Please, go." My strangled words came out wrapped in a sob. "Just go, Josh. I don't want to see you right now."

"Then answer your phone. Talk to me."

"I have nothing to say."

I heard his exhale through the door, and a soft thud indicated his head met the cold metal. "Then will you at least listen to me?" When I didn't respond, he continued. "I'm sorry, Lee. God, I'm so fucking sorry. I didn't mean it. I get so amped up at fights, I don't do or say the right things. It's hard for me to lose the adrenaline that fast. I just got so excited thinking about celebrating with you tonight, and then it's like you cut me off at the knees when you rejected me. You know I don't deal with rejection well. Please, babe…forgive me."

I turned around and slid down the door with my back pressed against it. My knees curled up to my chest and I wrapped my arms around them. I dropped my head and cried into the space between my legs.

My sobs must've been louder than I thought. "Lee, please don't cry. You know I hate it when you're hurt. I don't want you to be sad, and I hate myself for knowing I'm the cause of it. I just want to make everything right again. I want to make everything better."

His apology sounded sincere. But I couldn't ignore the nagging thought comparing Josh to Killian. Twenty-four hours ago, I'd explained my reason for being with Josh, saying I'd chosen him because he was the complete opposite of the person who'd wrecked me. And that was true. But I wasn't sure the price was worth it. Yes, they were nothing alike. Where Josh was hard, Killian was soft. Where Josh was demanding, Killian was pleading.

Where Josh was angry, Killian was loving.

I loved Killian. Always had. More than likely always would. And I knew what I felt for Josh wasn't the same. It wasn't love. Most of the time, it wasn't even lust. The real reason I was with him was because I knew if he ever left me, if he ever decided to walk away without a word, I wouldn't be devastated. My life wouldn't be over. I'd get up the next morning and go on living.

I couldn't do that with Killian.

Although, with that came a different kind of pain. One I'd never been used to before. The hurtful words and callous actions. I'd traded one tear for another. Albeit, Josh made me cry for completely different reasons, but cry nonetheless. I didn't know how much longer I'd be able to keep up this charade. How much longer I'd be able to lie to myself.

Especially with Killian near.

"Baby, say something. You're scaring me." His voice through the door brought me out of the mental agony I'd been in—for who knows how long. "Are you still there? Did you leave? Just hear me out. Listen to me. Please."

"I need you to go, Josh. Before you wake up my neighbors."

"Fuck your neighbors. I don't care about them. I only care about you."

"Can we talk about this tomorrow? You woke me up. I'm tired."

There was a moment of silence, and then a thunderous whack on the door—more than likely from him slapping it. "Who's in there with you? Who do you have in there? Tell me, Lee. Open the damn door and just fucking tell me."

I stood up and unlocked the door, fury motivating my every move. By the time I yanked the door open, my tears had turned from grief to anger, lining my face that probably burned bright red due to the breath I held in my lungs.

He tried to step inside, but I blocked him with my arm and stilled him with my glare. "Don't you dare. Don't come here and accuse me of cheating on you. I'm alone. In tears. Because you're an ass who doesn't know how to treat me right."

"He's here, isn't he? The guy from your past. You lied to me!" he roared, pounding his chest with his fist as he pushed past the barrier I'd placed between him and my apartment. "You've been different since you came back from your parents' house. I knew better than to let you go there."

"*Let* me?" I mocked and rolled my eyes.

"Yeah…let you."

"You need to leave," I said with a calmness that surprised even me.

He turned in a circle, craning his neck to see every inch of available space. When he pointed to my room, he asked, "Is he in there? Do you have him in your bed? Maybe he's hiding in a closet."

Before he could move closer to the open door, I grabbed his upper arm and pulled him back with all my might. "Get out, Josh. I won't allow you to do this. You said you came here to apologize. Well, this isn't showing me you're sorry. This made it worse. You need to leave."

He turned his vibrant eyes to me, anger embedded in his features. He looked nasty and scary. The creases lining his forehead deepened as well as the ones next to his mouth. His nose scrunched up, accentuating the jagged scar along the bridge. And his lips pursed, forcing his heavy, panting exhales through his nostrils.

"I'm done. I can't do this anymore. You need to get out before I call the police. Don't bother trying to reach me. Don't wait around to hear from me. We're over. Through. I refuse to let you treat me this way."

His expression turned softer in the blink of an eye, like he'd morphed from Jaguar to Josh right in front of me. His breaths became more labored, not so much out of rage any longer. "You're leaving me?"

"Yes," I said with my shoulders pulled back in confidence—even though terror flowed through my veins. "This was the last straw. I shouldn't have put up with half the things you've done or said to me—especially lately. Forcing my hand down your pants in front of others, talking about fucking my mouth in front of Dalton. Shit…" I hissed. "I shouldn't have been okay with letting you do that to me to begin with. You made me feel like garbage, worthless, guilty for trying to turn you down. Next thing I know, I'm on the floor, on my knees, with your dick in my mouth. And then you go and say something so ugly about it in front of Dalton."

"You know I'd never force you to do anything you didn't want to. If I believed you truly weren't into it, I would've never made you do it. You're acting like I raped you or something. I didn't. I'd never do that, and you know it. I've never pressed for more than you're willing to give." His tone was calm, smooth, but his words insinuated accusations against me, and they left me angered. "I'm sorry for saying something around anyone else. You're right. That wasn't okay, and I'll never do it again."

No words came to me. I had so much to say, but nothing formed. Instead, I stared at him with wide eyes, wondering where my courage had fled to. He was delusional if he thought he could change my mind, but for some reason, I couldn't utter those words. I couldn't reiterate my need for him to go, make him understand how serious I was about us being over.

He moved to the couch and took a seat. I followed, but remained standing in front of him, arms crossed, not sure how things had turned so quickly. One minute, I was enraged and kicking him out, threatening to call the cops if he didn't leave. And the next…he was in my living room with his head in his hands, every bit the lost boy he knew I couldn't refuse.

"I know I've upset you. I haven't treated you the way you deserve to be treated. I'm man enough to admit that. But please, baby, give me another chance. Let me prove to you I can change. I can be what you need…what you deserve." The utter sadness in his tone simmered my fight.

"I don't think you can do that, Josh. I hate to say it, but I don't think you're capable of changing. This is who you are, and that's fine. I don't ever want anyone to change for me. Just like I'd never want anyone to ask me to be someone I'm not."

He grabbed my hand and pulled me to the cushion next to him, his knee touching my thigh. In this moment, he seemed small. Not at all the same guy who could make my couch look tiny just by sitting on it. But here he was, vulnerable and weak, on display. For me. And I wondered if this would be the time he'd finally open up. Finally give me enough of himself so maybe I could understand him better.

"You're scaring me, Josh."

"No," he whispered and closed his eyes for a brief moment. When he found my gaze again, I couldn't help but become lost in his bright, intoxicating blue eyes. "Don't be scared. Please. I never wanna frighten you. I love you, Rylee."

I gasped, having never heard him say those words before.

"I can't lose you, too. I can't do it."

His words drifted into my ears, flowed into my brain, and then swarmed around until they played on repeat. Each time I heard them, more confusion plagued me. Over the course of our relationship, we discussed the bare minimum of our lives before meeting one another. He knew about the boy who'd broken my heart, the one who'd kept me from dating. He knew where I grew up and was familiar with my relationship with my parents. I'd mentioned my brother a few times, but it wouldn't have surprised me if he didn't remember his name. Other than that, he knew about school, about my degree, my job, and my need to help children in the system—children who'd suffered through horrific situations. However, he never asked and I hadn't confessed why. Even though he'd known about Killian, about the boy who'd lived next door to me, I never told him the whole story. It wasn't my place to offer up secrets that didn't belong to me, not to mention, I refused to admit my future had been paved by the boy from my past.

With as little as Josh knew about me, I knew even less about him. At the beginning, it was insignificant. He was the first man I'd dated since I was seventeen years old, and I enjoyed the easiness of our relationship. After I learned about his fights, I became interested in his life now, not at all caring about how he got here. But sitting on the couch with my hand in his, seeing his pain haunting him through the bright, almost translucent windows to his soul, I found myself curious about where he came from. Of how he became this man—*Jaguar*. So vicious, so closed off, so…cold.

"Too?" I cocked my head at him after coming out of my trance. "What do you mean? Who have you lost? And why have you never told me this before?"

"I did tell you. My mom."

I thought back to any mention of his mother, recalling him admitting how she was no longer alive. But that was it. I'd asked about her once, and he'd shut down the topic quickly. It had never been brought up again.

"Josh…" My moment of compassion seemed to have vanished. Maybe it was impatience. Maybe it was the feeling of being played. Whatever it was, I blew out a sigh so weighted down with frustration I nearly felt it fall into my lap. "If you're trying to guilt me into staying with you, it won't work. You can't compare me leaving to your mom dying. Nor can you hold her passing against me and make me stay."

"That's not what I'm doing."

"Then why are you comparing me to your mom?"

He released my hand and wiped his face. Even though I tried telling myself this was him manipulating me, I could see in his eyes that wasn't true. "My mom was my hero. My best friend. It wasn't always good times, but even when it was hard, it was always the two of us. And then one day…she left me. She—"

"Josh, she didn't leave you. You can't possibly think she chose to die."

His gaze locked on mine, and in them, I found inconceivable agony. "She did. When I was fifteen, she killed herself. It was her choice. No one shoved that bottle of pills down her throat. No one made her do it. It was *her* decision. She left me all on her own, knowing what it would do to me. And here you are…leaving me. Not allowing me to prove I can be better."

The backs of my eyes burned with sympathetic tears. I'd worked with children and families in the past who'd dealt with the loss of a loved one due to suicide. The grief and turmoil of those left behind is unmeasurable. The guilt they harbor can linger a lifetime.

"I had no idea. You've never told me anything about her before."

He shook his head and took a deep breath, as if steadying himself to finally offer me something. "When I was eight, she got pregnant. It was the happiest I'd ever seen her. Before that, she'd cry sometimes, thinking I didn't know. But our house was small, so I always heard her. It was mostly at night. But when she was pregnant…she was different."

"You have a brother or sister?" I was shocked by the imparting of this hidden knowledge.

"No," he said solemnly. "I don't understand it—never did. Anytime I'd call it my brother, she'd correct me and say it was *her* baby. Sometimes she'd say weird things that didn't make sense to me, but she'd just tell me I was too young to understand and leave it at that. I figured it had to do with my dad. They had shared custody, and I think she never felt like I was hers. So this baby was her way of not having to share it with anyone."

"I'm confused…who was the father of the baby?"

Josh shrugged, but then continued with his story. "I was eight, Lee. I don't remember much about it. Really, the only thing I vividly recall is her coming home after having the baby. She cried all the time. Worse than before. She no longer hid it from me, and eventually, my dad had to step in. I ended up living with him most of the time because my mom was so lost."

"Postpartum?"

"No. She never brought the baby home."

Confused, I narrowed my gaze at him and asked, "What happened?"

"Apparently, the father of the baby was married. He showed up at the hospital and took the kid from her. He refused to let her see her own child. I tried begging my dad to help her out, to help her get the baby back, but he wouldn't do anything. I hated him for it. I still hate him for doing that to her. I've never understood how someone could sit back and do nothing, just let a man steal a baby from its mother."

"Josh, that doesn't make sense. Something's not adding up. There has to be custody and courts involved. You can't just walk into the hospital and take a baby away without going through the proper channels."

"My mom had a lot of issues. She was bipolar, and as I got older, my dad told me she also suffered from paranoia." His gaze fell to the coffee table, and his shoulders dropped. It was as if he became defeated by his own words. "I was diagnosed when I was seventeen."

"Diagnosed? With what?"

"Bipolar disorder. It was after my mom killed herself. I'd gone to live with my dad full time, and started getting into the wrong crowd. Doing drugs. Masking the pain of losing my mom. He couldn't take the moods anymore and made me go to a psychiatrist. I fought him on it, but eventually gave in. It turned out to be a blessing in disguise. I'll always have moments of anger; I don't think that'll ever go away. But being in the ring helps control it. It gives me a place to work it out— a safe environment."

"But sometimes you're angry even when you're not in the ring."

When he turned to me, I saw sheer vulnerability through the glistening tears in his eyes. "I know...and for that, I'm sorry. I swear, Lee, I'll work on it harder. I'll try harder to be the man you thought you got when we first met."

I stood up and walked around the couch, needing a moment to clear my head. Had Killian not been in the picture, I more than likely would've given in. But unfortunately for Josh...I was no longer the girl he thought he'd gotten when we first met, either.

Josh came up behind me and placed his hands softly on my shoulders. "Give me a chance, Lee. Please. I'm begging you. I fucked up and I know it. I'll be better. I swear."

"I'm moving," I blurted out, instantly regretting the decision when his grip tightened. I shimmied out of his hold until we faced one another. "Well, it's not finalized yet. But I've been thinking a lot about it."

"Where are you going?"

"I don't know yet. I just started looking at options. I'm trying to work it out with my job first, but more than likely, back home to Tennessee."

His lips thinned and his nostrils flared. Anger had set into his expression, but when he spoke, his words were steady, only slightly strained. "For him? You're going back home for him? Is that what you're trying to tell me?"

Peering into his hardened stare, I couldn't help but wonder if he possibly suffered from the same paranoia his mom had. If this had been the first time he'd ever mentioned Killian, I wouldn't have thought twice about it. But it wasn't. Ever since I'd returned from my parents' house, he'd brought it up in almost every fight. What I originally assumed was jealousy, now seemed to reek of obsession and delusions.

"No, Josh. I really wish you'd stop bringing him up. You don't know anything about him or our relationship. I want to be closer to my family. It has always been the plan. You know this. I've stayed this long because of you."

"So what's changed? I'm still here. Why leave now?"

"Because I can't keep doing this with you."

"I told you I'd change. I'll be better."

"And although you might believe that…I don't. I can't sit around and wait for you to reverse thirty-one years of learned behavior. You can't make the anger go away overnight. You're still Jaguar inside that ring, and no matter what you say, you'll never be able to walk away from the fights. It's who you are, and I understand that. It helps you manage your daily emotions. It evens you out for the most part. But it's just not enough for me."

"Will you at least stay until after the tournament? Let me see where things go from there? I can start my own club and—"

"It won't change anything, Josh."

He stepped up to me and grazed my cheek with the back of his battered knuckles. "Sleep on this. Think about it. You're tired and shouldn't make these kinds of decisions without a proper night's sleep." He kissed my forehead while holding the sides of my face gently in his large hands. "Goodnight, Lee."

I stood stunned, rooted in place, while he turned and left my apartment. He closed the door behind him, as if this were any other night. I knew this wouldn't be the last of him, and that thought petrified me.

I wanted to be done with him.

But he made it clear he wasn't done with me.

TWENTY-THREE

Killian

I'D MADE IT THROUGH four weeks of fights, and this was the last weekend before the final match. Every week I advanced, so did Josh, and I couldn't have been happier. The only reason I made it this far was because of my need to meet him in the ring again.

The only times I saw Rylee were on Saturday nights as she stood in the crowd next to Josh. I eventually had to stop looking at her. The light in her eyes was gone. Her natural beauty seemed to be hidden behind a mask of pain and withdrawal.

Without a doubt, I knew he was to blame.

The competition became tougher as the tournament progressed. The man standing in front of me, sweat lining his brow, refused to go down. No matter how many times I silently begged him to just give up so I could stop hitting him, he refused to comply.

My knuckles ached, my muscles burned, and my head throbbed with the effects of the punches he'd landed. When he charged at me again, I bared my teeth and swung, throwing my entire body into it. His head turned at the last minute, offering up his ear to my clenched fist. Blood spurted and he dropped to the spring board.

He didn't get up.

He rolled to his side and moaned, holding the side of his face. My stomach knotted at the sight of glistening crimson leaking between his fingers, and in an instant, I was eight years old again. I was in my parents' bedroom, trying to comprehend what was in front of me.

I grabbed a towel, not caring who held it out, and pressed it to the guy's ear. His eyes were clenched tight and his breaths were short and shallow. It was clear he was in a lot of pain. His body was rigid, making it difficult to get him into a seated position.

"Hap! Come on! He has people to tend to him. Get out of there," Cal called from the side of the stage. Glancing over my shoulder, I shook my head in response. I wasn't about to leave this man behind. Not after I'd been the one to do this to him.

"We need to get him to the back room," I heard someone say next to me. I didn't know who it was, and I refused to turn to find out. Instead, I helped him to his feet and assisted him out of the ring.

Ignoring Cal's rants, I walked next to my opponent, leading him down the hall and into his room. Once we had him situated on the clinic table, I carefully lifted the towel off the side of his face. There was so much blood I thought I would vomit. My stomach revolted against the sight before me.

"He'll be okay now. Thanks for your help." A hand moved into my line of sight. When I followed it to the arm it was attached to, then the chest, and finally, settling on his face, I recognized him as Dalton, Josh's coach.

I nodded and took his offered hand, shaking it.

"You should probably get back to Cal before he has a coronary."

I released his hand, stepped away, and left the room. Josh stood against the wall with his foot propped behind him. The sneer on his face tested my restraint. I wanted to knock his ass out, lay him out on the floor and listen to him beg for mercy. But I knew that'd have to wait another week. Providing he won his next match—which he was almost sure to do—I'd see him behind the ropes. Where no one could save him. No one could protect him from my wrath.

Rather than play his game, I continued past him until I found Cal, fuming. "I swear, kid…you're gonna put me on blood pressure medication before this thing is over. I can appreciate your concern for others, but could you not do it in front of the entire crowd?"

My jaw tightened and I could feel the muscles tic in response.

"Fine...don't answer me," he said with the smallest grin. "You need to get back to the room so someone can take a look at that." He pointed to my forehead. With the adrenaline pumping through me, I hadn't the faintest idea what he meant.

I ran my fingers along the sheen of sweat on my brow, and when I pulled my hand away, blood tinged the tips. My sight met Cal's and I shook my head. I didn't need medical attention for a scrape. Nothing I couldn't handle on my own. I'd had worse than that, and survived. I only wanted to exit the gym, to put it behind me for one more week.

The stagnant night air hung around me, but it felt ten times better than inside. All the bodies crowded around left it stifling and muggy—what little breathable air existed was polluted with musk. My keys jingled in my hand on my way to my car, but then everything fell silent when I spotted her.

Her back was to me, but I'd know her anywhere. I watched as she climbed into her car and started the ignition. It became a race to get to her. This was the first chance I'd had since the preliminary fight weeks ago to be near her. Every other time, she was wrapped in Josh's arms. That fucker never seemed to let her out of his sight. But now, she was alone.

I turned toward the gym, making sure he hadn't followed her, and then sprinted to my Jeep. Keeping up with her, I never let her car out of my headlights.

We both parked at the same time, my vehicle a few behind hers in an empty space along the curb. She glanced at me, but didn't speak. Instead, she walked to her building in silence. It was as if she knew I followed her every step of the way. Through the main door, up the stairs, to her apartment. Not once did she turn around.

She walked inside...and left the door open behind her.

My invitation.

I peered over my shoulder down the hall, one last effort to make sure Josh wouldn't pop up, and then followed her into the apartment. Not only did I close the door behind me, but I locked it, too.

Rylee stood with her hip against the counter in the small kitchen, her hand beneath the running faucet. Without a word spoken between us, she turned off the water and made her way to me. The cloth was cold, but eased the pain on my forehead.

"I don't think you need stitches. It doesn't look deep."

Her melancholy tone sent an ache through my body, far worse than the sting she tended to. There was something off about her, but I didn't know what. It gutted me to see her so lifeless. So down. So...

Broken.

I took her wrist and pulled her hand away from my face, forcing her to finally meet my gaze. "You're the one who needs to be taken care of. Not me. Let me take care of you." The flecks in her eyes shimmered. It took me back to a time when the sun would glint off them while I drew on her arm.

"You're bleeding."

"It happens. I've had worse." Guilt assuaged me when she flinched. She'd never hid her feelings from me, and I'd always known how sad she was over what had happened to me as a child. It was in her eyes. Her touch. The way she always tried to heal me with her love, as if she could've magically taken away the scars from my face.

And the reminders of how I'd gotten them.

It was amazing what facial hair could do. How it could hide what was beneath it. How it could change the way a person viewed you. When we were younger, my artificial smile had always been on full display, constantly reminding her of the pain etched into my skin. But now, with a full beard, it was as if she saw something different. As if she saw *me*, and not the product of a heinous act.

Running my fingertip from her temple to her chin, I asked, "Why are you with him?"

She cleared her throat and glanced away. "I'm not, but he won't take the hint."

"You looked like you were with him tonight. And last week. And the week before."

My tone caused her to recoil, and it deepened the ache in my chest. "I'm biding my time."

"I don't know what that means, Rylee. Biding your time for what?"

Her eyes lifted to mine, and the tears lining the rims spilled over. "I go with him on Saturday nights because it's the only way I get to see you. He doesn't know that, of course. But he refuses to accept things are over, so he makes me go with him.

I don't complain because you're there. I just have to finalize my plans to leave. He'll never let me go if I stay here."

As if in slow motion, I dropped my lips to hers, tasting her tears on my tongue. Her arms wound around my neck, and I took the opportunity to lift her off her feet, into my arms. Somehow, we ended up in her bedroom. She grabbed the bottom of my shirt and proceeded to lift it over my head. The material abraded my forehead and caused me to hiss in pain. It hadn't bothered me until then. It was as if I just realized the cut was there.

"You need to clean it, Killian."

"It can wait. You need me more."

She took me by the hand and led me into the bathroom. What I thought would be a quick cleaning of my cut turned out to be so much more. She started the shower and quickly took off her clothes. I did nothing but stand there and watch in wonder. In amazement.

She was a goddess.

Molded from the softest clay.

More beautiful than all my memories of her combined.

Once she was completely bare, she stood in front of me and looked into my eyes. Without glancing down, she hooked her fingers into the waistband of my shorts and tugged them down until they pooled on the floor at my feet. My boxers followed next.

I stepped out of my shoes, into her, and pushed her backward until the scalding spray met our overheated flesh. The water soaked into her hair while I ran my fingers through the wet strands, watching as they darkened and began to spiral.

"I miss your curly hair." My voice was husky, giving away my need for her as if she couldn't feel it pressed against her belly. "I miss your eyes—the way they light up. Your lips. The way they glisten when you lick them." My fingers grazed her shoulders and trailed lightly down her chest, over her breasts. Her nipples peaked and called—*begged*—for my attention. "I miss your body, and the way it responds to mine. The chills on your arms when I lick your neck. The way your stomach sucks in when I touch you"—I continued my perusal of her body until my fingertips found her clit—"here."

"Killian," she said with a gasp and closed her eyes.

I steadied her against the cold, tiled wall, not once relenting on what I did to her. "You come alive under my touch, Rylee." I slipped my fingers through her silky folds until I plunged them into her tight cunt. "Come alive for me," I whispered.

She lifted one leg and I took it, hooking it over my hip. It opened her up, allowing me to push deeper, feel her clench around my fingers. I added a third, pulling a grumbling moan from her chest.

I dropped my head to her shoulder and cupped her mound, pressing my palm against her clit while curling my fingers deep within her core. "You're so tight. I can feel it, Rylee. You're almost there. Come on my fingers so I can taste you."

That's all it took for her to fall apart against me. Her fingers threaded through my drenched hair, where she fisted her hands and tugged. The burn it left behind on my scalp had me rolling my hips into her, thrusting my cock against her stomach. She whimpered and called out my name, but I didn't relent. I continued my assault, desperate to pull another orgasm from her.

"Rylee…" I grunted her name when she reached between us and gripped my cock. With each thrust into her hand, I plunged my fingers deep within her. "I need to be inside you." As soon as those words left my lips, I removed my hand, lifted her other leg, and slammed into her.

In an instant, I filled her.

Her warmth covered me.

I was lost in her.

Pelvis to pelvis, I pushed into her, feeling her pussy hold onto me, stealing my breath. Draining me. Taking everything I had. With her arms holding me to her, she exhaled into my ear. Her breaths formed into words until they became the best sounds I'd ever heard.

"I love you. I love you."

I thrust one more time before spilling myself deep inside her. Her inner walls clenched around me as she rode out her own waves of pleasure. Her orgasm trembled through her body, every muscle coiled tight.

The words, "I fucking love you" sat at the tip of my tongue, but I couldn't utter them. She'd told me it didn't count if I was balls deep in her, so I made sure the next time I admitted my love for her, they'd count.

Soaking wet and shivering, we scrambled to the bed and collapsed beneath the covers. I pulled her close, her back against my chest, and we found warmth together. I refused to let her go. Needing her skin to skin. I hadn't felt this kind of peace in so long, and I wasn't about to lose it now.

"You mentioned you have a plan to leave," I started once we were situated in our cocoon. "Where are we going?" When she shifted to face me, I couldn't take my eyes off hers. The awe shining bright rendered me fucking speechless, but her gasp spurred something inside me. "I'm not leaving you, Rylee. I did that once before, and I'll never do it again."

"Then let's go. Me and you...just like we used to talk about. Let's leave. Tonight." The hope in her tone took me from cloud nine to six feet under in a matter of three words. *Let's leave tonight*. Defeat imprinted on her features, probably seeing the hesitation in mine.

"I have to wait until after next weekend."

"Why?"

"The fight." It was such an easy answer, one that made so much sense to me. But watching the hope drain from her eyes, the color fading from her cheeks, proved just how powerful it was. And not in a good way. "Rylee...I have to fight him. I have to do this."

"He won't let me go." She teared up. "I told him we were over, but he won't stop. It's like he doesn't hear me. If I wait—and then leave with you—he won't just drop this control he has over me. It'll make it worse." She quivered in my arms, and something told me it was worse than I'd originally thought.

"Does he...? Has he forced himself...?" I couldn't spit out the words.

Her shoulders lifted and she tucked her chin to her chest.

"I won't let that happen again."

"And how do you plan to stop him?"

"I'll kill him." I didn't think twice about it until she whipped her head back and stared into my eyes. Fear brightened the gold. Uncertainty darkened the brown. Her pupils enlarged and practically took over the irises.

Dread covered me from head to toe as I replayed my words back to myself in my head. Instead of covering them up, burying the truth, I closed my mouth over hers. My lips trailed to her jaw, her neck, her shoulder.

Her chest.

Her stomach.

Her hip.

I sank my teeth into the flesh over the bone, leaving an imprint of my bite. When she hissed, I spoke against her skin and said, "I'll mark you. He'll know you're mine." I moved to the soft skin on her inner thigh and sucked hard enough to leave a round, purple mark behind. She tugged at my hair, pulling me up her body until I found my lips locked around her nipple. I clamped down around the hard bud, causing her to buck against me and whimper into the silent room. Again, I left behind a purple mark on the underside of her tit. "You're mine. And he'll know it." I pulled away and sat back on my haunches. "One look at this body"—my fingertips grazed her skin like a brush on paper—"and there'll be no doubt who you belong to."

"I'm not property, Killian. I don't belong to anyone."

I fell onto my hands, caging her beneath me. "You own my heart, Rylee. All of me. I love you—yesterday, today, and tomorrow. Yes, you belong to me. Always have. Always will." And then I crashed my lips into hers.

I left no doubt in her mind who she belonged to.

TWENTY-FOUR

Rylee

"I DON'T HAVE TIME for this," I said to Josh, who seemed incapable of listening when I spoke. "Shouldn't you be getting ready for the fight? Not on the phone with me, arguing over the same things."

"I don't need to get ready. If anything, that fucker should be preparing for *me*. I've got his ticket. The only thing I need to practice is my acting. Sorry-ass bitch gets all emotional when his opponent is hurt. All I gotta do is pretend I'm in pain, and *bam*! I'll knock him on his ass."

"Josh…" I dropped my head into my hand, curling into myself over the sink. A wave of nausea rolled through me over his unyielding confidence. I'd seen them both fight, and even though Killian had beaten him the last time, I couldn't help the fear of this time being different. Josh was right. Killian had a weakness, and nothing would stop Josh from exploiting it.

"Babe…" He mimicked my exasperation, rushing his exhaled word through the line. "I've done everything you've asked of me. I've stepped back, given you space. I've left you alone the nights before a fight—despite how badly I've needed you—all because you've asked me to. Can't you just do this one thing for me?"

I scoffed, nearly choking on the saliva that pooled beneath my tongue. "You make it sound like you're asking me to pick up your dry cleaning, Josh. But you're not. You want me to suck your dick so you can be relaxed for this fight. I won't do that."

"You don't want me to be relaxed?"

"Go jerk yourself off if that's what you need, but I've already told you I'm not doing that for you anymore. In the past, I did it because I was your girlfriend, and I wanted to show you support. We're not together. I'm not your girlfriend. And I realize now, that wasn't me giving you support—that was you using me, and me giving up my dignity in the process."

"You may believe we're not together…but I know the truth." His paranoia had taken on a whole new voice. No longer did it make him sound like a jealous boyfriend. Instead, he refused to accept the fact we were over. He was delusional.

He'd gotten a little better over the last month. Less controlling when it came to me, no longer forcing me to give him head—we still argued over whether it was actual force or not—and he did give me space. Although, that was still debatable. There were times he'd say things about where I was or how long I was inside a store that led me to believe he'd been following me. But at least he kept his "distance." I still went to the fights with him; however, that was more my decision than his. I honestly only went to see Killian. With the fear of being watched, I never wanted to risk seeing Killian outside of the ring. And aside from last weekend, I hadn't seen him at all. It was too much of a gamble.

"It's not going to happen, Josh. If you need to get off in order to clear your head and relax before tonight, then either take care of it yourself or find someone else. I have plans and I'm not going to cancel them just so you can get your dick sucked." I slipped on my shoes and grabbed my purse from the hook next to the door.

"Where are you going?" he asked, completely disregarding the mention of having someone else tend to his needs. To be honest, it surprised me. When I'd mentioned it once before, he flipped out and told me he wasn't a cheater.

"I'm meeting with a co-worker. And no, I'm not going to tell you where."

"Fine," he bit out, his anger palpable. "But you'll be there tonight, right?"

I'd decided I couldn't watch the fight. Just thinking about it made my stomach twist and flip until a metallic taste coated my tongue. Josh and Killian were both good fighters, both had a chance of winning in the ring tonight. However, I couldn't risk being there in the event Josh won. I knew he'd stake his claim on me. He'd follow through with his celebratory promise—the one he made before this tournament round began. Before Killian came into the picture. The same promise I'd agreed to, long before everything became so murky.

But I couldn't tell him any of that. "Sure, Josh. I'll be there." I prayed he wouldn't be able to hear the lie. "Listen, I have to go. I'm getting ready to get in my car and head out. I'll talk to you later."

Before climbing into my vehicle, I glanced around the empty street, looking for any trace of Josh. Feeling confident he wasn't there, I tossed my phone into my purse and settled behind the steering wheel. My heart raced the entire drive, and I couldn't stop obsessively checking the rearview mirror. Josh had mentioned needing to be at the gym at two, saying Dalton required him to be there early to prepare and get in the zone. But I knew him. If he thought I'd lied to him, nothing would stop him from finding out the truth. He had an hour before he had to report to Dalton, and it wouldn't surprise me if he wasted it chasing me.

When I pulled into the diagonal space in front of the brick row houses, I took a moment to calm my nerves. With no sign of Josh, I wanted to believe I was safe, but I couldn't ignore the fear of his unpredictable paranoia. However, one glance at the open front door, at Killian standing there, leaning against the frame without a shirt on, I felt safe.

"What time do you have to be at the gym?" I asked once I made it inside and he had the door closed behind me. "I mean, not for the fight, but to get ready?"

Rather than giving me an answer, Killian took my hand and led me around the couch to his room. With the door closed, he seemed to find his ability to speak. "Cal said I just have to be there an hour before. He knows me by now, knows I'm better prepared when I'm here instead of punching a bag or doing drills."

"What kinds of things do you do here to get ready?"

"It's all mental, Rylee." He took the scratchpad from the mattress and shoved it beneath the bed. "If I don't have the strength or stamina by now, then I won't have it before tonight. I spend this time remembering why I'm here."

"So you draw? To remind yourself of what you're fighting for?" My heart skipped a beat when he nodded, his gaze glued to the floor next to his bed. "What do you draw?"

"You." His eyes met mine and glowed a brilliant, minty color. "You're my reason for being here. For doing this. For going in that ring tonight and coming out the winner. I mean…it's for me, but ultimately, I do it all for you. Everything I've ever done has been for you."

"Except leaving me," I mumbled beneath my breath.

He gently held my arm and waited until I met his stare before saying, "Even then, it was for you. I left because I needed to deal with the shit that happened to me. I needed to face my past head on. I needed to find my voice. All so I could be a man for you. So I could take care of you and provide for you."

My heart nearly dropped to my feet. Sorrow crept into my chest and confusion settled in my mind. "But, Killian, you haven't found your voice. You still refuse to talk to people. How will tonight make any difference?"

"I'm working on it. Do you trust me?" His gaze implored me to nod, which I did. "Then trust I'm doing the right thing. I've talked to Cal—like *talked*. It wasn't much, but it was something. This won't happen overnight, nor do I expect it to, but I know I'll get through it. And having you here gives me the strength to push even more."

I sat on the edge of the bed, the mattress dipping around me, and I leaned back on my hands. "Then sketch me." He'd always used his memory when penciling my likeness, never using me as a model. So this time, I wanted to offer him something new in the hopes it'd help him mentally prepare for tonight.

His neck bobbed with his thick swallow, causing the hairs to shift around his Adam's apple. Without wasting time, he moved to stand in front of me and tugged at my top until it was on the floor at his feet. After unhooking my bra and discarding that as well, he grabbed my legs, behind my knees, and moved them onto the bed, turning me to the side. I thought he'd take off my wedges, but he left them on.

However, he didn't leave on my long Bohemian skirt or panties. Those were off within seconds.

Lying in the middle of the bed in nothing but my shoes, I relaxed into the comfort of his scent and closed my eyes. I grew lost in the scratches of his pencil, the swooshes of his hands moving over the paper, the crinkles of the pad in his lap as he sat in front of me. Every now and then, I'd open my eyes and take in his brilliance. His furrowed brow. His long lashes. His teeth clamped down on his bottom lip. It was intoxicating to watch him study me. Every inch of my naked form. Every line, every detail, the remnants of every mark he'd left behind on my skin a week ago.

He glanced at me and his hand stilled. No longer sketching, he blinked several times in my direction, almost as if he couldn't believe I was here. In front of him. In the flesh. Like all this time I'd been nothing more than his imagination, and now…now I was *real*.

I sat up and reached for him. Rather than climbing on top of me, he tossed the pad of paper to the floor and pulled me off the bed. He spun me around in his arms until my back was to his chest, then he leaned into me, causing me to catch myself on the bed. His heated touch wrapped around the back of my thigh, just above the bend in my knee, and he pulled it up and propped it on the edge of the mattress. His leg grazed mine, widening my stance. I was bent over, bare as the day I was born, all while he silently manipulated my body into the position he sought. I wasn't sure if he planned to draw me like this, or if this was his way of telling me he'd had enough of the penciled version of me and needed the real thing.

Either way, I let him call the shots.

I let him take the lead.

I followed.

A burst of humid air landed on the small of my back, just before the moisture of his lips cooled it down. His fingertips danced on the sensitive skin around the curve of my ass. And before I knew what was happening, his tongue slid through my folds from behind. I tried to buck against him at the sensation, but he held me still. He drove the tip of his tongue into my entrance, but before I could explore the sensation, his fingertip grazed the tight ring of my backside. My body grew hot, and desperate need flowed out of me in untamable moans and grunts. I could no longer hold myself up and fell onto my elbows, conceding to the things he did to me.

"Killian..." I moaned his name, hoping he heard the longing in my tone.

His mouth vanished, although his touch remained. There wasn't enough time to discern what he was doing before I became completely filled with him. His initial thrust took me by surprise, eliciting a gasp, but he stilled long enough for me to acclimate to him. I was convinced I'd never get used to his size, no matter how many times I was with him.

"You're so perfect, Rylee," he said from behind me in a strained voice. "So perfect, like you were made for me." He slowly dragged his shaft out until only the head remained wrapped in my warmth. Stilling for a beat, he said, "No one else," and then he pushed deep into me until his pelvis slapped against my ass.

Two thrusts in and he had already found my G-spot. I clenched around him and tilted my hips back, offering him more reach. With my face buried in the comforter, I held my breath, pressed my eyes tightly closed, and bore down for the impending orgasm building low in my belly as I met him thrust for thrust. But Killian wouldn't let me catch it.

I couldn't register anything other than him sliding out of me until he had me flipped onto my back, my legs bent and spread wide for him. Rather than filling me with his dick again, he plunged three fingers inside and cupped my mound while staring directly into my eyes. He bent at the waist with his mouth hovering over my heaving chest.

While continuing his assault on me with his fingers, his tongue peeked out and flicked my hardened nipple. "By the time I'm done with you, you'll be begging to get off. But"—he switched to the other breast and took his time tracing lines of moisture around that nipple—"I'm not going to let you come until I do." He nipped at me. "We're going to come hard. Together."

What he was doing to me was almost too much to bear. I couldn't take it any longer and gripped the comforter while riding his hand and arching my breast into his mouth. The onslaught started all over again, forming low in my gut and spreading to the fried nerves in the small of my back.

Again, he stopped just as I reached the cusp of my orgasm. He stood between my parted legs and stuck his fingers in his mouth, slowly dragging them out while holding me hostage with his stare. I don't think I'd ever been more turned on in my life. Once he was done sucking my arousal off his fingers, he took hold of my wrists and pinned them to the bed above my head. And with the pace of a snail, he entered me.

Unlike before, his movements were drawn out, unhurried as he withdrew and slid into me again and again. We were face to face, eye to eye. His breaths warming my cheeks. His chest barely inches from mine as he rolled in and out of me, slowly bringing me back to the edge.

"I can't take it anymore, Killian. You're killing me. I need to come. Please…"

He closed his eyes just before his lips met mine. His ministrations hadn't changed, hadn't waned or sped up while he lovingly massaged my tongue with his. When we were younger, there were times he'd be slow and gentle, making love to me the only way a teenager knew how. Then there were the times we'd be wrapped up in impatience and desperate need, when it'd be fast and punishing. However, no matter the pace or the circumstance, he was always loving. Always concerned with me. With my pleasure. He'd always held this air of control, even when he seemed uncontrollable. Regardless, I never felt unsafe with him. Even now…his control seemed more refined, more dominate, yet he still showed me this was about me. His gratification would come when mine did. And I never doubted that.

The way he ground against my clit, even with the slow pace he kept up, my body began to hum with pleasure once again. I wanted to hide it from him, act like I wasn't on the verge of coming apart, because I didn't want him to stop again. But if there was only ever one truth to our story, it was that I could never keep anything from him.

He knew.

He felt it.

And he stopped it.

Releasing my wrists, he slid back, pulling away from my body to stand between my legs again. He gripped the backs of my thighs, my knees bent over his hands, his dick still deep inside me. "You'll come *with* me. And I'm not ready to end this just yet," he said through gritted teeth as he dragged himself almost completely out of me. Then, without warning, he slammed into me again.

My back arched off the bed, offering him a deeper angle. I was incapable of doing anything other than gripping the material of the bed beneath me and letting him take me. I couldn't stifle my moans or muffle my needy cries. I gave it all to him. Letting him love me in his own way. Loving him with everything I had.

Everything I ever was.

Everything I'd ever be.

After he'd cut off so many orgasms before they could even begin, the urge to come became stronger, more unbearable than ever before. It was no longer simply a wave of heat washing over my skin or burning nerves at the base of my spine. My legs shook, my chest constricted. A deep ache took over my entire being, suffocating me in the inferno I'd found myself trapped in. My knuckles ached with the grip I had on the bed. Every muscle in my entire body wound so tight I didn't think I could move without breaking apart into a million pieces.

Relief flooded me when his tense, gritty voice resounded around me. "Give it to me, Rylee. Fucking come for me." I gave in and exploded around him. Wave after debilitating wave drowned me in a sea of pleasure. Ecstasy consumed me, stealing my breath, silencing my screams, burning bright and hot enough to set every molecule on fire. His garbled words were music, and I danced to the unintelligible lyrics.

His body collapsed on mine.

His exhales mingled with my heavy pants.

His perspiration added to the sheen on my clammy skin.

We were one.

Always had been.

Always would be.

TWENTY-FIVE

Killian

AFTER FILLING RYLEE WITH my need for her, I had to force myself to leave. She was in my bed, sound asleep. The images of her chest rising and falling with each contented breath followed me all the way to the gym.

I was calm.

Like the eye of a storm.

On the verge of becoming deadly when it's least expected.

As I stood in the back room, in front of the mirror over the sink, I ran my hands over my face and let my eyes fall closed. Adrenaline began to spike, but I wouldn't let it. I needed an even head going into this match, and the only way to do so was to replay the images of Rylee behind my eyelids.

I hadn't stopped with her once we finished. It took a moment to catch our breaths, but once we did, I found myself settled between her legs, my lips covering every inch of her perfect body. I'd even grabbed a marker and drew my name on the curve of her pelvic bone, just like I'd done so many times before. She didn't stop me, just laid there while I marked her. Between the black ink and the purplish mark—forming faint bruises—there was no doubt who she belonged to, even though she hated it when I said that.

But it was the truth.

It wasn't me staking ownership over her. It wasn't some claim of my control over her. No. It simply meant she belonged to me. And I belonged to her. We were made for each other— we belonged together by design. Two halves of the same whole. She wasn't a possession, but something valuable—

something *invaluable*. An heirloom you can't part with, a memory that can't be taken away. Priceless.

That's what she was to me.

Except now, she wasn't just a memory. She was real. Tangible. Living, breathing, in my life once again. Just like it was meant to be. Josh meant nothing. The years I lived apart from her were meaningless. The pain we'd endured through our separation no longer mattered. Because it was all over with now. She was mine again. And my heart was where it belonged.

I opened my eyes and caught my reflection. I studied it, like I hadn't seen it in a while. This time, instead of adrenaline coursing through me, excited anticipation covered me like a warm, welcoming blanket.

"Happy! C'mon! Time to get out here!" Cal called from the door around the corner.

When I approached him, his mouth hung open and his eyes widened.

I grabbed the zip-up hoodie from behind the door and exited the room, completely prepared for the fight. For the ring. For Jag. Excitement danced in my fingertips as they flexed by my sides, knowing just how ill-prepared he was for me.

He thought he was.

But he had no idea who he would step into the ring with.

With the hood pulled over my head, my gaze on the ground in front of me, I stepped to the side of the stage. All the lights in the room had dimmed, other than the ones directed inside the ring, and the excitement was felt all around. People buzzed in their seats, murmurs, screams, claps, and cheers of support filtered around me. Everything I'd done up until this point had all been for this moment.

Cal clapped me on the back, signaling it was my time to step up. Josh was already inside, bouncing around to the sound of his name being hollered out from the stands. I turned to face my coach, took the jacket off, and looked him square in the eyes.

"I couldn't have done this without you," I said to him, unsure if he could even hear me over the ruckus. But he must have, because his gaze softened and he offered a short, jerky nod.

Keeping my head down, I made my way through the ropes, my back to Josh. I stood on the other side and nodded to Cal. Then I glanced around me, noticing the size of the crowd for the first time. Every Saturday night, if I peeked out beyond the ring, it'd only been to find Rylee. But not this time.

She wasn't here.

She was in my bed.

Waiting for me.

So for the first time since this all started, I took in the atmosphere. No matter what, this would be the last time I'd set foot in this place—or any place like it. I came for a reason, and I'd leave with a purpose. With my girl. With my voice.

This. Was. It.

As if in slow motion, I turned to face Josh. His gaze wasn't on me, but grazing through the heads in the crowd, probably looking for Rylee. I felt content, knowing she wouldn't be here to witness this, and even more relieved to know he'd never touch her again. I waited in place, never taking my attention off the asshole in front of me. Waiting for him to face me.

And then he did.

There are no words that could ever describe the expression on his face when he looked at me. The way his chest stilled, no longer working to pull air into his lungs. The paleness of his skin. The intensity and awareness in his eyes.

I simply smirked and waited for the officiant to call it.

* * *

Rylee

I STRETCHED MY ARMS over my head and felt every aching muscle in my body pull taut. With it came the memory of Killian and what he'd done to me. Glancing at the clock, I realized the fight would begin soon, and it took everything in me to not jump out of bed and go hide in the crowd, just to make sure Killian was okay.

My bladder needed to be relieved, so I wrapped myself in the sheet and headed to the attached bathroom. On my way out, I noticed the edge of his sketchpad sticking out from beneath the disheveled covers. As I reached for it, I found a box beneath the bed, and decided to sit on the floor while looking through his drawings. He'd said he used me to relax before a fight, and I found myself curious as to whether he depicted me from when we were younger, or from now.

I started from the beginning, admiring his talent as I flipped through image after image of my likeness. The first few of them were of my younger self, but as I continued through the pad, I found my face, as it was now, staring back at me. However, most of them had me with curly hair, even though I didn't wear it that way anymore. I smiled at the thought of him saying he missed it, and decided he would come home to find me naked, in his bed, with spiraled hair draped over his pillow.

When I finished going through that notebook, I pulled out the box and began to sift through the belongings in search of other drawings of me. More pads of paper, pens, a set of charcoal sticks, and a container of markers sat inside. Beneath it all lay a yearbook, the same one I'd seen in his room when he was younger. Leaving that in the box, I opted for one of the other sketchpads.

Nothing—and I mean *nothing*—prepared me for what I found inked on those pages. Gory depictions of death. Blood. Lifeless bodies. Guys dressed in dark clothes. I flipped through each page, not looking too closely at the images. In the back, Killian had newspaper clippings. No pictures, just words—I couldn't stop myself from reading them. Needing something—*anything*—to take my mind off the images I'd just witnessed.

Jameson Richards, age thirty, found dead in home. Apparent cause of death seems to be overdose, although authorities haven't released official report as of yet. I skimmed the article, wondering why Killian would have this in his possession, but stopped when I came across the line that read: *Richards grew up in New Hope, Pennsylvania.*

Picking up another article, I realized it was about the brutal slayings of Killian's parents. In it, I read about the vicious attack on the couple's eight-year-old son. Other than what he'd told me in the past, this was the first time I'd gotten any real account of the incident. And it left me running for the toilet.

I washed out my mouth and returned to the box. Somewhere deep inside, the need to know more drove me further. Another article, not about his parents but of yet another death—this one seemed more gruesome than the first. *Lance Parsons was violently stabbed behind a nightclub. Nineteen stabs wounds in all. His body was found by a bartender, who'd gone outside to throw out a bag of trash.* And again, a little farther down, I found that he, too, had once been a resident of New Hope.

With nothing else to go on, I dug through the box and took out the yearbook from the bottom. On the front was the familiar tiger, along with the name "New Hope" in gold lettering. Flipping through the pages, I eventually found the names and pictures of both victims—teenagers smiling at the camera in their black-and-white photos. Part of me was confused; albeit, a very small part, only because I didn't want to believe what I was reading. Reason told me these were two of the intruders from so long ago, but I tried to ignore it, knowing that meant there was still one more out there.

I went back to the sketches and found an uncanny resemblance between the penciled faces filled with color and shadows, and the small, grainy photos in the yearbook. I flipped to the next drawing and gasped.

Blue eyes.

A cut on the bridge of his nose.

Thin lips adorned with a sharp Cupid's arrow.

My stomach rolled as I sat hunched over the yearbook, dry heaving with tears flooding my eyes. Through warped vision, a small face came into focus. It was identical to the one on the paper next to me—different expression, different clothes, but same face. And next to it, the name Joshua Disick.

Bile rushed up my esophagus as I ran into the bathroom again, only making it to the sink this time. My abs ached with each heave and the hot tears refused to submit. A blazing fire scorched the back of my throat as I emptied what remained in my stomach into the porcelain sink.

I couldn't think.

Had zero rational thought.

All I knew was I had to make it to the gym to stop Killian. He knew who Josh was—had known this whole time. I was the fool who thought he'd come here for me. Never, in my wildest dreams, had I imagined he'd shown up in Baltimore for someone else. Especially for the man who'd killed his parents.

Slaughtered his parents.

I couldn't even wrap my head around that.

I had to push that thought to the back of my mind and focus solely on getting to Killian before the fight began. I couldn't imagine the rage he must've had filling his veins. Thinking about how I'd kissed Josh's lips, let him hold me, done things with him... I couldn't. It sickened me and left my skin prickling like I had thousands of roaches crawling all over my body.

The drive was a blur. I couldn't recall even getting dressed or finding my keys, let alone every turn and stop between his place and the gym. I pulled into the first spot I came to, knowing there wouldn't be anything available closer to the front. Two steps into my sprint, I had to stop to remove my wedges. There was no way I could run without falling or twisting my ankles, not while frantically trying to get to Killian.

It started with a pinch in the soft part of my bare foot—the arch. The pain didn't register through the adrenaline. It wasn't until I'd almost made it to the front door before realizing I'd even cut myself, rather than just stepping on a sharp rock like I'd assumed. The trail of blood and sticky warmth gave away how bad it was, but I didn't waste the time examining it. I didn't have a single minute to spare. Not a second. Millisecond. Nothing.

Either the doors were heavy or I'd somehow lost the vast majority of my strength between parking the car and this spot. It was hard to pull open, but I managed to get inside and head straight for the ring in the center. The lights were lowered, but the stage was lit like a Broadway show...only this wasn't a play.

This was reality.

A nightmare.

My fingertips tingled and my knees felt numb, just beneath the kneecaps. The room seemed to dim again and all the sounds began to fade into the distance. My movements were sluggish, but nothing would keep me from making it to Killian. Stopping the fight.

In front of me, raised four feet off the ground, stood Josh and Killian. Jag and Happy. Josh's eyes were wide, his mouth hanging open in shock. Surprise. Awe. Whatever it was, for the first time in as long as I'd known him, he appeared to be afraid. Fear paled his cheeks, trembled in his hands, and struck him still. Killian's face was cleanly shaven, his scars no longer hidden beneath the growth of facial hair. A smirk tugged at one corner of his mouth and his soft green eyes lit up with…vindication maybe. It was hard to tell.

"Killian!" I screamed, but I doubted he could hear me over the hollering in the room. People were going crazy—yelling, clapping, stomping. I stepped closer to the stage until my hands came to rest on the flooring. It was against the rules, but I didn't care. I needed to be seen. Heard. I needed this to end. "Killian!"

It must've been enough for him to hear, because he turned his focus to me. Instantly, his expression fell and concern laced his features. No longer the smirk, now a frown. The glint in his eyes had vanished and the color had darkened. His brows dipped and firmed. All in a split second. In two long strides, he was in front of me, kneeling down to bring himself closer to my face.

"Don't do it. I know why you're here. I know about Josh. About your family. I saw… Please, Killian, don't do it. It won't make you feel better. It won't erase what he did to you. It'll only make everything worse." I tried to get the words out, but they sounded sluggish even to my own ears. The confusion deepening in his eyes let me know it hadn't just been me. "Don't do it," I repeated, hoping he'd hear that part, if nothing else.

"Happy," the officiant called from behind Killian and pulled his attention away. "You ready?"

He took one last look at me and mouthed, "I'm sorry" before standing and reclaiming his spot in the ring. His fists clenched, his jaw tightened, but when he found me out of the corner of his eye, he seemed to go soft.

Killian must've missed it. I know I sure as hell didn't hear it. But while I observed my fighter, the officiant must've asked

Josh if he was ready—which he must've said yes. Because without warning, he swung his fist through the air and landed a hard punch to the side of Killian's chin. His head snapped back and his feet faltered, offering Josh just enough time to step up to him and land another punch to Killian's ribs.

A thud rang out just as the boy who owned my heart fell to the floor.

The room became almost silent, but I didn't know if that was me or if everyone had quieted down. A strange warmth covered my body until I felt like I'd been swathed in a fuzzy blanket. The room darkened again, and small black spots danced in my vision. I felt weak—even breathing took conscious effort, labored and desperate.

The last thing I saw before I blacked out was Killian flipping Josh over onto his back. He climbed on top of him, pinning Josh's arms beneath Killian's legs, and then he stuck his thumbs into the sides of Josh's mouth, pulling the skin until it resembled a clown's smile.

And then he turned his head toward me.

A second was all I had before the lights completely went out.

TWENTY-SIX

Killian

ANOTHER NURSE CAME IN with a tablet in her hand and crossed the space to Rylee's bed.

No matter who came into the room, they all looked at me with a level of disgust in their expressions. The swelling on my face and the way I winced when I moved or took a deep breath probably had a lot to do with it. But I really wished they'd stop being so concerned about me and start doing something for Rylee.

The clock on the wall said it'd only been about forty-five minutes since we'd been in the hospital. I knew it had to have been wrong. It felt more like days. Each second ticked by without a single person giving me any information.

Rylee had started to stir, and now, her eyes opened. They were nothing but slivers of gold, out of focus. She groaned, but I couldn't imagine it was out of pain. They had to have given her some kind of medication to alleviate it. I didn't remember much about the time I'd been in the hospital when I was younger, but the pain medicine was something I'd never forget—or should I say, I'd never forget that feeling when it would start to wear off. Maybe that was the problem. Maybe whatever they gave her wasn't working and she needed more.

I didn't bother trying to talk to any of them.

It was useless.

They wouldn't tell me anything, anyway.

"Sir," the nurse said, repulsion lacing her tone, "I'm going to have to ask you to step out for a moment, please. I need to discuss some things with Miss Anderson."

Rylee's head rolled to the side, and the second she saw me sitting in a chair next to her, her eyes fell closed and a long, ragged exhale slipped out. "No," she rasped and then opened her eyes again to find mine. "Stay."

"Are you sure that's what you want?" It was clear this nurse didn't want me here. She'd asked me to go to the waiting room beyond the curtain separating Rylee from the other patients in the emergency room, but I could tell she really wanted to ask me to leave the hospital completely.

Isn't gonna fucking happen, lady.

Rylee looked to the woman in scrubs on the other side of the bed. "He stays. With me." Her words were filled with air, the spaces between used to refill her lungs with oxygen. "Whatever you have to say can be said in front of him."

"Okay..." She dragged the word out and focused on the tablet in her hands. "You came in with a large, deep laceration on the instep of your right foot. We cleaned it out and stitched it closed, but you won't be able to walk on it for a while until it heals. Straining it or stretching the wound will cause the sutures to rip, and therefore, reinjure the tissue and possibly the tendons as well."

There was a long pause, as if to let that information sink in before she offered more.

"You were also unconscious from the blood loss. We were able to give you a transfusion to bring your levels up, but we were unable to give you any narcotics to offset your pain."

"Why?" Rylee croaked out, stealing the thoughts from my head.

The nurse glanced at me and then at Rylee again. "If you're asking, then I should assume maybe you don't know. When was your last menstrual cycle, Miss Anderson?"

Rylee turned her head to stare straight ahead, but closed her eyes. A single tear rolled down her cheek before I swiped it off her jaw with the back of my finger. She licked her lips and then whispered, "I don't remember."

"We ran your blood because your...friend here...couldn't provide your blood type to us."

Rylee squeezed my hand. I hadn't remembered she even held it. I was so absorbed in what this woman said, utterly confused as to how Rylee's blood type had anything to do with her not receiving medicine for the pain she clearly had.

"From the hormone levels in your blood, we're looking at around six to eight weeks. Does that sound about accurate?" she asked, but only got a nod from Rylee. "At this time, all we can offer you is Tylenol. Would you like me to bring you some?"

Again, Rylee only nodded, her eyes still closed and her hand still gripping mine.

Without another word, the woman vanished through the thick blue curtain, leaving me alone with a somber Rylee. "What's going on? What did all that mean?" I whispered, too worried to speak any louder.

She barely opened her eyes, not looking at me but focusing on our joined hands. "She can't give me any pills because I'm pregnant."

All the air had been sucked out of the room. I couldn't breathe. Couldn't process her words. Couldn't hear any sounds around me. No beeping machines. No shuffles of feet on the other side of the curtain. No coughing, crying, moaning from any of the other beds.

"Y–you knew?"

"No, Killian." Her eyes finally found mine, and they shone with truth. Honesty. "I didn't know. Trust me, I swear to you, I would've told you had I known. Everything's been so crazy lately with Josh and moving and finding a new job...with you showing up. Being with you. I guess I wasn't paying attention to my periods."

The words, "Who's the father?" sat at the tip of my tongue when the nurse walked in again and stole them away. She handed Rylee a plastic cup of water and two white pills, which Rylee took and swallowed down. And again, the nurse left the room without another word spoken.

"Josh can't know." Her voice was so soft, yet filled with so much terror.

I no longer needed to ask the question.

She'd just given me the answer.

The *wrong* answer.

"What happened tonight? With the fight?" Her meek voice broke the stifling silence.

I ran my palm down my face, still not used to the smooth skin on my cheeks. "When you passed out, I walked away."

"So no one won?"

I shook my head. "No…he won." *Everything*.

My gaze trailed up her covered legs, thinking about all the places I'd touched her. All the ways I'd made her mine. I was her first, and for two years, I was her only. I had no right to be angry at her for moving on. I'd left her. But that didn't stop the overwhelming jealousy from clogging my throat or stilling my heart. When my eyes moved to her stomach, I couldn't seem to look away. Inside, a baby grew. Life. Not mine. It belonged to the man who'd taken my family. Taken my childhood. And there was no way in hell I'd let him take this baby.

The thought of raising his child sent a cold shiver through me.

I wasn't sure I could love it the right way.

Not with his blood running through its veins.

"It was only supposed to be for a year. Not five," I mumbled to myself.

"What was? What're you talking about, Killian?"

I found complete desperation in her eyes and decided to answer. "When I left. I never meant to be away from you for so long. I thought I could find them within a year and be there for you by the time you graduated. Then we could resume our plan of being together. But it didn't happen that way. I never expected them to be so hard to locate."

She blew out a long exhale and blinked her eyes, as if warding off tears. "That was so stupid, Killian. I know you wanted to face Josh. Hurt him. But you shouldn't have done that. He could've hurt you. It all could've backfired and he could've taken you away from me."

When I saw Rylee fall to the ground by the ring, her skin as pale as sand, everything had vanished. I'd forgotten all about the fight. About Josh. About Rylee knowing the truth. I only cared about making sure she was safe, getting her help. I couldn't lose her. I *refused* to lose her.

"How'd you find out? How'd you know it was him?"

"Your sketches. I found the articles, the yearbook. It wasn't hard to figure it out after seeing it all together." She paused to lick her dry lips. "Those newspaper clippings…the guys who were found dead…"

My heart sank. I hated the thought of her seeing that. My past. My present. My nightmares and demons. I wished I could've changed it, made her un-see it all. It was ugly and painful and fucked up. But she knew. There was nothing I could do about it now.

"Were they the guys from when you were younger? From your parents' house?"

I could only nod, unsure of how much information I wanted to tell her.

"And now there's only one left…Josh."

I nodded again, but decided to speak. "He's the one who killed my mom."

Her gasp was sharp. "He's the…the one who did…?" She pointed to my face. "Oh my God. I can't believe he…can't believe it was him. And I…"

"Don't, Rylee. You didn't know, so don't even think about it." I moved from the chair to sit on the edge of the bed with my hand on her thigh. "He won't come after you. He won't come after your baby. I promise you. I'll make sure he never bothers you again."

I'd kill the motherfucker.

• • •

RYLEE WAS QUIET THE entire drive to her apartment. I wanted to take her to Cal's, where I knew she'd be safe, but she wanted to be in her own space. Plus, I knew Cal wasn't too happy with me. He'd sent a few texts while I was at the hospital, asking about the fight and what had happened. It was very obvious I wasn't myself from the moment I'd stepped into the ring.

I didn't feel like answering his questions.

He'd know everything eventually.

I sat her on the edge of the bed and turned to open a drawer for a clean T-shirt. Only the lamp in the corner lit the room, and it set a level of gloom over us. I was filled with sadness, anger, frustration, and…utter defeat. There were so many things I wanted to say to her, but I couldn't get a single word out past the lump in my throat.

She stood, putting weight only on one foot, and held onto my shoulders. I slipped her skirt off her hips until it pooled on the floor at her feet, then helped her to a seated position on the mattress. Her shirt slithered up her body, over her chest and head, and I nearly lost my breath. But then she reached behind her and unhooked her bra. And I started to choke. I couldn't get the T-shirt over her head fast enough.

Not because I didn't want to look.

Because I wanted nothing more than to look.

Stare.

Touch.

But I couldn't. Everything seemed so different. Her. Me. *Everything*. And I hated it, hated me, hated Josh. Hated the entire situation. I knew this wasn't something that could break us—*nothing* would ever be able to tear us apart. We'd get through it, figure it out, make it work. It'd take time and effort, but we'd do it. However, that didn't mean things weren't tense or strange or...*off* between us now.

Rylee leaned into the pillow and situated herself while I elevated her injured foot. I ran my fingertips along the smooth skin on her legs, slowly tracing invisible lines from her ankle to her thigh, where I paused to take it all in. The bumps forming on her flesh, the small gasps, the way her spine arched slightly off the bed while the tips of my fingers lingered along her underwear before making it to her soft stomach.

I flattened my hand and stared. Her belly rose and fell with each shallow breath she took, and I could only think of the life she harbored inside. The life that didn't belong to me. The one I didn't put there.

"What's wrong? You look mad." She stilled for a moment, her body turning rigid with fright. "*Are* you mad?"

"No," I said to calm her worry. "I don't know how I feel, but I can tell you I'm not angry."

"But you're not happy."

I sighed and sat down on the bed next to her, my hand on her lower belly. "It's kind of hard to be happy, Rylee. I won't lie. I always thought I'd be the one to do this to you. To put a baby in you. To make a family with you. I never, not once, thought you'd do this without me."

She pulled herself up onto her elbows, but I didn't let her interrupt me.

"But I can't be mad. Not at you. It's not fair to you, because I was the one who left in the first place. I was stupid thinking I'd be able to hunt those fuckers down just because I knew who they were. I didn't take into account it'd been ten years, and people don't stay in one place. I thought I'd be able to find them, take care of shit, and move on. Find my voice and come back to you. Instead, I fucked everything up."

Sitting all the way up now, Rylee took my hand—which had fallen to the side with her change in position—and placed it over her stomach once more. She didn't move, didn't speak until I looked right at her. Into her eyes.

"You did put this here, Killian. *You.*" She shook her head and giggled, her eyes falling closed. "Considering your obsession with coming in me, not pulling out, I don't know why you'd even question it." Then she cupped my face and gazed into my eyes. "It's only ever been you, Killian. Only you. No one else."

Her words echoed in my head. I tried to make sense of them, yet they jumbled up the more I replayed them. Only me. "You mean...? You and Josh? *Never?*" I needed clarity. This wasn't something I could afford to misunderstand.

"No," she answered while shaking her head. "There were...other things. But never sex. We've never been together like that. He tried—my *God* did he try—but I never could. It was like my heart knew you were coming back to me, and it wouldn't let me give myself to anyone else."

I crushed my lips to hers until she was lying flat again. But I couldn't let the kiss linger too long. Not only could I not allow us to get so worked up we wouldn't be able to stop, considering she was in pain and had just gotten home from the hospital, but I had something else that needed my attention.

I lowered myself down her body until my mouth hovered over her lower stomach. My lips grazed her soft skin, the little bit between the bottom of the T-shirt and her underwear. This was mine.

Ours.

I did this.

The best thing I'd ever done in my entire life.

TWENTY-SEVEN

Rylee

I WOKE TO THE SOUND of the front door. I couldn't tell if Killian had left or had just come in from somewhere, so I laid in the silence of my room and listened. I figured out rather quickly that he hadn't gone anywhere by the shuffles coming from the kitchen. Then the bangs.

Then the voices.

"What the fuck are you doing here?" It sounded like Josh, but I prayed to God it wasn't, because nothing good could've come out of him being here. With Killian. In my apartment. "You've got to be kidding me."

Then his words stopped. A loud, hollow thud resounded through the space, filtered through the bedroom door that was left ajar, and echoed around me. If death had a sound, that's what I'd heard. I immediately pulled the blanket off my body and reached for the set of crutches leaning against the wall next to the nightstand. It took a lot of effort to steady myself, but I managed to get out of bed and make it to the door just in time to hear more.

"You're a fucking monster, and you're gonna get what's coming to you." That was Killian. I'd know his voice anywhere. But there was no reply, and that was what worried me. "The other two fuckers are dead. You're the only one left. The only other person who broke into my house, went into my parents' room, and murdered my family. And your time is up."

I knew now, without a doubt, it was Josh in my house.

With hoarse, strangled words, he said, "We were fucked up."

"No fucking shit."

"No." Josh cleared his throat, and I paused by the door with my foot throbbing in pain, waiting to hear what he had to say. "I mean, we were fucked up on PCP. We were high. It's not an excuse—I'll never try to excuse what we did. To you or your family. It was wrong, and I've spent the last fifteen years living with what I did."

"If you felt so fucking guilty about it, why didn't you ever turn yourself in?"

Josh didn't answer. Instead, another hollow thud rang out.

"What did my parents ever do to you? Huh? What did *I* ever do to deserve what you did?"

"Your parents stole you from my mom!"

My heart stopped beating. Right then and there, the entire world stopped turning. My life stilled. Time meant nothing. His words pierced through me like tiny arrows, puncturing every viable organ on their way out.

Finding the courage I didn't know I had, I exited the bedroom and stopped behind the two men. Killian had Josh up against the door facing him, away from me, with his hands around Josh's neck. I couldn't see his expression, but he stood straight with his spine rigid. Taut. Anger and vengeance rolled off him like the waves of an ocean.

"My mom carried you for nine months, went into the hospital to deliver you, and never brought you home. They kept you. She cried for you every night. It was like I stopped existing, because her new chance at having a child that was all hers was stolen from her. The only peace she ever found was through a bottle of pills and death. She killed herself because of your parents."

"That's a fucking lie!" Killian roared in his face.

Josh didn't flinch. He didn't try to move away or even blink, as if he'd expected it.

"Oh my God…" I covered my mouth with my hand, but they'd heard me anyway. Two sets of eyes turned to find me standing there, in shock, shaking like a leaf. No longer did I feel the throbbing pain in my foot. Sleep no longer weighed me down and fear didn't knot my stomach.

I felt nothing.

Absolutely nothing.

"Baby, are you okay?" Josh tried to come to me, but Killian pushed him away. The force caused his head to reverberate against the door, the hollow thud echoing louder than before. "Get the fuck off me, man. She's my girlfriend."

Before I could say anything, Killian spoke up, his threatening tone loud and clear. "She was never yours. She's always been mine. *Always*. Stay the fuck away from her, or I will end you right here and right now. You got lucky in the ring tonight. But don't think that'll happen again."

Josh took one look at him, then me, questions dancing in his eyes. "Him? This is the boy? Your old neighbor?"

I nodded.

"I won't repeat myself." Killian moved to stand between Josh and me. "Get the fuck out and stay away. This is your only chance to not end up like your buddies. To not end up on the wrong side of life. This a courtesy, considering you and your friends slit my mom's throat open, stabbed my dad nineteen times, and then carved my face into a fucking smile. If I ever see you again, I can promise you there won't be any mercy shown on your behalf."

It was as if I'd just been punched in the chest. Stabbed in the back. Had my legs knocked out from beneath me. All at once. *Stabbed my dad nineteen times*. No matter how many times I tried to tell myself it was a coincidence, I couldn't be convinced of it. Because every time I'd tell myself *This can't be true*, I'd hear Killian say, "This is your only chance to not end up like your buddies." *Dead*. Both of them. One found stabbed...*nineteen* times. Just like his dad.

Seconds after the door closed with Josh's exit, the crutches fell to the ground with a loud clatter. Weight fell onto my foot in a desperate attempt to catch myself, but the pain was too much and sent me careening to the floor in sheer agony. It radiated up my leg until it blended with the ache in my chest. My head felt heavy, filled with uncertainties, denial, conviction. I refused to believe it—any of it—but when Killian came to help me up, to console me, the truth burned so hot I pushed him away for fear of being set on fire by his touch.

He called out my name, the desperation thick in his voice. The worry heavy in the air around me. But I ignored him and attempted to pull myself up and hobble to my bed. My weak stomach felt ready to empty itself with every movement I made. I swallowed it down and forged on, ignoring Killian's presence behind me.

"Y–you killed them!" I held my hand out to ward him off and silence his arguments. I couldn't bear to hear his excuses just yet. "The other two...the articles. You killed them. It was you. You didn't find them dead. You left them that way."

"Just let me explain," he pleaded.

"*No!*" I curled into myself against the bed's headboard and wrapped my arms around my legs, as if protecting me from the monster who stood in front of me. The monster who'd once been my savior. "There's nothing you can say to make it right."

His chin dipped and he ran his fingers through his hair, pulling on the strands until they fell down around his face. "They killed my parents, Rylee. They fucked me up for years. I'm still fucked up because of what they did. What I had to witness. What I had to live through."

"An eye for an eye."

"Exactly." He looked at me, his eyes bright with triumph.

But they quickly dimmed with my next words. "Except that never works, Killian. Never. They hurt you and your family, so you go after them. But did you ever stop to think that maybe they'd have family whose lives would be ruined by *your* revenge? And then what? It's okay for one of their family members to come after you or someone you love? What if one of them had a brother, now suffering the loss of a loved one, and comes after me to get back at you? Or worse...comes after our baby? When does it end? There's always another eye, another person to make pay for the pain left behind."

"They needed to pay for what they did. I needed to find my voice, reclaim my life. I needed to stop living with the torment of that night. The night *they* caused. The night *they* walked away from. Meanwhile, I've been living with it every single fucking day of my life."

"So you killed them to find yourself? Are you saying this person"—I pointed at him—"sitting in front of me right now is who you really are? This is the real you?" I waited for an answer, but he only nodded. "Then there's no hope for us. Because I was under the impression the real you was the boy who used to draw flowers on the backs of my hands. The one who'd lay in the grass with me and stare at the moon and stars without saying a single word. The boy who'd sneak into my window at night and hold my hand while I talked about my day at school. Who had kissed my entire body, every inch of me, after taking my virginity, because he didn't want me to be in pain."

"That is me."

"No, it's not." I cut him off, needing him to hear my words more than I needed my next breath. "The man in front of me right now just hurt me so deeply, there isn't enough kissing to ever make that pain go away."

He sat on the edge of the bed and dropped his head into his hands. He didn't look at me while he spoke. His words sad, his voice gritty and raw. Emotional. "What if I don't want to let you go? What if I want to fight?"

I remained silent for a moment before he turned his attention to me. "I'm tapping out."

"No, Rylee. Please don't. Let me make this right."

"There's nothing you can do to make any of this right. You can't give them life again. They're gone…because of you. You're no different than they are, Killian. You're a killer. A murderer. Just like them. You can't fix that."

"But…I love you."

I wiped tears from my face and straightened my spine, pulled my shoulders back. "You're killing me. Breaking me. I never thought in a million years, even after you walked away, that you'd be the one to smother the life out of me." A hiccup got stuck in my chest. "You don't love me, Killian. If you did, you never would've gone after them. You never would've believed you needed to get revenge in order to be whole. You've had your voice this entire time. They didn't take it from you. You're the one who silenced yourself."

His pain was so visible, so tangible, I had to close my eyes to protect myself from its assault. I wanted him to leave. I wanted him to stay. I needed him to make it right, but at the same time, I knew he couldn't. It'd be a lie if I said I wasn't relieved to know those men no longer walked the earth, or that I wasn't crippled with fear at the knowledge of Josh and the things he'd done to the only man I'd loved. The only man I would *ever* love. But it didn't make it right. It wasn't his call to make. Killian wasn't God, and it wasn't his decision to end their lives—just like it wasn't theirs to end the lives of Killian's parents.

I told him I needed him to go.

His weight lifted from the bed.

He left.

It was what I wanted. What I needed.

I guess I never imagined how much it'd hurt.

TWENTY-EIGHT

Killian

I KNOCKED ON THE door and took a step away, waiting for her to let me in.

As the seconds ticked by, I couldn't stop comparing this time to when I'd gone to Cal's place after leaving Rylee on her bed. Alone. In tears. Pained and gutted by my actions. My head was in a fog, jumbled up, nothing making sense. Nothing meaning a damn thing anymore. So when Cal opened the door and found me on the top step in tears, I practically fell into him.

I'd expelled my truth to him in words I couldn't make heads or tails of. I didn't care how he took it or what he'd thought of me. Rylee had turned me away, so I no longer cared about the opinions of anyone else. However, his compassion had surprised me. It pushed me to keep going instead of giving up. He'd convinced me that there was more out there. There was more to live for, to fight for. To win.

So I packed my things and drove home. To Elise's house. Where I knew I belonged. Where I knew I was safe from the demons chasing me and the heartbreak threatening to cripple me. I was lost, but here, I was safe. It may not have been the house I'd lived in, but it was where Elise lived, and that was all that mattered.

She gasped and covered her lips with both hands. We'd spoken often throughout the years, but I hadn't returned since the day I walked away. I hadn't seen her, not once, in five years. And in an instant, I regretted it all.

Every last thing I'd done since I turned away from Smithsville.

"Don't just stand there, come in." Elise held the door open wider and made room for me to enter. As soon as the door closed, her arms wound around my neck, pulling me into her for a hug. "Are you staying? Did you bring a bag with you? How long are you here for?"

I'd thought of the many ways I'd fill her in, all the different words I could've used. Aside from the one time I'd spoken to her on the night I snuck out, she'd never heard my voice. All our conversations since then had taken place through continuous text messages. So settling on an explanation proved to be harder than I'd originally thought.

"Here…I think there's a pad of paper in the kitchen. Come on in." She led me farther into the house and stopped at the counter separating the kitchen from the living room. She took a small notebook, probably used for grocery lists, and slid it in front of me.

With the paper and pen in my hand, I glanced over to her and said, "Was I adopted?"

This time, there was no gasp. No hand covering her gaping mouth. Her eyes were wide as saucers and it seemed her breathing had ceased. I wasn't sure if my question or the fact I'd spoken instead of written it out caused her reaction.

"The guy who killed my mom…the one who cut up my face…he told me my parents stole me from the hospital. That I didn't belong to them."

Tears filled her eyes and leaked down her face faster than she could wipe them away. "Killian—" My name hiccupped in her throat and she had to take a pause to regain her composure. "You know who it was? You spoke to him? Who…?"

"I'll tell you that in a minute. Right now, I really need to know about my parents. I really need the truth. I feel like I know nothing. I can't make sense of anything. You're the only person who can give me any answers. Please, Elise. I need to know."

She shook her head, but not in response, more of a way to clear her mind, if I had to guess. When she rounded the corner of the counter, she took a seat in a barstool and inhaled deeply. "Your mom couldn't carry a child. They'd tried so many times, and even though she could get pregnant, she'd lose it. Her body rejected pregnancies, treating them as foreign objects that

223

her immune system fought off. So they decided to use a surrogate."

"So my parents are really my parents?"

Her glassy eyes met mine. "They are. They only used a woman to carry you. But your parents' blood runs through you. Your mom knew a woman—they were friends—who offered to help them. Toward the end of the pregnancy, they had to get a court order to keep her in town, and for the hospital to notify them if the woman went into labor. They were concerned she was going to try to keep you. Everything got really messy after that. After your parents died, I was convinced it was her, but then I found out she had killed herself a year before."

"It was her son," I said and waited for that piece of information to sink in. "His name is Josh and he went to my dad's school. He said his mom killed herself because my parents stole me from her, so he blamed them. He said it was their fault his mom died."

"Did you turn him in? Call the police? Let the authorities know? What about the others? Weren't there three of them?" Elise flung question after question at me. She didn't wait for me to answer one before moving to the next, eager and impatient for the answers she'd waited fifteen years for.

I touched her arm to quiet her long enough to speak. "The other two are dead. One overdosed on heroin, and the other was attacked behind a strip club. Josh is the only one left. And no...I didn't turn him in."

"How'd you find him?"

"I've always known."

The defeat in her eyes could've been seen from the moon. "You've known all along and yet you've never said anything? You never told the police?"

"I was eight, Elise. I was there and saw what they did to my mom. To my dad. It wasn't just a threat of 'speak and I'll kill you.' I knew firsthand what they'd do to me if I told anyone."

"But you would've been protected. The police wouldn't have let that happen!"

I tried to calm down, knowing my anger wasn't directed at Elise. "I was eight. Just a fucking kid. I had my mouth sliced open, literally hanging on only by my jaw. I'd seen my mom's throat slit, almost decapitated. My dad had been stabbed nineteen fucking times. There's not a damn thing anyone could've done to convince me I was safe."

More tears fell. More hiccups clogged her throat. "So…so what did you do? What are you gonna do about it?"

I shrugged. I didn't have an answer. No matter how much thought I'd given to Josh, what I should do about it, I couldn't come up with anything. Cal never asked, never tried to convince me of anything. It was my decision—and now Elise's.

"You don't have to do this alone. You aren't alone, Killian. You never were. I've always been here for you…and so has Rylee. But you just never wanted to see it. Now, you don't have to take this on all by yourself. Let me stand by your side."

"I don't deserve that," I answered in a growly whisper.

"Deserve what? Support?"

"Any of it. Rylee gave up on me. And once I tell you the truth…you will, too." I couldn't bear the thought of losing both women—the only two women who'd been there for me every step of the way since it all started.

She stilled with her stare boring holes into my face, as if waiting for me to say something. But I couldn't. Even if she asked, I wasn't sure I could give her the brutal truth. She'd turn her back on me, just like Rylee had. And I couldn't chance that happening. I couldn't be alone.

It started with me telling Elise about Rylee—about finding her in Baltimore.

Then the baby.

When she questioned why Rylee would walk away—*push me away*—after finding out about carrying my child, I had to tell her the truth. It was hard and painful and scary as fuck, but I started at the day my parents were killed. I told her how I found out who they were, about my promise to myself to make them all pay restitution for the damage they did—the lives they stole. To me, they'd walked away from it all and never gave it a second thought. They'd gone off to live their lives, off to a land free of consequences, and I refused to let that be their final destination. I told her about the day I left, about leaving Rylee alone in her back yard. When I got to the part about Jameson and Lance—the two men who were found dead—she cried. She held my hand while I exposed every detail, every gritty bit of truth. But anger quickly took over when I got to Josh's role, both then and now. I explained who he was. What he'd done.

She insisted on retribution.

I agreed, but I didn't know what to do.

"Do you trust me?" she asked, sounding confident and determined.

I nodded, because I did. I trusted her. Although, that didn't mean I would like what she had to say. Which…as it turned out, I didn't. I fought against it. Pleaded with her to let it go. But she refused. And eventually, I agreed.

It wasn't the easiest choice.

It wasn't the hardest.

But, it was the right one.

• • •

ELISE WAS right. She remained by my side through it all. Held my hand. Comforted me. Spoke when I couldn't, listened when I *could*, and waited through the moments in between.

When she first told me what we would do, I had my doubts. I didn't believe her—I didn't *want* to believe her. I didn't want to accept that there might've been another way around it all. I refused to believe there were other options.

Options that wouldn't have taken me away from Rylee.

Options that wouldn't have made her push me away.

Options that wouldn't have left me with blood on my hands.

But in the end, she was right and I was wrong. Through it all, I'd learned that vengeance doesn't make the best support system. When it's nothing but you and your anger, the healing never comes.

If only I'd learned that five years ago.

Ten years ago.

Fifteen years ago.

It all would've been different.

"All rise…" The baritone voice echoed through the small room, followed by the sounds of everyone rising from the wooden pews. There were sniffles and coughs, but no one spoke. The door behind the large bench opened, and out came a woman with white hair, wearing a black robe and red-rimmed glasses.

I turned around and caught Elise's eyes. They were teary and her lips trembled as she attempted to offer me a smile. It didn't work. The comfort she so desperately tried to provide me was lost, swallowed up by her grief. Her pain. Her loss.

Seeing me in that courtroom, I knew she was reliving it all over again.

So I turned around to keep her from seeing my fear. I didn't want her to worry about me, as well. She had Steve by her side, her hand in his. His support was all she needed. He truly did love her, and I was happy she didn't have to deal with this alone. Didn't have to sit there and hear it all by herself. But it didn't stop me from thinking about how alone I was. Without Rylee, I was *so alone*. No matter how badly I'd wanted her here with me for this, I knew she couldn't be. She had enough to deal with, and this shouldn't have been added to her plate.

So here I sat. Alone.

In New Hope, Pennsylvania. Alone.

In the courtroom. Alone.

Facing the judge. Alone.

Awaiting sentencing.

Alone.

TWENTY-NINE

Rylee

"WHEN ARE YOU GOING to give that man a chance, Rylee?" my mom asked as she sat at the kitchen table next to Dad. He set his newspaper down and eyed me. Having one parent corner you first thing in the morning was bad enough. Being cornered by both of them meant this day wouldn't be a good one.

When I'd shown up at their house four months ago with my bags packed and a job lined up in Smithsville, they didn't ask questions. I simply told them Josh and I didn't work out and I was ready to move on with my life. But when they found out I was pregnant, there was no way to avoid telling them the truth—or, at least, a simplified version of it. At first, they assumed the baby was Josh's. They weren't so supportive once they found out Killian was the father. They demanded he take responsibility. But when I explained to them his absence had been my decision, they started to quiet down.

Then Killian showed up.

Two and a half months ago, I started receiving packages by the front door. They hadn't been delivered through the post office or UPS. They'd been delivered in person, by one man. Killian Foster. They always contained little gifts—baby shoes, a keychain of a moon, sketches of a forest at night…little things to let me know he wasn't going anywhere. And somehow, my parents started showing support. *For Killian*. They believed he deserved a discussion, but I refused. I wasn't ready yet. There were still so many emotions and convictions I had to deal with first.

Even though I hadn't seen him in person or spoken to him, he proved he wasn't going anywhere. Along with the packages, he'd also left me letters stuck between the screen and my bedroom window. Love notes, if you will. Apology letters. He'd given me space, yet remained close. Day after day, he wore me down. Little by little. I knew I wouldn't be able to stay away for long, especially now that my parents seemed to have taken his side.

"It's not that easy, Mom," I said with my back to her while I grabbed the carton of milk from the fridge. "I can't really explain it, but I need more time."

"More time?" Her voice went high, as if what I'd said was utterly ridiculous. "Honey, you're having a baby. You don't have that much time left. You're halfway through your pregnancy, and at some point, you're going to have to let him be a part of it. Whether you decide to forgive him or not, he's going to be a father, and he has every right in the world to be a part of that baby's life. Not just once it's born, but now. You can't rob him of this experience. It's not fair."

I set my now empty cup on the counter and wiped my mouth. "I'm not planning on keeping it all from him. I have my ultrasound in a few days and had thought about asking him if he wanted to go with me. But I'm scared."

"Scared of what?" The entire time my mom grilled me, my dad sat next to her and watched, as if this was some kind of evening news program. Any moment he might get up and make some popcorn to go with the show. "Is there something you haven't told us about this fight you two had? I mean, you say you're mad at him for abandoning you all those years ago, but you must not have been that mad if you slept with him."

My eyes rolled on their own. It'd become a habit I couldn't break whenever I was around her. There was only so much I could tell them about Killian, and why I'd decided to push him away wasn't one of them. "I haven't spoken to him since we found out I was pregnant. So I'm sorry if the idea of going to his house and knocking on the door terrifies me."

At the end of the street, there was a house being remodeled. It was an older home an elderly couple had lived in for decades, never updating anything. I saw Killian's Jeep parked along the curb every day. It was no secret he was there. Not to mention, he'd told me so in one of the letters he'd left for me, saying he was fixing it up for us. For me. For the baby.

That letter left me in tears for days.

"Not to mention," I added with a finger in the air, "I haven't heard from him in a while. As far as I know, he's tired of trying. He's given up. So to go to him and put myself out there like that isn't the most comforting idea."

He hadn't been around for over a week. No letters. No boxes left on my porch. No Jeep parked outside the house. He'd made no attempt to reach me or tell me where he was going. Two days ago, on my way home from work, I noticed he was back. And still, I hadn't heard a peep from him.

I knew I needed to make a decision, but I was torn. Him disappearing really opened my eyes, though. I realized I didn't want him *gone*. I just didn't really want him there. At least, not yet. But my mom was right—I didn't exactly have scads of time to waste. I needed to make a decision, and soon.

"We're not saying we want you to be with him. That's obviously your call. We want you to be happy. But more than that, we want our grandchild to be taken care of. If that means child support, then fine. If it's Killian being in the baby's life, great. Either way, we only want what's best for you and the baby."

"I appreciate that, Mom. I'm trying my best. I'll stop by his house on my way out to see if he wants to go to the appointment. If he says no, then I have my answer."

It was easier said than done. The entire way back to my bedroom, my body shook with nervous anticipation.

When I got dressed, my stomach flipped.

When I slipped on my shoes, my chest tightened.

But nothing came close to the anxiety that consumed me when my phone rang. I was seconds away from leaving the house—the car was cranked and my hand rested on the gear shifter—when my phone lit up with a Baltimore area code. I didn't think my "hello" was even heard as it barely slipped out. Fear of it being Josh ate at me. I hadn't heard from him since he left my apartment after his altercation with Killian, and I knew he'd come back at some point.

He couldn't stay away forever.

"Lee?" a deep voice asked through the speaker.

I stilled, my heart in my throat. "Y–yes."

"Hey, it's Dalton." He almost sounded relieved, which didn't do much for my anxiety. "Listen...I wanted to call and apologize. Josh had me completely fooled. I had no idea of the things he was capable of."

"W–what are you talking about?" I hadn't kept up with anything since I left Baltimore. I had no idea what Josh had been doing, so Dalton's apology threw me for a loop. "What do you mean by the things he's capable of?"

"He wasn't always good to you, and I never stepped in. I feel horrible for letting him speak to you the way he did. I just thought he was trying to sound good in front of other people. I assumed you never would've stayed with him if he truly treated you that way. So I'm sorry."

"You called me to say that? It's fine, Dalton. Nothing to apologize for. I'm okay."

"Well, at least now you won't have to worry about hearing from him."

"What does that mean?" My heart skipped a beat.

He sighed, and I swear his pauses lasted for eons. "You haven't heard?"

"Heard what? Stop talking in circles and please just tell me."

"He, um...he's gone. He's dead."

"*What*? How? When?"

"It happened a few days ago...that's why I thought you might've heard."

"No. I left Baltimore. I've been in Tennessee and haven't kept up with him. How? How did he die?" My words came out so fast I didn't think he'd understand me, but I couldn't slow it down. I couldn't slow down my breathing or my heartbeat.

"He was stabbed to death in—"

"Stabbed?" A harsh ringing only I could hear pierced my ears. I grew lightheaded and had a hard time pulling in enough oxygen to clear the haze surrounding me. "You said this happened a few days ago?"

"Yeah. Three days ago."

I couldn't stop the train my thoughts had hijacked. All I could think about was Killian. How he'd been gone. How I hadn't seen him or heard from him. For over a week. How he'd come back two days ago. One day after Josh was stabbed. *To death*.

It couldn't be.

It couldn't be.

My phone fell to my lap, the call disconnected, and I bent over the steering wheel to catch my breath. I needed to put things into perspective. I needed to believe Killian wouldn't have done something like this. But he would. *He had*. The other two men who'd broken into his home when he was a child were…dead. Murdered. And Killian had admitted to being the one who ended their lives.

I flew into action without an ounce of thought as to what I would do. I had no idea of the words I'd use—if any. I wanted answers, but I also didn't think I'd be able to hear it come from Killian. I didn't think I'd be able to handle knowing the truth.

When I'd gotten into my car before the phone call, I knew I had a decision to make, and I was prepared to make it. I was prepared to accept Killian for who he was, despite some of the things he'd done, because I could understand—on some basic human level—why he felt it was necessary. But now…now there was no way. There was no excuse for what he did. None.

My decision had been made.

And it wasn't the one that would lead to him being a father to my child.

I stomped up the front steps and stormed into the house. The front door had been left wide open, as well as all the windows on the first floor. The only sound filling the empty space was banging, maybe a hammer and a nail. Adrenaline drove me to the back of the house where I found Killian nailing a piece of wood to the wall.

He was shirtless with only a pair of jeans slung low on his hips, a tool belt hanging from the waistband. His tattoos were on full display and a sheen of sweat clung to his bare skin, reflecting off the light through the window at his side. Had this been any other day, any time other than moments after Dalton's call, I would've been in a puddle at his feet. But it wasn't. I'd known the truth, and there wasn't a thing he or his hard body could do to break me down.

When I came to stand behind him, leaving six or seven feet of space between us, he turned around to face me. His eyes bore into mine—confusion and relief swirling around in the pale-green color. But he didn't speak. He stood there, frozen in time, reminding me so much of the man I'd seen in the gym that first night.

"So do you feel better now? You feel like you got your revenge? Found your voice?" My words shook with the tears threatening to spill down my face. They were a mixture of anger and sadness. I was pissed at him for so much, but mostly for what he did to Josh after I'd made it very clear how I felt about what he did to the other two. And then I was sad. Because I felt as if I'd completely lost the image of who I'd always seen him as. He was no longer the man of my dreams. The one I thought I'd love for the rest of my life. That man was gone. He'd left me standing alone in my back yard over five years ago and never returned.

Killian nodded and blinked a few times, clearly confused by my reaction to him.

"Why?" I cried. "Why'd you do it?"

"Wait." He stepped forward, causing me to take a step back. Over and over again until I met a wall and couldn't retreat any farther. He stopped an arm's length away and furrowed his brow. "What are you talking about?"

"Josh! You think I wouldn't find out? Did you really believe I'd never know what you did?"

"Rylee," he whispered my name and shook his head. "I thought you'd be happy about that. I thought that's what you wanted."

"You thought I wanted you to kill him?" I shouted with tears streaking my face.

"*Kill* him? No. I didn't kill him."

"Then what did you do? What are *you* talking about?"

He huffed and hung his head, running his fingers through his hair. A few strands fell forward and swayed against his heavy breathing. When he looked back up, into my eyes, I saw something, but I had no idea what. To me, it seemed like pride. But that didn't make much sense to me.

"I went to the police," he admitted and waited for my response, which I didn't give him. "Elise and I went to the authorities in New Hope. I told them everything. I told them about the night my parents were murdered—everything they'd asked me when I was a kid but I wasn't able to tell them. I gave them Josh's name and turned him in."

"B–but…he's dead. Josh is dead."

Killian nodded and bit his lip. "Yeah, but I didn't kill him."

"So what happened?"

"I told you. I turned him in. They went to him and asked him a few questions, and he confessed. He admitted to killing my parents and attacking me. I didn't think he would, but he did. He died in prison—one of the other inmates stabbed him. Rylee…no matter what you may think of me, what I've done to make you hate me, I'm not that kind of person. I never would've killed him no matter how badly I'd wanted to."

"But…you were gone. You weren't here. And he died. Where were you?"

"I had to go back to New Hope for his sentencing."

I was so confused, and the more answers he had, the worse it got. Nothing made sense, yet at the same time, it was completely clear. I felt like I was stuck in a dense fog, trying to find my way out, getting lost over and over again. "What about the others? You killed them."

He shook his head and took a step back. "You're right. I have their blood on my hands. But it's not what you think. I'm not innocent. But I'm not a monster, either." He paused, more than likely to see if I'd stop him. When I didn't speak up or move, he continued. "I tracked them down after I left here. In my head, they got away with destroying my family and stole my childhood. I wanted to see what kind of life they had. I wanted to show them my face and let them know what they had done to me. I needed them to see—as adults—the chaos their actions had left behind.

"Jameson wasn't easy to find. He was a junkie. Addicted to heroin. But I eventually located him. I sat with him in his living room—which was in this nasty, rundown apartment building occupied by other lowlifes and junkies. He was high, fucked out of his mind, but he knew who I was. I couldn't understand too much of what he said, but it was enough to know he didn't walk away clean. He didn't leave my house that night and go on with his life."

"That doesn't explain how he died, and why you say you have his blood on your hands."

"Jameson was the kid who stood back that night. He was the one who didn't stop the others. When Josh came after me, all Jameson did was stand there and beg Josh not to kill me. But he didn't stop it. Jameson didn't turn his friends in or do the right thing. So when he stuck the needle into his vein, I didn't do anything to stop him. I sat back and watched, exactly what he did to me. I knew he was high. I knew he was already on something, but I didn't stop him from injecting that shit into himself. And when his life faded away, I didn't call for help. I didn't do anything other than sit there and watch him die."

Tears came on so fast I couldn't see beyond them. His silhouette was nothing but a blur. "What about the other one? What happened with him? What did you do to him? He was stabbed, Killian! Nineteen times! Just like your father. That's not a coincidence."

"No...it's not."

THIRTY

Killian

SHE PRACTICALLY BEGGED for me to lie to her. To tell her I had nothing to do with either death. That I was the man she always thought me to be. But I couldn't give her that comfort. I refused to stand there and lie to her while looking into her tear-filled eyes.

The truth gutted me.

But it was all I had to give.

"When I found him—Lance, the one who'd stabbed my dad—I didn't know what to expect. He wasn't an addict like Jameson. In fact, he wore business suits and lived in a nice house. He had a good job and seemed to have done well for himself. It pissed me off, because that was the image I'd had in my head all those years. He'd ruined my life and then went on to live in the lap of luxury. I hated him. But I never went there to kill him."

"Then what did you go there for?"

"To show my face. To speak to him. Let him hear it all from my mouth so he would have to live with the sound of it for the rest of his life. I wanted him to see my pain. Hear it. Feel it. But I didn't want to kill him—well, obviously I wanted to, but I never would have. What had happened with Jameson was bad enough. It made me feel dirty, like I was no better than they were. But I continued to try to justify it to myself. Jameson was a junkie, ending his own life."

I stepped away even farther, needing the space in order to tell her the truth.

"I'd followed him to a strip club several times. Each time was the same as the last. He'd sit against the far wall and drink

236

water. I never once saw him drink anything with alcohol in it. Each night, one of the strippers would go to him, he'd pull her to the back, and then he'd return about ten minutes later. I wasn't stupid. I knew what he went back there to do. But one night, he didn't return to his seat. So I went after him, wondering where they'd gone. There was an exit at the end of the hallway he'd disappeared down, so I went out the front and snuck around the side of the building. It was dark, but there was just enough light to see where I was going. Between the moon and the dim, flickering bulbs off the top of the building, I was able to see enough. Like the stripper on the dirty ground with her arms wrapped around her legs. And the man propped against the brick wall, hunched over with his limp dick hanging out of his pants."

Rylee gasped but didn't say anything. I gave her a moment before continuing.

"The woman was hysterical, her makeup was smeared all over her face, her mascara running down her cheeks. She just kept repeating it wasn't her fault, that he'd attacked her. That's when I saw the knife sticking out of his neck. I told her to run, and once she was gone, I took the knife and stabbed him eighteen more times. I didn't even think about it. The only thing I saw was a horrible man who'd killed my dad and then attacked this innocent woman in an alley. All I could think of was the number of times he slid his knife into my father's chest. It wasn't until I'd reached the number eighteen that I even realized what I'd done."

"Was he…was he…?

"Yes," I said to spare her from finishing her question. "He was already dead before I got there. It was a small pocket knife, but big enough that when she stuck it in his neck, he bled out. He didn't have a chance by the time I got back there. He was already gone."

"So you just left? You fucking stabbed a man—dead or not—and just left?"

I nodded, not even having an excuse for my actions. "I found out later that the woman was stopped a few blocks away. She was covered in blood, and someone had called the cops. When they started their investigation, other women from other clubs came forward, claiming he'd done the same thing to them."

"Then how come no one did anything about it?"

"One woman did. She'd called the cops on him, but nothing was ever done about it. I guess the others were too scared or strung out to say anything." I sighed and leaned against the wall. "I know a thing or two about not coming forward with information about a crime. I can't blame them for not talking."

Rylee glanced at her feet and twisted her hands in front of her. "So, about Josh. You turned him in? And he confessed?"

"Yeah. I didn't think anything would be done about it since so much time had passed, but Elise promised me that if I came forward, I'd feel vindicated. That if I said something, told the authorities about what he'd done, I'd find some semblance of peace again. But that didn't happen. I didn't feel better when he was arrested or when he pled guilty in front of a judge."

I crossed the room and took her hands in mine, urging her to look at me.

"I didn't feel better until I stood in front of that same judge, in front of a roomful of people, and told my story. That's when I felt vindicated. That's when I was no longer silenced. At his sentencing, telling everyone the things he did, what he said, the scars and nightmares I've lived with ever since then…that's when I found my voice."

More tears cascaded down her cheeks, except these weren't formed by sorrow or anger. Her brows no longer pinched and her eyes didn't squint. They were round and soft. Full of contentment and peace. Pride. Love.

For the first time since she kicked me out of her apartment, I started to believe I had a fighting chance. I'd bought a house, worked night and day to fix it up, sent her gifts and letters in the hopes she'd forgive me. But not once did I allow myself to believe it could happen until this moment. This very second.

"How did you do all that without the cops knowing you were there when the other two died? How did you not get in trouble for that? I don't understand. Didn't Josh say anything? Didn't he try to turn you in?" Her voice was so soft, barely a whisper.

I shook my head. "They were already closed cases. Their names did come up when I gave my statement, but no one ever questioned anything. And I guess Josh didn't feel it necessary to do or say anything about it. I found out he suffered from delusional paranoia. He'd been medicated, and had gone off and on his meds several times."

"He told me his mom suffered the same thing."

"His dad was there. He spoke after I did. I thought he'd ask for leniency, which he kind of did, but not the way I'd expected him to. He told the judge Josh was safer in custody—to himself and to others. He was sentenced to life, but while they were getting ready to transport him to a different correctional facility, one of the other inmates got to him." I tilted my head and asked, "You thought I killed him?"

"Well, yeah. I'm not saying what you did to the other guys is all right, but it's not at all what I thought. I thought you...*killed* them." It was clearly difficult for her to admit that. "It's a hard pill to swallow, Killian. Like, how can I be okay with you murdering them, but hate Josh for what he did? If I hate him for stealing the life of another, shouldn't I feel the same about anyone doing it? I love you, and that will never change. No matter what you did or didn't do, I will always love you. But sometimes, love has nothing to do with acceptance."

"I don't think I know what you're saying."

She sighed and glanced at the ceiling for a moment before meeting my gaze again. "I've always hated seeing the parents of murderers come to their defense. I understand love. I understand how blind and stupid it can be. But to say the love *you* have for someone holds more weight than the love of a victim's family...that's just ignorant."

"I understand." My heart sank. I could barely breathe. What she said made sense. It was real, raw, and honest. It was the truth. I turned around, because I couldn't bear to see her walk away.

I couldn't watch her give up on me.

It was hard enough hearing it.

"I have a doctor's appointment on Thursday. It's an ultrasound, so we'll get to see the baby. Would you like to go?"

Her words were soft, yet firm, no hint of them shaking with fear or rejection. If anything, they were surrounded by hope.

I spun around so fast I almost got whiplash. "You...you want me to go with you?"

Her smile brightened the entire room. "Yeah. A baby is a new beginning, right? What better way to start it off than with pictures of the life we created? I want you there. I don't know what'll happen between us or where things go from here, but I do know I don't want to do this without you."

"Tell me when and where and I'll be there." It'd been so long since I'd felt any level of joy, so what ran through me right then practically made me high. It made me believe my darkest days were behind me.

I just had to continue with what I was doing.

Building us a life with my bare hands.

Loving her every single day, and reminding her of it.

And like the night waits for the moon, I'd wait for her.

THIRTY-ONE

Rylee

I'D BEEN NERVOUS for days.

After asking Killian if he wanted to go to my appointment with me, we hadn't spoken. He'd left one letter that night, but other than that, it'd been radio silence. I'd wanted to go to him, day after day, but for one reason or another, I decided against it. So as I got dressed Thursday morning, my stomach knotted and my hands trembled.

When I pulled into the parking lot of the doctor's office, I spotted Killian right away. He stood next to the front door with his back against the building, waiting for me. The sight of him made me smile and relax. He wore a pair of dark jeans and a light button-up shirt. As I approached him, I could tell he'd gotten a haircut since the last time I'd seen him. He still wore it pulled back, but the underneath was shaved closer to his scalp. And God, did he smell good—the same scent I always remembered belonging to him was back.

"Are you ready?" he asked and opened the door for me to enter.

"Ready for what?" My face flamed with the stupidity of my question. I couldn't recall a time I'd been more nervous. It was ridiculous, considering this was Killian. I'd known him since I was ten years old. He was my first. My only. Hell, I was having a baby with the man. Yet for some reason, his presence and the sound of his voice rendered me stupid.

"Don't we get to find out what we're having today?"

We took our seats in the waiting room after I signed in. "Do you want to know what the sex is?" Honestly, I hadn't thought much about it. My health and the health of my unborn child were always on the top of my priority list, but everything else seemed to have fallen to the wayside. The gender, names, colors…none of it mattered to me.

Killian looked me right in the eyes, not a hint of emotion on his face, and said, "Of course."

"Oh, I didn't think it was that important."

"I mean, I want to make sure the baby is okay. That's the most important thing. And of course, make sure you're okay. But after that, I'd like to know what we're having. I'm doing the baby's room next, and I'd like to know what color to paint the walls and what kind of mural to put up." The confidence in which he spoke, as if it was already written in the stars that we'd be together and living in that house, sent my heart into a slight arrhythmia.

I opened my mouth to speak, but the nurse came through the door and called out my name. Killian stood and pulled me up by my hand, even though I wasn't big enough to need the help. He kept our fingers laced together while we followed the woman to a back room where an examination table sat next to an ultrasound machine.

"Don't you have to get naked or something?" Killian asked after the nurse left the room.

I giggled and settled back onto the white paper lining the bed. "No. The ultrasound wand goes over my stomach. All I have to do is lower the band on my pants and pull up my shirt. Sorry to disappoint you."

He scratched his chin, the short hairs bristling beneath his nails, and examined the computer next to me. Then he turned to face me before lifting my shirt just enough to see my stomach. Laying on my back, I didn't look pregnant—in fact, even standing up I barely showed. I just looked like I'd packed on a few pounds and had a soft belly. But Killian looked at me like I was the sexiest woman in the world.

It'd been a long time since I'd seen that look.

And it stilled my heart for a beat.

He placed his hand over my warm, sensitive skin, and ran his thumb from side to side. "What do you think it is?" he asked, not once taking his sights off my stomach, as if he could see through me to the baby I harbored.

"I'm not sure. I haven't really thought about it."

His eyebrows pinched together when he shifted his gaze from his hand to my face. "Not at all? I can't stop thinking about it. Well, about the baby in general. Are you not happy about it? Do you not want this?"

Pain struck me hard in the chest at the thought of Killian thinking I didn't want this child. Or want it with him. Quickly, I shook my head and said, "No. That's not it at all. Of course I want it. Of course I'm happy and excited. There's just been so much going on…and it's hard to think about it all."

He nodded and licked his lips, as if contemplating his next words. "I think it's a boy. A beautiful, healthy baby boy. And he's going to be happy and loved and taken care of." He continued to stroke my belly, practically speaking to the child inside me.

"Hey, Killian?" I cleared my throat, trying to rid myself of the nerves. "How did you learn to work on houses? Like…where did you learn how to do all that?" It was something I'd wanted to know since I found out about the house down the street, but I never had the gall to walk over there and ask him. I hadn't been ready for it yet. But now I couldn't find a reason not to ask.

"After I moved away, I worked at a few construction companies. I started just helping out for a few bucks. Over time, I was able to learn a few things until they were giving me more responsibilities and tasks. I really enjoyed the alone time. I was able to do a lot of thinking. Before finding…Josh…I was in a town about three hours outside Baltimore for a little over two years. That's where I learned most of what I know now. It's also where I learned to box."

A knock sounded at the door before it opened and a young woman walked in, interrupting our conversation. The grin on her lips never faltered, even after introducing herself to Killian. There are no words to express the joy and contentment I felt watching him interact with someone comfortably. It was what I'd always wished for.

As the woman took measurements and pictures of the baby, she pointed to the screen and said things like, "here are the fingers and toes," and "the little nugget's legs are crossed." While she pointed everything out, Killian sat right beside me, my hand in his, with his attention glued to the screen in front of us. Occasionally, he'd turn to catch my eye, but most of the time, he was too absorbed in the images of our unborn child to do anything else.

"So, are you ready to know what you're having?" the woman asked with a gleam in her eyes. It was obvious she enjoyed her job as she never seemed to stop smiling. When we both nodded, Killian pulling himself out of his chair, she said, "It's a boy."

I was beyond excited, but Killian was ecstatic. He fist-pumped the air and let out a celebratory "hoorah!" It made me giggle, but more than anything, it filled me with pride. This man, who'd spent over half his life in silence, couldn't contain his eagerness over our big news. Words flowed as if he'd never gone a day without speaking. Excitement laced his hollers.

He obviously wasn't silenced anymore.

"This…" he said while pointing to the black-and-white printout of our baby after the sonographer left the room. "This is my inspiration. To be the man this child needs. To be the father this baby deserves."

I pulled the strap of my purse over my shoulder, but paused when he grabbed my arm to stop me from leaving. "What is it? What's wrong?"

"I never truly apologized to you, Rylee. And you, more than anyone, deserve it. I wasted so much time chasing the revenge I thought was necessary to move past what'd happened to me. But that's not what I needed. *You* were. You've always been exactly what I needed, *when* I needed it. And I turned my back on you. I listened to my anger and resentment, when I should've listened to my heart. My heart has always led me to you. It always will. I'm sorry. For so many things, but mostly because I hurt you. I'll never do that again. I swear."

He wiped a tear off my cheek and pressed his lips to my forehead.

"I will do right by our baby, right by you. Be who you both deserve."

"I don't…" I started to speak but the words became clogged in my throat and wouldn't come out past the emotion building inside.

"You may not think you know what you want right now. You may believe you need more time to figure it all out. But I'm not worried at all, and do you know why? Because I love you. And you love me. And despite everything we've been through, we belong together. I knew that the moment I laid eyes on you. The moment I spoke to you for the very first time. I have no doubts. I'm not giving up, and I won't let you do it, either."

As I stared at him, I couldn't help but fall in love all over again.

In so many ways, he harbored horrible brutality no one should ever experience, but with me, his innocence was blind and beautiful—perfect.

• • •

THE REST OF THE day was hectic, fitting a full schedule into one afternoon.

But I'd finally made it to the last appointment of the day.

The little boy in the chair across from me continued to color in his book without looking at me. He did this often. Sometimes, he just sat there, staring at the walls. He spoke, but not much. Mostly, it was stories about his group activities, never anything regarding his case. It broke my heart to see him so quiet, so withdrawn. He reminded me so much of Killian it was sometimes hard to separate the two. Eleven is never an easy age—so many things changing—but it was worse when you've lived through a tragedy.

Tyler McHugh had a good life. His parents loved him, his grandparents were always around. He did well in school and had plenty of friends. But life has a way of laughing in your face, reminding you things aren't always perfect. Reminding you of the evil inside others. And that's exactly what happened to Tyler less than a year ago.

It was the middle of math class on a Wednesday morning. His teacher stood at the board, explaining something Tyler couldn't remember. He couldn't recall what time it was—just after eleven thirty—or what he'd eaten for breakfast that morning. But the things he could remember would more than likely stick with him for the rest of his life.

The door opened and his teacher turned around.

She wore a yellow sweater over a white dress.

Everything became "loud and quiet at the same time."

And then Mrs. Landrey's dress was no longer white.

Her sweater was no longer yellow.

They were soaked red.

Kids screamed and ducked beneath their desks, and from Tyler's hiding spot, he watched as some of his friends cried, some shook with fear…and others were motionless. Lifeless. Those were the images he'd never forget. The ones that would haunt him forever. The ones he'd told me about when we first met.

Since then, he didn't speak about much.

Today, he just sat there with his tongue peeking out past his lips while he concentrated on his coloring. It was something I offered to a lot of the kids—art. Tyler wasn't the best at staying inside the lines or drawing accurate depictions of things, but that didn't matter. The important part was to express himself. In his own way.

I moved to sit next to him, to see what he was so intent on. I'd found a lot of the children who came to my office had to be led into talking. Simply asking what they were coloring or drawing or building really helped them open up. Even if they didn't talk about their nightmares or feelings, at least they were talking. And to me, that was the most important thing they could do.

On his paper, he'd drawn a big smiley face attached to long sticks for the body, legs, and arms. "Is this you?" I asked and pointed to the paper. He wasn't a little kid, so I tried to speak to him without the softness in my tone. Compassionate, but not condescending.

"No. He's my friend from the group." Tyler, as well as several other kids who had been through traumatic experiences, belonged to a city-run youth program. Three times a week, they'd get together and learn how to interact in a healthy environment. It was something I was passionate about, and encouraged all the children who came to see me to be a part of it—or at least something like it, be it the YMCA or the Big Brothers and Big Sisters Club. I was happy to see Tyler really take to it and enjoy his time there.

"So you've made friends? What's his name?"

"Happy," he said without taking his eyes off the paper.

My heart skipped a beat, then stopped, then overcompensated and sped up. "His name is *Happy*? Or is that just a nickname?"

Tyler shrugged.

"Is he your age?"

"No," he answered with a slight shake of his head. "We see him when we go to the children's gym on Mondays. He teaches us how to box. They have one of those big punching bags there, too. And we get to wear gloves."

There was no way.

It couldn't be true.

I had to have been hearing things.

"He teaches you how to fight?" My voice seemed to have been stuck in my throat, because my question came out sharp and off key.

Tyler finally stopped coloring and looked over at me. "No...well, kinda. We don't learn how to fight people. That's bad. It's only okay if we need to defend ourselves, but there are other ways to do that before fighting. Happy just teaches us about ways to get the anger out. Like when we're really mad about something. He taught us how to calm down, how to breathe better so we aren't so mad."

"And he does that while teaching you how to punch a bag?"

Tyler shook his head and laughed. Laughs didn't come often with him, so I took a moment to enjoy the sound of this one. "No, silly. Boxing is for learning control. Happy says we're the only ones who can control how we feel and what we do. It helps center us while giving us exercise."

"And he tells you this, or someone else does?"

He quirked his head and peered at me through the sides of his eyes. "He tells us. Why wouldn't he tell us if he's teaching us?"

I offered him a smile and said, "I don't know, that's why I asked...*silly*."

Again, he rewarded me with laughter.

And I couldn't help but think Killian had something to do with it.

THIRTY-TWO

Killian

AS THE SUN LOWERED in the sky, the temperature dropped. But nothing could cool down the excitement coursing through me over the day I had. Seeing my child, my *son*, sent me on a high I never wanted to come down from. Touching Rylee again made me feel like an addict who'd tasted their drug of choice for the first time after years of sobriety. But as I made my way into the neighborhood, drawing closer to her house, my nerves kicked up. I couldn't explain it, but the thought of her rejecting me again did something to me. It made me anxious. Although, more than anything, it made me determined.

I'd never lose her again.

I wouldn't allow it.

After one knock, the door opened. Rylee's father stood in front of me. I hadn't seen him in years, although he didn't look much older than I remembered. As he stared at me, his gaze narrowed and he pulled his shoulders back. I knew he didn't care for me very much, especially since his daughter was carrying my child and she didn't have a ring on her finger. Not to mention the way I'd left her when she was only seventeen.

I expected him to hate me.

What I didn't expect was for him to stand there with the door open, giving me a chance to speak. But that's exactly what he did. With his arms crossed over his chest, he watched me, waited for me to make the first move.

The first word was always the hardest. It terrified me the moment my top lip met my bottom row of teeth or my tongue connected with the roof of my mouth to form the first sound of the first word. Speaking to new people wasn't easy, but this wasn't just a person who'd never heard me talk before. This was Rylee's father. The man who'd seen me as a boy. A broken, lost, scarred boy. And now, I stood in front of him as a man. A man who was in love with his daughter, and I wouldn't allow anything to get in the way of that. Not even the hoarse, groggy notes of my first words to him.

"Hi, Mr. Anderson." Rylee's mother came up behind him, her eyes wide and her mouth hanging open. "Mrs. Anderson. I'm sorry to just drop in uninvited, but I was hoping I could speak with Rylee."

"Well, it's about time you come here and do more than just leave a box by the door." He shifted weight onto the other foot and made room for his wife. "Listen, I don't presume to understand what's going on with you two, and to be honest, it's not really my business. But I think you and I"—he turned to look at his wife—"and Holly need to have a chat first."

I nodded and took a small step back, expecting him to come outside. "I agree. I actually have something I'd like to talk to you about as well."

He remained in place and let his arms drop. "Okay, but us first. We want to make sure you're planning on taking care of that baby. This isn't some game where you get to pick and choose the responsibilities or when you get to take them on."

"I know that, sir." I held up my hand to stop him from continuing. "From the moment we found out she was pregnant, there hasn't been a single thing I've done that hasn't been for them. For both of them. Rylee and the baby. My *son*. There hasn't been a day that has gone by since I was eleven years old that I haven't loved your daughter. And there won't ever be a day I don't. I'm trying to right my wrongs. I may not know what I'm doing most of the time, but I can promise you I'm doing my very best."

"That's all we ask for," he said, yet he didn't move.

"I also want to apologize to you and Mrs. Anderson. I'm sorry for the way I left when I was eighteen. I'm sorry for hurting your daughter. I'm also grateful that she has both of you to lean on. She's incredibly lucky to have parents who love her the way you two do."

Mr. Anderson cleared his throat while his wife blotted her eyes.

"I will do right by Rylee. And that's the reason I'm here." I paused to take a breath, not necessarily needing the courage, but searching for the right words to say. "I want to marry your daughter—*no*." I shook my head. "I *will* marry her. I know I'm supposed to ask for your permission, but if I'm being honest, I don't want to. I don't want to risk you saying no, because that's an answer I won't accept. I mean no disrespect to either of you. I'm just in love with Rylee and I can't take the chance of her not being my wife. For any reason. I'm doing what I can to earn her trust back, and I'll continue to do that until the day I die."

They looked at each other, speaking without words. It was that kind of communication I used to have with Rylee, and I prayed to God we still had it. Being apart from her for months, not having much contact with her, left me unsure. Yet hopeful.

"How exactly do you plan to support her? Financially? And I know you're fixing up that big house down the street, but how are you affording it?" They were logical questions, especially coming from a father.

"I have a job, sir. Once the house is finished, I will be going to work for a construction company here in town. They've already hired me, but they're giving me the time to get settled in with the house and everything. Their crew is actually helping me a lot. In the meantime, I have money in the bank. You don't have anything to worry about when it comes to the finances. I was an only child, so my parents' estate went solely to me. They'd set up a trust that I've had access to since I was eighteen. When I turn twenty-five, I'll have complete access to it all. But I don't plan to use it for more than needed—such as the house. Everything else will come from hard work. I won't let you down. I promise."

Finally, they both took a step back to offer me space to enter the house. "She's in her room. Let me go get her for you," Rylee's mom said with a soft yet shaky tone.

"If you don't mind, I'd like to go to her."

When she nodded her approval, I had to slow my movements to keep me from bolting through the house. I needed to get to her. It'd been too damn long. When I made it to her bedroom door, I had to control my knock, because I was ready to beat it down. Patience was never my strong suit. Half a second later, I invited myself in, not at all waiting for an invitation, and found Rylee in a state of undress. I quickly stepped inside and closed the door, twisting the lock on the knob behind me.

"Killian...what are you doing here?" She held a T-shirt over her chest and stood in nothing but a pair of underwear. She was the sexiest thing I'd ever seen, and I couldn't take my eyes off her. In fact, I couldn't do anything until she repeated herself, asking me why I was there.

I didn't bother answering her, only crossed the room until I was in front of her with my hand on her small, slightly rounded belly. Then I held her by the back of the neck and brought my lips to hers. It was the softest kiss I could manage with her being half naked in my arms, her body pressed against mine.

When it ended, I held her hips and gazed into her eyes. "What are you doing tomorrow?"

"I have work, why?"

"Cancel your appointments. Or reschedule them. Have a sick day or something."

"Why?" she asked again, more cautious this time.

I smiled as my heart sped up, each beat trying to break through my chest to get to her. "Because we're getting married. Tomorrow. We'll get a license and then go to the courthouse. I can't wait another day to make you my wife."

She giggled and lowered her head. "Aren't you supposed to ask?"

"Maybe, but that would be a waste of words. Although..." I sealed my lips over hers once more and leaned into her, pushing her down onto the bed. "If you want me on bended knee..." I took the shirt from her hand and dropped it to the floor. Then I hooked my fingers beneath the elastic band of her underwear and pulled them down her legs while she lifted off the mattress just enough to get them over her hips. Finally, I bent down on one knee, between her legs. "Rylee Scott Anderson, I've loved you for what seems like my whole life."

"Killian," she said with a sniffle.

But I interrupted to finish my thought. "I didn't exist until I met you." I kissed a path from her knee, up her inner thigh, until I reached her core, already glistening and ready for me. "I can't lose you. Not ever. You're my home, Rylee."

I ran my tongue through her folds and she dropped back onto her elbows.

"Keep your eyes on me." I licked her again, my focus solely on her. "Don't look away." And then I covered her pussy with my mouth, kissing her the way I would her lips, before pulling away and slowly raising myself over her on the bed.

With a slight adjustment, I shifted her up the mattress, giving me enough room to kneel on the edge between her legs. My lips on her skin. Her taste on my tongue. "You're my better half. My *best* half. The greatest part of my life." I met her eyes and held her gaze while I freed myself from my shorts. "Looking at you, I see my whole life. Marry me."

I pushed into her.

She arched her back.

But she kept her eyes on me.

"Say yes," I said with a gentle thrust.

"Yes." It was one word—the best word I'd ever heard—wrapped in air.

"Say you'll marry me."

"Yes, Killian. I will marry you."

"Tomorrow," I prodded.

"Yes. Tomorrow," she repeated.

I covered her mouth with mine and pushed all the way into her until my pelvis met hers. I trailed kisses down her cheek, pausing to lick the edge of her ear, and whispered, "Now, I need you to be quiet so your parents don't hear us." Then I rested my face in the warm space between her neck and shoulder. My favorite place in the world.

I eased out before carefully sliding back in.

Over and over again.

Until she was breathless.

Until I was complete.

● ● ●

RYLEE SLEPT IN MY arms all night. It was strange being in her bed, in her parents' house, and waking up with sun. I had to constantly remind myself it was okay, I would not have to climb out the window this time. Ryan and Holly had talked about it, and they offered for us to stay there instead of a hotel.

Their decision probably had more to do with us getting married so soon, and less to do with hospitality, but I wasn't about to argue.

From now until the house was in livable conditions, we'd be staying in their home. Sleeping in her old bedroom, on her old bed, and showering in her old bathroom—together, after Ryan and Holly left the house or went to sleep.

"What are we doing?" Rylee asked when I parked in front of the jewelry store. I made sure to get there as soon as they opened, which meant we woke up early. I didn't want to waste another second, although I didn't exactly want to leave the bed, either.

"Did you not want rings?" I stepped out of the Jeep and waited for her around the front.

"You're going to buy my ring in front of me?"

I smirked and opened the door for her to enter first. "No. I already have yours. We're here so you can pick out mine." I handed the salesman who approached us my credit card and said, "She can pick out any ring she wants."

They sized my finger and then I kissed her forehead before walking out.

Less than ten minutes later, Rylee got in the Jeep with a smile on her face.

That smile remained until we got to the Clerk of Courts office.

"Hey," she said and grabbed my arm to keep me from getting out of the car. "I found out something yesterday, and I wanted to talk to you about it." She waited for me to nod, giving her permission to continue before speaking again. "What do you do on Mondays?"

I shrugged and hoped she wouldn't notice how her question worried me. "I work on the house and go to the gym. Why?"

"Why didn't you tell me about the work you do with the kids?"

I swallowed and focused on my hands around the steering wheel. "I don't do it to get brownie points, Rylee." I glanced at her seated next to me. "I do it because they need to see someone who understands them. I'm not there because I have to be, or because I have some fancy college degree. I'm there because I was them—I *am* them. They need to know vengeance isn't okay. Anger and resentment only feeds more anger and more resentment until there's nothing left. And they need to hear it from someone who's been in their shoes."

"I really wish you had told me."

"Why? What difference would it have made? I didn't do it for you or to win you back."

"I know...but it's a helpful reminder of why I love you. There were days I needed that. Nights I couldn't sleep because I didn't know what the next day would bring. I had started to believe you weren't the same person, so knowing that would've reminded me you were. You *are*."

"I got lost for a bit. But you found me. You were always right there in front of me the whole time. I was just too blinded by rage. Too stuck in my own nightmare to see you. But you never stopped seeing me, and I think that helped me find my way back sooner."

"I'm just glad you did."

"I'm glad I did, too."

THIRTY-THREE

Rylee

MY HANDS SHOOK inside Killian's large palms.

We stood in the courthouse, in front of an officiant, facing one another. Ready to take on the world together. To vow to love each other for the rest of our lives. There shouldn't have been any nerves, yet I seemed to be full of them.

However, they weren't born from fear.

They were derived from excitement.

After all this time, everything we'd been through, I couldn't believe we were standing here together. Ready to take this next step. I'd prayed and hoped and dreamed of this day for so long. Although I never expected to be in a courthouse. I'd always imagined I'd be in a church, standing in front of hundreds of family and friends in a white dress with flowers. The whole dream wedding every girl plans from the time they're young.

But here I was.

In a long skirt, plain white maternity top, and a sweater.

Because Killian didn't want hundreds of people to look at me when I became his wife. He wanted it to be just the two of us. No one else. He wanted to be the only one watching me when he took me as his. And when I took him as mine. I'd agreed because…it made sense. It was always just us, so our future should've begun the same way. Not to mention, he promised I'd have my wedding if it was really what I wanted. *After* this.

Killian wore dark jeans and a button-down shirt. He didn't appear nervous at all. In fact, he held an air of confidence that settled and calmed me. After we got our marriage license,

Killian drove as fast as he legally could, holding my hand between us, and offering side glances all the way to the courthouse. My parents and Elise, as well as her husband, met us there to serve as our witnesses. Killian didn't want anyone there, but relented when I informed him we needed someone to stand by our sides.

"Do you have your own vows?" the man beside us asked.

I was ready to answer him, tell him we did not, but Killian smiled and gave a different answer. "Yes, I've prepared something to say."

"Really? When did you do that?" I asked in a whispered voice.

His smile said it all. "I've known practically my whole life what I would say to you on the day you became my wife."

"Very well. You may proceed." The officiant held out his hand to instruct Killian to begin.

With his hands holding mine, his gaze steadied on my eyes, he started the speech he'd prepared long ago. "My dad always told me you can salt food and hide clutter in a closet. He said finding a woman who could cook and clean wasn't important. I needed to find a woman who would love me to the end of days, support me like a rock, and treat me with the respect I deserved. He told me I needed a woman who would be my best friend, my soul mate, my shoulder when I needed one. My mom told me I needed to be a man. A man a woman like that deserved, because it was more than just finding love. It was about being *in* love.

"You, Rylee, are that person. You are my best friend. Always have been. You've been my rock, my shoulder, and you've loved me more than I ever thought possible. You take me as I am, yet you don't let me wander down the wrong path. You keep me good. Because you are my good. You're everything good in my life."

He licked his lips and blinked when his eyes started to mist.

"So as I stand here right now, I promise to love you through all the tomorrows. I promise to love you until the moon stops lighting the night, until the stars stop leading the way…long after my last breath. I promise to be the man you deserve every day of your life. I'll never stop loving you, Rylee. Never."

When his pause was longer than a simple break, the officiant turned to me.

I cleared my throat and glanced around the room. But Killian squeezed my hand and forced me to look back at him. "I don't have anything prepared. I didn't know we were doing our own vows."

"It's okay. Speak from your heart. That's all I did."

A calmness settled over me when I gazed into his eyes. The color of pistachios. And then I opened my mouth to let whatever I felt come out into words. "I've always known it was you. Not once, not one single day have I doubted my love for you or yours for me. Even in your absence, my love never wavered. It never weakened or broke. It was the one thing that got me through each day. My heart continued to beat in my chest, and that's how I knew you still loved me. That's how I was able to carry on, and wait until the day we made it back to each other.

"You've always talked about the moon. It's always been your thing. You used to say you wanted to steal it from the sky and freeze time. But I think that was our past. I believe our future belongs to the sun. To grow, nourish, warm us. We deserve to flourish beneath the rays, in the open, for all to see. We no longer need to hide in the night, but dance in the day. So as I stand here, I vow to love you until the sun no longer rises in the east and sets in the west. I promise to love you until it stops burning in the sky. Until there is no more day or night. And even then…I'll still love you."

Killian didn't wait to be prompted before kissing me. He held my face in his hands and brought our lips together. It was instinctual. Perfect. His thoughts, feelings, and impulses all wrapped up in that one kiss.

When the officiant cleared his throat, we finally parted and giggled with the excitement of teenagers. "Do you, Rylee, take Killian to be your lawfully wedded husband? To have and to hold through sickness and health? For richer or poorer until your dying breath?"

My heart pounded against my sternum. "I do."

He asked Killian the same question, to which he answered, "I do."

"And now for the rings." He waited for us to nod before continuing. "Killian, please place the ring on Rylee's finger and repeat after me."

Killian pulled out a plain gold band attached to a single solitaire diamond ring. I gasped, having never seen it before, and wondered when he would've gotten something that brilliant, that perfect. "It was my mother's," he answered in a hushed tone. "I got it when I turned eighteen and it's belonged on your finger ever since."

He pushed the rings over my knuckle and repeated after the officiant.

"With this ring, I thee wed."

And then it was my turn.

I pulled the brushed titanium band from my pocket and slid it over his finger. I knew it belonged to him the moment I spotted it. Along the circumference, etched into the metal, were starbursts, representing the rays of the sun we would grow under.

"With this ring, I thee wed."

"By the powers vested in me by the state of Tennessee, I now pronounce you husband and wife. You may kiss your—"

Killian didn't wait until the words were spoken before lacing his fingers in my hair and pulling my face to his. He took my mouth with fervor, obviously not caring about the people standing around. My parents. His aunt. The others waiting their turn. None of it mattered. It was as though we were the only two in the room.

In the courthouse.

In the world.

Just us.

No one else.

EPILOGUE

Killian

I SAT ON THE edge of the bed with my sketchbook in my lap, a charcoal pencil in my hand. The grey image in front of me didn't compare to the real thing, but I had to get it out. I had to mark this moment, watching my son sleep in the arms of his mother. Watching my wife hold the best part of me.

"We have to come up with a name, Killian. We can't call him 'him' forever."

For months during the pregnancy, we'd tossed around ideas, but nothing ever felt right. Rylee had suggested naming him after my father, but I didn't care for that idea. I believed he needed his own name. I didn't want my son coming into this world with expectations he'd have to live up to. I wanted something strong, something uniquely him. So we ended up agreeing to wait until he was born. To look into his tiny face. We thought we'd just know once we saw him.

Well, we saw him.

And we still didn't know.

"Nothing feels right," I said while continuing to draw the two loves of my life.

"We can use our middle names. Scott Owen or Owen Scott. Or we can mix our names like my parents did with mine. Rylan." She ran the tip of her finger over his face and smiled at the way his nose scrunched up.

As I sat there and watched it all, watched the way she was with him, I couldn't help but think about her vows. She was right. All my life, it'd always been about the night. But Rylee gave me the day. She gave me the sun, the warmth. She was my brightness. And now she'd given me a son.

"Blaise." The name rolled off my tongue while I stared at my son in my wife's arms.

She glanced at his sleeping face and smiled. "I think that's perfect. Blaise Foster. But what about a middle name?"

I couldn't hold back my grin. "I like your idea of mixing our names. Rylan. He can be Blaise Rylan Foster. And our girl can have Kylee as a middle name."

"Killian…we just had this one less than twelve hours ago. Can we hold off on thinking about the next baby? Maybe give me a year or so?"

"A year? I was thinking more like a few months. Tops."

She huffed out a giggle and shook her head. "My vagina still hurts. There will be no talk of sex or babies until that pain goes away."

"I know how to make it go away."

Rylee laid her head back on the pillow and blinked at the ceiling. "You're impossible."

"I'm impossibly yours."

"Always."

"And forever," I added.

"Until the sun stops rising in the east."

"And stops setting in the west."

She took my hand in hers. "I love you."

I had it all. Everything. Whether I deserved it or not, I had it.

LEDDY'S NOTES

Oh, these are my favorites to write. I love to talk about why I wrote a book or where things came from, yet I feel like no one cares. So I get to put it all in here and let whoever read it, read it haha.

Almost a year ago, my man and I decided to binge watch the show *Lie to Me*. (If you haven't watched it, you totally should. It's on Netflix and has 3 seasons...it doesn't air anymore *sniff sniff*). The whole premise of the show is about a guy who is a human lie detector. He watches the way people react and can tell if they're telling the truth or not. Anyway, I loved that idea, but started wondering how people would be able to do that. Then I thought about how people who can't hear would be able to do that because they'd rely more on visuals and facial expressions. Then I started thinking like a writer and wondered about a character. However, I didn't want someone who couldn't hear, because the whole sign language and no speaking thing gets a little hard for conversations. Dialogue would be nearly non existent. So...I pondered about a character who could hear, but not talk. Yet I was still in the same boat with conversation, so it became a character who *could* talk, just didn't. Which, in retrospect, totally negates the whole human lie detector part. Oh well. I digress. Once I got to that point, I then began to question why he wouldn't talk, and almost immediately, I saw Killian's scars. Oh, boy...was the journey from conception to completion a long one.

I saw Killian as an adult. A fighter. But I knew I didn't want a fighter book. I don't watch the sport, and honestly, I don't know too much about it. I didn't want the whole UFC thing. But I couldn't figure out how he got there, or why. All I knew was he was there, he was angry over something that had happened to him as a child, and he ran into his girl, the one from his past. I knew she was dating a fighter, but that was about it. It wasn't until a friend helped me take a step back to see his childhood, that I was finally able to see his whole story. And once I did that, there was no stopping it.

I remember sitting down to write the prologue, telling my friend Steph how I saw it going. She told me, "I don't know how you're going to pull that off" and I said, "I don't know either, but I'll sure as hell try." Then I wrote the first word. Then the next. And they never stopped coming.

I'll always refer to this book as Killian's book. His chapters came so easily for me. I'd sit down and they'd pour out of me without any thought given to them. Rylee's chapters were harder, and there were some I literally had to skip over because I wanted to get back to his. This is also the first book I've ever written in alternating points of views. I have the hardest time flip-flopping between characters, and I feel if you don't stay in one person's head, both characters end up sounding alike. So I typically avoid it since I never felt confident doing it. But for some reason, these two had no problems differentiating themselves to me.

I don't know what it is, but there's something about Killian that has tied him to me in ways other characters never have. I believe I'll always have a strong connection to this book, and I hope you do, too!

In a nutshell, I watched a TV show, questioned it to death like any over thinker would, breaking it apart and dissecting it until something else is created, then agonized over his youth for a solid six months before spending a few weeks pouring it out onto paper.

Don't ask me to fix your dishwasher...I'll give you back some contraption that is nothing like what it used to be. Oh, and I'll probably mark it up to give it "character." ☺

HEY YOU!!

I'm gonna make this quick…

I couldn't do any of this without my family. Nor could I do this without all the readers. You guys are amazing—the new, the old, and the returning. Amazing, I tell ya!

Lauren Runow…without Trevin and Lily's story, I doubt I would've been able to sit back and see Killian and Rylee as kids. So thank you for opening my eyes, even when you had no idea you'd done so lol.

Stephie…this is normally where I call you a whore, so why change things that aren't broken? Thank you for your notes, your talks, and your amazing feedback. You're the greatest whore of them all.

My TWOTs…I can't imagine doing any of this without the six of y'all. Thank you for being there when I needed someone to sprint with, or when I just needed help organizing my thoughts.

Sarah and Joy…I can't even begin to tell you how valuable you both are to me. You make my crazy life a little easier to manage.

Emily…probably my biggest supporter through this whole thing. I can't thank you enough. I love you more than you can possibly know, and I honestly don't know where I'd be without you.

Josie…thank you for making my words pretty.

Robin…Oh dear Lord! Even though I probably made your life hell with my cover changes, you rocked my socks like always. I can't imagine ever putting out a book without your covers again. You are like Monet with book covers. So sorry this one was such a pain in the ass, but nothing compares to the reaction I got when I saw this one. Thank you!

Readers, bloggers, people of the world…I can't say thank you enough! Honestly, you keep me going when I don't always feel like I can. Thank you for everything!